TRIPLE *Power* PLAY

JESSICA LYN

Copyright © 2025 by Jessica Lyn

authorjessicalyn.com

All rights reserved. No part of this book may be reproduced in any form or by any electronic or mechanical means, including information storage and retrieval systems, without written permission from the author, except for the use of brief quotations in a book review.

This book was not created with AI. This is a work of fiction. Names, characters, businesses, places, events, and incidents are used in a fictitious manner and are a product of the author's imagination. Any resemblance to actual persons, living or dead, or actual events is purely coincidental.

This book series was originally published in September 2023 on Kindle Vella.

Edited by Studio ENP and EJL Editing

Copyediting and Proofreading: The Fiction Fix

Cover Photo by Michelle Lancaster @lanefotograf

Cover Design by Lori Jackson @lorilovesbookjackson

Interior Formatting by Sarah Symonds @dragonflyreads

AUTHOR NOTE

This book series was originally published, unedited, in September 2023 on Kindle Vella.
The characters are the same. The plot is the same.
However, new chapters have been added and scenes rewritten (a dozen times).
For those unfamiliar with Kindle Vella, it was a serial platform.

Thus, this series is a fast-burn and may not read the same as a typical novel.
Enjoy!

WARNING: PLEASE READ!

First and foremost, your mental health is important.

This book series is a dark romance,
and although not as dark as others,
it does contain themes of mental illness and addiction,
including intrusive thoughts and ideations,
past trauma, and substance use.

Please visit authorjessicalyn.com for a full list.

The characters of this series are imperfect.
The men are manipulative and over-the-top.
The sex is explicit.

Please do not read if that is not your thing.

That being said,
if obsessed, jealous, stalkerish, Dom vibes are your jam,
you've come to the right place.

*For those who dream of a villain
to chase away their nightmares.*

ONE
JACKSON

I slam the beer bottle on the bar, gesturing to the bartender. She smiles and gives me a finger wave as she settles the tab with two guys. They nudge each other, sizing me up and whispering.

Fuck, I'm too sober for this.

I don't know why I accepted the beer when Grant handed it to me. I prefer vodka. It gets me where I need to be faster than this grassy shit. The burn is nice too.

That familiar craving claws at my insides, and I taste the poison on my tongue. I wave at the bartender again, this time with less patience.

She saunters over with desperate fuck-me eyes and a lopsided grin. I bet she thinks that's sexy. Newsflash—it's not.

"What can I getcha, handsome?"

When she takes the empty beer bottle, she runs her fingers over mine suggestively. Fucking vomit.

I jerk my hand away. "Vodka tonic. Double. No lemon. And don't touch me."

Her face falls, then hardens. Typical. "No reason to be a prick."

"No reason for you to touch me. Do your fucking job and get my drink."

My agent would hate me right now. My father too, but for very different reasons.

Thoughts of the asshole have me scanning the club for him. I know he's here somewhere, kissing ass with the team's owner, Richard or Dick or whatever the fuck his name is.

Robert.

My father, Kyle, is somewhere, most likely sucking Robert's dick. Not literally—Kyle prefers his toys on the illegal side.

The drink crashes beside me, liquid splattering across my black button-up. If I didn't want this vodka so badly, I'd throw it at her.

I snatch the drink. "No need to be offended. It's not you, it's me. I don't fuck whores."

Grant elbows me in the ribs. "Dude. Chill. Before you get us kicked out of our own party."

There is no *chill*. This is my worst nightmare. The music is loud, bright lights flash in the dark, and bodies rub against one another. I don't touch people. I don't dance.

In fact, I dislike people. *Period.*

"Captain and alternate captain, we're not getting kicked out."

I down the vodka tonic in one go, temporarily easing the craving. I glance back at the bar. There's no other bartender in sight, and I'm not ordering another drink from that bitch. I'll have to go elsewhere.

Grant juts his chin. "Here comes the new rookie. Klawasaki? Kaluzinski? How do you pronounce his name?"

"No clue," I mutter.

He raises the beer bottle to his lips and nearly chokes on the watered-down piss. "Oh, shit. Check out his girl."

I have no interest in who's dating who, but with nothing better to do, I follow Grant's line of sight to see Rookie dragging a girl behind him. He's pushing his way through the crowd, her hand in his, not at all paying attention to the people touching her.

What a douche.

And I swear, she mouths "Sorry" to everyone she bumps into.

A smile tugs at my lips. It's amusing, how she doesn't belong.

Not because of looks. No, this girl has to be the hottest in the club. Not just hot—*perfect*.

Despite the terrible lighting, I can see she's stunning, with long dark hair and a warm complexion. Her dress is white, a beacon under these black lights. The top is a damn corset, the tight fit highlighting her full breasts but not obscenely. The skirt blooms at her curvy waist with teasing layers, ending mid-thigh, showing off her toned, mile-long legs.

She glances back to apologize again, and my gaze catches on the slender straps crisscrossing over her exposed back, tying off above her round ass—a gift from Heaven.

They break through the crowd and stop in front of us.

I don't acknowledge him; I can't take my eyes off her. She peers over at the rookie, waiting for an introduction, but he's too busy kissing ass with Grant. Her gaze drops to her feet, timid.

I extend my hand and lean in so she can hear me over the music. "Hi. Jackson."

She's wearing strappy high heels, putting her at about my chin.

Placing her delicate hand in mine, she gives me a shy smile. "Aurora. Nice to meet you." Polite, too.

Aurora. Interesting. Her name is the color of my eyes. She's basically named after me. It's fate.

I hold her hand far longer than socially acceptable. She has bubblegum-pink fingernails. Cute. Her hand is small in mine, and her skin is incredibly soft. I inhale her intoxicating sweet scent and groan internally. I wonder if she tastes as sweet, and my cock stirs.

Huh, I thought that part of my body was no longer functional, the same as my heart.

With reluctance, I release her before my arousal becomes obvious. Our gazes meet, and I'm enchanted by caramel eyes both innocent and wicked. I glance lower at her pouty, cherry-red lips. She's eye candy from head to toe, and I happen to have a sweet tooth.

Dragging my eyes away from her sinful mouth, I turn to Grant. "Hey, let's go upstairs."

We exchange *the look*, and his brows nearly hit his hairline. "That's a code violation."

Typically, it's the other way around. I struggle to suppress laughter at his awkward attempt to pick up some chick.

"This doesn't count."

I'd break Bro Code for this girl even if she was dating Grant. Shit, she could be dating the coach for all I care. I'd still go after her.

He guzzles the rest of his drink and sets the bottle on the bar. "Lead the way."

I lift my chin to get the asshole's attention. "Hey, Rookie. You wanna take this up to VIP?"

He holds her hand, leading her up the stairs, and I hate it. I want to tear them apart, but I remain behind her, hands itching to grasp her waist and prevent her from falling in those heels.

I'm rewarded with the sway of her hips and a view of her glorious ass.

We find a booth in the VIP area, and I hang back to ensure I sit across from her. Grant and Rookie go to the bar for drinks, and I waste no time getting to know her.

"Aurora, where are you from?"

"LA," she says with a touch of sass.

"What part of LA?" I smirk, fully enjoying myself.

"San Fernando Valley. Yes, I'm Hispanic. No, I won't speak Spanish for you, and no, I don't cook. Is that what you want to know?"

No, I'm obsessed. I want your location in case I need to find you.

"That's disappointing. I love eating."

She shakes her head and giggles, the sound infectious, and I can't help but laugh along with her.

"Since we're discussing stereotypes, do you live on the beach, drive a Jeep, and surf?"

She's talking about my dirty blond hair, green eyes, and summer tan.

Then, it hits me: *she has no idea who I am.* It's liberating.

"I live on the beach when I'm not working. No to the Jeep, but that sounds fun. I'll get one if you want."

She rolls her eyes at my attempt at flirting, but it's not an exaggeration. I'll buy a fleet of Jeeps if it gets her to go on a date with me.

"And I surf a few times a year. I used to surf a lot growing up."

"What do you do for work?"

I'm tempted to lie, but I want to know her beyond tonight. "I play on the same hockey team as the rookie you came with."

Pink flushes her cheeks, and she lets out an adorable chuckle. "Oh. Yeah, that makes sense."

"I'm glad you don't know me."

She tilts her head. "Why?"

"Stereotypes." I grin.

"Ah, yes. You poor thing. Those horrible hockey player stereotypes. At least you have all your teeth."

Her sarcasm has me laughing again. It's weird not having that constant agitation in my chest, the one that helps me pop off whenever needed, the wall protecting me from giving a fuck.

Grant and Rookie return, ruining our playful banter. Rookie hands Aurora a glass of champagne, but she politely thanks him and sets the drink aside, her fingers tracing through the condensation.

She doesn't trust the drink or him, which tells me everything I need to know.

"Aurora," Grant says, handing me another fruity beer I'm not interested in, "I hear your best friend is dating our goalie, Killian."

She flashes him a friendly smile. "Emily. Yes."

"So why are you here with him?" I nod toward the rookie.

She opens her pretty mouth to respond, but he rudely interrupts. "She's my date."

I shoot him a glare. "I didn't ask you." I turn back to Aurora. "What are you doing here with him?"

"I'm his date," she mimics with a hint of teasing.

"You're his date, or you're *dating*?"

"Is there a difference?" Fuckface asks, far too cocky for someone so recently drafted.

"There's a clear distinction. Maybe you should've gone to college instead of declaring for the draft."

"Fuck off, O'Reilly."

I ignore him. "How long have you been together?"

All humor drops from her face, and I fear I've embarrassed her or pushed too hard.

Before she can reply, he stands, seizing her arm and tugging. "Come on. Let's go."

She gapes at him, her eyes wide with shock, and I see red.

This kid just signed his death warrant.

Violence surges in my veins, and I relish the sensation.

A deranged grin stretches across my lips.

"Fuck," Grant curses.

My dickhead fuse is short, and my tolerance is miniscule. People who know me don't touch me. They only fuck around and find out once.

And for whatever reason, this girl feels like an extension of myself.

I reach over the table and snatch his hand from her arm, twisting and squeezing at the wrist. "I'll break your fucking hand if you ever touch her again. Then your wrist. Then your shoulder. And if you open your mouth one more time, I'll knock your fucking teeth out. You'll be watching games from a hospital bed while sipping meals through a straw."

His nostrils flare, and a deep shade of red spreads over his face and neck. "Come on, man. We're on the same team here." All bravado is gone from his tone. Pathetic.

I release his hand, and he sits back down.

"Don't sit. You're not staying."

He lingers at the front of the booth, jaw clenched tight. "If I leave, she's going with me."

The balls on this guy. I'd rather be skinned alive than see her leave with this prick.

A massive body appears beside Rookie. "What's up, fuckers?" Kill singsongs before he cuffs the back of Grant's head.

The slender blonde with him must be Aurora's friend, Emily. She's bleach-blonde and plastic—your typical puck bunny or jersey chaser.

She slides into the booth beside Aurora, glancing between us. "What's going on?"

Aurora peers over at me helplessly.

"Fuckface put hands on Aurora, and now he's leaving," I say, more than willing to be her voice.

Brows furrowed, Emily scans her best friend. "Hands on her *how*?"

"He grabbed my arm. That's all." Aurora's tone is quiet yet rushed, her gaze nervously flitting around the table. She doesn't enjoy the attention.

Her anxiety calls out to me. I want to wrap her in my arms and protect her from this harsh world, keep her to myself and hide her where no one can find her.

Okay, that's a little unhinged, but what the hell do I know? I've never given a fuck about anyone before.

Except for my mother, who's dead, and I deliberately avoid thinking about.

Emily murmurs something, and Aurora quickly shakes her head.

"She's not leaving with you." Emily gives Rookie a dismissive nod. "Go find someone else."

This girl's BBE, Big Bitch Energy, is solid. I don't hate it.

His dark eyes flick between me, Killian, and Grant as if he's contemplating the consequences of arguing before he storms off.

I shoot him a smug smile and a childish wave. "See ya on the ice, Rookie."

He tosses me the middle finger, and I'm almost giddy as I face the most beautiful girl I've ever seen. "Okay, where were we? Oh, right. You were saying you wanted to leave." I pull out my phone and check the time. "If we hurry, I know a fantastic place to eat."

"She's not leaving with you, O'Reilly."

That BBE focuses on me, but Emily is in for a fight. I never give up. I always get what I want—always—and I want Aurora. I don't understand it, but I'm not letting her slip through my fingers while I figure it out.

"I think she can make her own decisions."

"She doesn't know you."

"And you do? This is the first time I've met you."

"That you know of—you're always drunk, which is why Aurora isn't leaving with you."

I turn to the girl I'm already obsessed with. "I've had three drinks. We'll take an Uber, and I won't drink the rest of the night. I swear."

Unfortunately, Emily can't resist intervening. "She's not your type."

"That's hilarious. What's my type?"

Only Grant has seen me leave with a girl, which was a mistake I haven't repeated. I admit, that night, I was far beyond intoxicated and unable to do anything besides black out. When I woke, all my shit was gone, including my favorite pair of boots. I miss them far more than I miss wasting time chasing tail.

Ain't no piece of ass worth risking a pair of broken-in Iron Ranger Red Wings.

Emily points across the room, and at first, I'm confused. I don't see any girls I'd be even remotely interested in. Then, I see him, his beady eyes staring in this direction.

Shit. The last thing I need right now is my father's attention.

He's sitting with a group of middle-aged men, his flavor of the night beside him. My skin burns as that familiar agitation returns to my chest, rage twisting in the pit of my stomach. I fucking hate him, and I hate being compared to him.

I clench my jaw, struggling not to lose it on Aurora's friend.

Thankfully, Grant steps in. "You're wrong. You don't know what you're talking about. You need to go back to your table and mind your own fucking business."

Kill shifts on his feet. "Emily, come on."

She leans in, ignoring him. I'll give this girl props; she doesn't back down. "I know exactly what I'm talking about. I worked for that agency. I know the girl who's with *your* father."

My head spins, putting the pieces together. Panic sets in, but one thing's for sure. "Have you ever seen me touch a girl? Any girl at all?"

"Not while I was there," she grumbles.

"I don't do that shit." That's the truth. I'd rather take a rusty butter knife to my balls than follow in my father's footsteps. "If I did, don't you think I'd be over there?"

Her lip twists in disdain, and she glares at me, not believing a word I say.

I don't blame her. He's still my father, whose connections I benefit from, right?

If I get popped for a drug test, he'll make it disappear.

I'm untouchable—the entire organization fears him. No cop in LA would dare give me a problem. As long as I provide my father with money and notoriety, I can get away with murder.

But I'd never lay hands on a woman, nor do I mess with prostitutes or underage girls or whatever sick shit he's into.

"We got to go, Emily," Kill insists. "Come on. Let it be."

Emily narrows her eyes at me in warning before whispering something to Aurora, who nods. Then, thank fuck, she leaves.

Grant follows, and I'm finally alone with the girl whose warm caramel eyes don't look at me like I'm a piece of shit.

Aurora picks at her nails, a slight tremble in her voice. "I'm sorry. She's protective."

"I don't blame her. I'd be protective of you too."

Fuck, I already am. I was prepared to break a teammate's hand for touching her, and I'd do it again.

"You wanna get out of here?" I ask.

Her face lights up with a grin. "Yes, please."

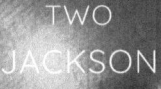

TWO
JACKSON

"This...is not a restaurant." Not budging from the curb, Aurora eyes the high-rise building with suspicion.

"I didn't say I was taking you to a restaurant. I said I'd feed you."

Her head whips around, panic written all over her face.

"Take out your phone. Send Emily your location. She knows my teammates, and they know where I live. I'm not going to hurt you."

Just kidnap you. Kidding. Maybe.

She places her hands on her hips, cocking her head to the side. "You said a fantastic place to eat."

"I have food on the way. My place is quiet and comfortable, preferable to eating out."

"What if I hate the food? I'm a picky eater."

"You won't. If you do, I'll cook for you."

She shivers, her arms prickling with goosebumps. It's an August night in California, so it's not cold, but she's not wearing much.

"Please don't make me beg. I'll get on my knees right here on the sidewalk."

I'll do it, too.

"I'm not sleeping with you."

I grin at her adorable attempt at being assertive. "I don't wanna sleep with you. You're hideous."

It's a blatant lie, and she knows it.

She presses her lips together to suppress her smile. "I'm serious."

I put my hands up in a placating gesture. "I won't try anything. I'll keep my hands to myself."

She releases a dramatic sigh. "Fine."

I swipe my keycard, and we step into the private elevator.

"Are you this way with every guy you date?"

"Is that what we're doing? Well, I haven't dated... much."

"Why not? Because you're hideous?"

That makes her giggle, and her smiles are pure oxygen in my lungs, breathing new life into me. "Because I'm nineteen."

Nineteen? *Nineteen?* Maybe that's why she skipped the champagne, not because she didn't trust Rookie. Oops.

"Shit, really?"

"For three more days, and I'm far too busy to date."

"Why? Are you in college?"

She drops her gaze and fiddles with a thread on her skirt. "No. I work a lot."

"Well, I'm twenty-three, didn't go to college, and also work a lot."

She shoots me a shy smile.

The elevator stops, and my stomach flip-flops. It's not that I'm messy. I'm not, and I have a cleaner. But I've never had a woman in my space, nor have I dated a woman even remotely similar to her.

Timid. Witty. Down-to-earth.

I worry my lifestyle will scare her off.

Being a pro hockey player with a political father, I've been around attractive women. Most have this air of entitlement I recognize immediately and despise. Not Aurora.

She clutches her small purse in front of her and follows me into the open living area.

"Wow." Wearing a dreamy expression, she gazes out the two-story corner wall of windows, where a vibrant pink sky outshines the downtown lights. "You can see the coast from here."

I bought this place primarily for the view. It offers an escape from the city when it all becomes too much.

But the skyline pales in comparison to those wide, innocent eyes.

I'm infatuated and try my hardest not to stare. She's quiet and gentle, and in my chaotic world, that's a blessing.

"Thank you. Have a seat." I nod to the white sectional. "Can I get you something to drink?"

Call me psychic, because I know exactly what she'll say.

Gingerly, she perches on the edge of the cushion, crossing her long legs. "Water is fine, thank you."

Knew it.

Going to the fridge, I scan the alcohol selection before I catch myself. I can't remember the last time I was so hyped about something that I wanted to stay sober—not since my rookie year.

"Sparkling or mineral?"

"Ooh, sparkling."

I've never seen a woman excited over water. She wasn't this excited over my eight-million-dollar penthouse. I'm not sure if that makes impressing her easier or harder.

I open the glass bottle and hand it to her.

"Do you live here alone?" she asks.

"Yep. Grant stays here often though."

Alone is my preference. Me and alone are best friends. Even Grant gets on my nerves half the time. He's always fucking happy.

Sitting on the large ottoman in front of her, I lean forward, resting my elbows on my knees, and reach for her ankle. That same bubblegum-pink polish is on her toes.

She shifts her feet away from me. "What are you doing?"

"Taking your heels off. They can't be comfortable. Relax, babe. I won't hurt you."

I unbuckle the strap, slowly pulling off her shoe to savor her soft skin against mine. I'm tempted to glide my hand up her leg, but I'm certain she'd kick me in the balls.

I set her shoes aside, contemplating hiding them. "I'm going to get changed. You want something to change into?"

Her brows furrow in confusion, and she scans me from head to toe. "I don't think I'll fit into your clothes."

Laughter erupts from my chest at her genuinely puzzled expression. So fucking cute. "I'll bring you a T-shirt and boxers. You can roll them."

Her face falls, and her cheeks blush. "Wow. You're used to this."

Her dismissive tone kills my amusement. "I had a girlfriend in high school. Did you not have a boyfriend who gave you his clothes to wear?"

Something passes through her eyes. Sadness or regret? "No." She sets the water bottle on the end table. "Sorry, I should go."

She moves to grab her shoes, but I snatch them and hold them out of reach.

"Why? You haven't eaten yet."

"I... This... No." She draws a shaky inhale. "You're too intimidating. Emily was right. I'm not your type. You won't like me, and I'm not going to sleep with you. There's no point."

Wow, that's a lot of word garbage. For someone so attractive, she's incredibly anxious. Not mere shyness—no, there's an aura of hopelessness surrounding her, something I'm all too familiar with.

"Why won't I like you? I liked you the moment I saw you."

Her eyes flicker to the door. "I'm... No. This is too much, and I work early in the morning."

She reaches for her shoes, and I hide them behind my back.

"Where do you work?"

Her tiny fists clench her skirt, and she lifts her chin. "Nowhere. Now give me my shoes."

Oh boy, even her temper is adorable.

"You work with Emily, right? That's why you were with the rookie?"

And why she became uncomfortable when I asked how long they'd been together.

"Yes," she urges, as if that'll push me away.

If it was anyone else, she'd be out the door, but the skittish girl in front of me isn't a professional escort. She's too nervous and inexperienced. Any other escort or puck bunny would be thrilled to land a professional athlete. They'd be moved in and planning our wedding already.

Yet Aurora watches the door as if gauging whether she can outrun me.

She can't. I'm the fastest player in the league. She won't make it two steps before I tackle her to the floor.

Let's hope it doesn't come to that.

"How long have you been escorting?"

"A month."

"How many dates have you been on?"

"Six."

My jaw drops. "In a month?"

"One guy booked me three times."

"I'm sure he did. Did you go home with him?"

She scowls. "No."

"To a hotel? Anywhere?"

"If you're asking if I sleep with my clients, the answer is no. My contract is strictly dating. I giggle and flirt." She shrugs, half-assed. "It's been easy...until tonight."

Giggle and flirt and then play hard to get. The innocent act—at least, that's what these guys are thinking.

But it's not an act. She's pure temptation, and I need to move fast before some guy gets any fucking ideas.

She's only allowed to have one stalker. Me.

"When was your last relationship?"

She hesitates, her eyes searching mine. "In high school. Two years ago."

"See, we're not that different. I haven't had a relationship since high school either."

Not that it was much of a relationship, and certainly nothing serious. There are only two things to do at boarding school: sports and girls.

"Yeah, okay," she mutters.

She doesn't believe me—likely assumes I sleep with a lot of women. You need trust to jump in bed with people. I do, anyhow.

I smirk. "Are you stereotyping me again?"

"Whatever." She rolls her eyes. "Can I have my shoes?"

"No. I'm not done getting to know you, and you haven't eaten."

My tone is nonnegotiable, and to my surprise, it works. Granted, she appears to be sulking, but at least she has relaxed into the couch cushion and isn't racing for the door.

"Fine. I live with my grandparents, raised by my grandparents. My grandmother is a seamstress, and my grandfather works in construction. I help my grandmother, work with Emily, and waitress. I have a shift in the morning. I don't date because I don't have time."

I know what she's doing, but there's nothing she can say to turn me away.

"Why do you work so much?"

"Always have. I'm sorry I wasted your time. I thought we'd go to dinner, and I'd go home. I didn't know you'd bring me here." After taking a breath, she adds, "And thank you for sticking up for me." Polite, even when annoyed.

With my fingers steepled against my lips, I sit on the ottoman and contemplate the beautiful girl staring back at me. She was okay having dinner with me and was fine when we first got here, but now, she's freaking out because I offered her a change of clothes.

Is she worried I'll pressure her into sex? She said she was intimidated by me, not my place or my lifestyle. Me. I laughed at her innocence, and I'll never do that again.

"I could stare at you all night, and it wouldn't be a waste of my time. You don't have to change. It was only a suggestion. I won't pressure you, but make no mistake, I want you. And if I have to, I'll get your agency information and book you." Fuck, that's it. The solution to keeping her is right in front of me. "You know what? That's what I'll do. That way, you'll know I'm serious about you. What's the agency?"

Her face scrunches up in horror. "Why me?"

I bite my lips to stop from laughing. "Why not you? You're the most beautiful woman I've ever seen, inside and out. Am I that terrible? Are you not attracted to guys? What is it?"

Not my most convincing speech, but no one ever said I was great with words. Aside from hockey, I have little going for me.

Other than being damn good-looking, of course.

"I'm attracted to guys...in certain places."

Certain places? What the hell does that mean?

"Where?"

"Books."

Did she say books? Yes. Yes, she did.

This time, I can't stop myself from bursting out laughing.

She glares at me, all pouty-lipped.

"Sorry, you're just too fucking cute."

No worry about this one cheating or being with me for money or popularity. No, she'll be home, reading and comparing me to fictional men. I can handle that.

"Well, you're in luck. I have everything you book girls go feral over. I'm six-three, play a professional sport, have tattoos and a motorcycle, and I'm cocky. So let's make a fairy tale, princess."

She shakes her head in amusement, her lips pressed into a tight smile.

"Give me the agency information. I won't stop until you tell me."

"Fine," she grumbles. "Elite Escorting. I'm a GFE."

I give her a blank stare.

"Girlfriend Experience."

Ah, that makes more sense.

The doorbell rings, and she jolts.

"That's the food." I stand and offer her my phone. "Here. Find the agency or whatever for me."

She peers up at me, unsure, and tentatively takes the phone.

"You won't find anything in my phone, trust me. Only close friends have this number, and my agent runs my social media."

I open the door for the concierge, grabbing all four bags before he enters the penthouse and further intimidates Aurora. While in the entryway, I turn on the AC, because this girl makes me sweat. Every time she glances at me, I feel hot all over.

I lay the containers on the coffee table, pointing to each one. "Chinese, Mediterranean, Greek, Thai, burgers and fries, Italian, or I can order pizza."

Her eyes widen, and her mouth drops open.

"Go ahead. Pick."

She returns my phone. "You need an account. It'll be pending until your background check clears."

I plop on the couch, pulling at the collar of my shirt, which is still sticky from the bartender incident, and create an account with Elite Escorting, something I never saw myself doing. Ever.

Aurora opens each container, growing happier and happier. She loves food, books, and sparkling water. Can this get any easier?

I upload a picture of my license and a selfie and pay extra for expedited processing, which allows me to schedule her. I book her for three months, pending her approval, hoping to have her moved in by the end.

"You take care of your grandparents?" I ask.

She holds a hand over her mouth, finishing her food. "I pay my share of rent, utilities, food, and all that, yes."

I read the fine print, where it provides for a tip or allowance. It says the money goes directly to Aurora, with no commission taken. I compute everything in my head. She doesn't have to be with me twenty-four hours a day. Technically, she could still work. That's disappointing. I wish she was required to stay right here in my penthouse.

My goal is to give her enough money to quit her other jobs but not enough to ghost me afterward. I want her dependent on me. Is that wrong? Perhaps. Does the end justify the means? Absolutely.

I go with a hundred grand. That seems low, but I'll give her more if needed.

I carefully read a lengthy list of rules. Unless she explicitly agrees otherwise, only light touches are allowed. Any violence, assault, harassment, or roughness immediately ends the contract, and no money is returned.

And that's it. She's mine. No one else can book her—if she agrees, which she will. I'll make sure of it.

THREE
JACKSON

Aurora is sitting on the floor on her knees, eating over the coffee table. She's fucking adorable...and hungry. She's picking at the vegetables and salmon and the pita and hummus.

I bet the asshole didn't feed her and she was hangry. He's definitely getting hit for not feeding my girl.

"I'm going to get changed. Eat whatever you want, babe."

"Umm..." Those shy, innocent eyes peer up at me.

I stand over her, and a shiver runs down my spine.

Don't get hard. Don't get hard.

"Can I have a hoodie?" she asks. "I'm cold."

"You keep looking at me like that, and I'll give you my last breath."

She glares at me, but there's no heat behind it.

I cut to my room before she sees the prominent bulge in my pants. I change, wash up, and grab clothes for her. "Brought you some joggers. Maybe you can tie or roll them. If not, there's a pair of boxers and a hoodie. You can use my bathroom or the guest bath near the kitchen."

She changes in the guest bath, because of course she does, and comes out wearing my team hoodie and, I'm guessing, my boxers, though I can't see them.

The hoodie is enormous on her, reaching mid-thigh, and she's barefoot.

I have the urge to pick her up, wrap her legs around my waist, and cuddle her. Hard. Against the wall.

Jesus, what's wrong with me?

I take her dress to hang up as an excuse to get control of my never-ending boner. My dick hasn't had so much as a chubby in months, and now, it won't quit.

Curious of her size and where she shops, I check for a tag, but there isn't one. Calling out, I ask, "Where did you get this dress?"

"I made it," she yells back.

"What? No way."

I twist the dress this way and that way—it's flawless. I press the material to my nose and inhale like a fucking weirdo, and my eyes nearly roll back, not at all helping my erection.

When I return, she's in the same spot, only cross-legged.

Feeling lucky, I sit behind her and cradle her with my legs. I reach around her and grab a fry, popping it into my mouth. "The dress is unreal. I would've never known."

"Thank you." She tosses a smile over her shoulder. "I told you, my grandmother is a seamstress. I've been doing it forever. I take dresses from thrift shops and remake them. It's not hard."

She shrugs, but I can tell it's an accomplishment she's proud of.

"Is that something you wanna do? Make clothes?" I wrap an arm around her, and my traitorous cock jerks.

Fuck it.

"It's a dream of mine, yes."

Her words are breathless, and a nervous excitement rushes through my stomach, a sensation I only get before big games.

"You're great at it. Now how am I supposed to shop for you?"

She glances back at me, eyes full of apprehension, but I don't miss how they flicker to my lips. "You don't have to buy me anything."

"No worries, babe. I'm going to spoil you anyway."

I place a kiss below her ear, and a shudder runs through her. I know she can't be cold, and I do it again, grazing my teeth against her delicate skin.

"Stop it." She elbows me playfully. "You're a menace."

"Oh yeah? I'll show you a menace."

I tighten my arms around her, peppering her face and neck with kisses while she giggles and attempts to wriggle free.

Her giggles are the sweetest fucking sound.

She falls to the side, rolling onto her back, and I drop on top of her. I can't remember when I last laughed or smiled this much.

Her body against mine is heaven and hell all at the same time. There's no way I can hide an erection in these sweatpants, and I know she isn't giving me relief anytime soon.

It doesn't help that she's gazing at me as if I'm some god.

I wasn't lying when I said I could stare at her for hours, memorizing it all. Thick lashes, freckles, gold flecks surrounded by warm caramel, Cupid's bow lips...

Reaching up, she runs her finger along the curve of my neck, tracing my tattoo and eliciting goosebumps. "What's this one?"

Black, rough-sketched wings extend across my shoulders. In the middle, down my spine, is the date of my mother's death, the day she got her wings—not that I believe in that stuff, not for me, anyhow. With my T-shirt on, Aurora can only glimpse the tips of the feathers.

"They're wings."

She purses her lips. "I see that. Do they have meaning?"

"Everything has meaning."

She takes the hint and doesn't press further. "They're beautiful."

"Thank you. Not nearly as beautiful as you, though."

Her fingers glide into my hair, and I melt into her.

My dick throbs so hard, I'm a teenager again, touching a girl for the first time. "If you keep doing that, I'll have no choice but to kiss you." Now it's me who's breathless.

"Maybe I want you to kiss me."

Her words are barely above a whisper, and I'm on her before they even finish registering in my obsessed brain. I cup the back of her head, and my body surrenders to hers the moment her soft lips meet mine.

I try not to crush her, keeping my weight on my forearms, but every part of me wants to devour her. I deepen the kiss. I can't get close enough. I'm drunk on her.

She's addicting.

I've never wanted anything more than I want to be inside this girl, and not simply to fuck her. No, I want to be attached to her, know her every move and thought.

My hips shift on their own, grinding my aching cock into her core. She breaks the kiss far too soon. Still wanting more, I trail kisses along her jaw and throat.

Her body tenses, and I sense the moment something changes between us. Her fingers loosen in my hair, and her heart races against mine.

"What's wrong?" I rest on my elbow to give her space.

"I... " she falters.

"It's okay. If you want me to stop, I will. Just tell me."

I slide my hand under her hoodie to caress her stomach, and she grabs my wrist.

"Sorry." I pull back and intertwine our fingers. "Fuck, I can't get enough of you."

"I've never... I've only done this once." Her breathing stops, as if she's bracing for my reaction.

Does she think I'll reject her? That's fucking stupid. The thought of her with another guy infuriates me, but nothing more.

"I hate that someone else got you before me, but I guarantee I'll reach places he never did and make every inch of you mine."

She searches my eyes, and I let her see the truth in each syllable.

"I-I'm sure you'd prefer a girl with more experience."

"Nope. No, I wouldn't. Stop trying to talk me out of being with you. I want you. You're gorgeous. You're sweet. You're real." She wants me too. I heard her little whimpers as we kissed and felt her body trembling beneath mine. Her fingers are still in my hair, as if she doesn't want to let go. "But you need to know one thing. I don't plan on this being casual. If we have sex, I'm going to expect you to be mine. Only mine."

She narrows her eyes at me. "And what about you?"

I can't stop myself from kissing her. "It goes both ways."

She returns my kiss, our tongues quickly intertwining and picking up where we left off. She makes those delicious whimpers, and I swallow them up.

Then, a thought hits me. "You said you had sex once, not with one person. Once?"

She swallows hard and nods. A wary expression fills her eyes.

I hesitate to ask, but I need to know. "You didn't enjoy it?"

Her face flushes from more than our kiss. "It was my first time. That means nothing."

"Not for you, no. Did he hurt you?"

"*It* hurt, and then it was over." Her stiff shoulders rise in that fake, half-ass shrug.

A familiar haunting darkness churns in my gut. "I'm going to need his name."

"What?"

"Give. Me. His. Name."

"What? Why?"

"Because he hurt you."

"Maybe not on purpose. Are you always this intense?"

There's a defensive edge to her tone I don't follow. The world is cruel—*men* are cruel. She's perfect.

I can't understand her embarrassment—it's an emotion I rarely experience—but I'm not about to fuck this up and mock her innocence again.

"The tattoo is for my mother. She was killed when I was fourteen, and you saw my father. He's an asshole. There's nothing you should be ashamed of, not with me."

With a sigh, the tension leaves her body, that shy gaze staring back at me.

"Now, can I show you something?"

She raises her chin. "What?"

I grin. "Don't worry. It's not my dick."

"What are you going to do?" She's suspicious, but a hint of a smile plays on her lips, her walls slowly crumbling.

I kneel between her legs. She has my boxers rolled at the waist, and I reach for the hem.

"Give you an orgasm, and we're not arguing about it. It's happening." I whip the boxers off before she can stop me, dragging the material past her feet and tossing them aside.

I place my hands on her knees, and she sucks in a gasp, clamping her legs together.

"Relax, I won't hurt you."

"Yeah, that's not what I'm worried about," she says, more to herself.

"What are you worried about?"

Soft, vulnerable eyes meet mine. "You. This."

"Whatever *this* is between us, I feel it." It's sharp and tangible, a flutter of butterflies in my stomach, a surge of hope blossoming in my chest, a dark possessiveness pulsing in my veins. "And I don't want to fight it. You're meant to be mine—I know it down to my bones."

Her legs loosen, letting me take control. "You better be good, O'Reilly."

The cocky grin on my face could blind someone. "Oh, I'm always good, baby."

I glide rough palms over the smooth skin of her inner thighs, following with my lips until I'm lying on my stomach, her pussy spread out before me.

Fuck me, she's bare and glistening.

"Goddamn, you're perfect. Every inch of you."

Ravenous, I dive in to taste her. With my tongue pressed flat, I lick from opening to clit.

My mouth waters, and a groan rumbles from deep within. "Your cunt is fucking sweet."

"Oh my God," she whispers.

My lips stretch into a smirk against her. I could do this all night. Shit, I could spend all my days buried between her legs.

She's a high I'll chase for the rest of my life.

I flick and circle her clit until she writhes underneath me. "Does that hurt?"

"No."

Moving lower, I slip my tongue inside her, curling to find the right spot. Her legs relax in my hold, her back arches slightly, and her fingers weave through my hair.

Running a hand along her flat stomach, I palm her breast and pinch her nipple. Her hips flex in response, needy moans echoing in the room.

I withdraw, teasing her clit with my thumb. "Does that hurt?"

She bites her bottom lip and shakes her head, her glassy eyes begging for more.

I close my mouth over her pussy, sucking and licking, before inserting my middle finger into her wet heat. Fuck, she's tight, and my cock throbs with envy.

My gaze never leaves her face. Her pupils are blown, her lips parted as she takes quick, shallow breaths.

"Does that hurt, baby?" My voice is husky, thick with desire. It'd only take me about three pumps to come.

She swiftly shakes her head, and I add a second finger.

"What about now?"

"No," she whines so sweetly, rocking her hips. "*Please*, Jackson."

The way she pleads my name goes straight to my dick, precum leaking in my sweats.

I'm not about to refuse her, but there's one fact I need her to know. "I could pound you into the floor, and you'd love it. It should *never* hurt. You understand?"

She nods emphatically. I'll find out who he is, but it's the last thing I want to hear right now. I'd much rather listen to her lusty moans and whimpers.

"Come for me, babe." I double down, sucking and tonguing her clit while fucking her with curled fingers.

Her thighs quiver against my shoulders, and she grips my hair, keeping me where she wants me.

A cry of pleasure rips from her throat as she throws her head back in ecstasy. Her walls squeeze me tight, and then, to my utter shock and fucking awe, her pussy creams my fingers.

I lap it up like a starving man, not wanting to waste a single drop of her.

For as long as I live, I'll never forget the sensation of her cum dripping down my inner wrist.

Her body settles, and when I glance up, she's gaping at me with the same wonderment. A sense of urgency comes over me. I need her—every part of her.

I need to make her mine.

Our lips collide, and I tangle my fingers in her hair. She clings to me just as fiercely, our tongues intertwining and desperate moans resonating between us.

Maybe there is a god, because this girl is straight from Heaven.

Or maybe she's the devil sent to claim my soul.

Regardless, she consumed every part of me the instant I laid eyes on her.

And no matter where the rest of our story leads, she'll always be mine. I'll always be hers.

Our souls will always be one.

FOUR
AURORA

Two Years Later

THIS IS A MISTAKE.

I can't do this.

I have no choice. I *have* to do this.

To make matters worse, I'm late. Late to meet my first substantial client in nearly two years.

My clicking heels come to a halt on the sidewalk. There's no turning back now. There he is—leaning against an idling limo, arms crossed over his broad chest, giving off a vibe of annoyance as he drums his fingers on his bulging biceps.

Great.

And, of course, my date is gorgeous—in an older, unrefined, rugged kind of way. In an all-black suit with dark wavy hair, Ethan Blackwood oozes confidence, a demeanor that teeters on the edge of arrogance.

Why couldn't he be ugly? Ease my crushing self-doubt and insecurity for once?

He's tall, a handful of inches over six feet, and has the undeniable physique of a professional athlete, well-defined muscles stretching the fabric of his tailored suit. Since we're attending a charity gala hosted by LA's professional hockey team, the Huskies, I shouldn't be surprised by any of this.

I set myself up for this disaster.

His surly behavior is almost endearing, but I'm far too nervous, my bubbly mask struggling to stay affixed. Reentering the dating scene after a disastrous relationship has me walking on eggshells. Add the high likelihood of seeing my worst mistake at the gala tonight, and I'm wavering on the precipice of a panic attack.

I take a deep breath and urge myself to focus. I push aside thoughts of attractive older men, my tumultuous ex, and the shitty nursing home where my grandmother is currently confined.

I can do this. I've meticulously perfected each and every aspect of my appearance, all for tonight's purpose.

Dressing for revenge and killing this date.

The model image is simply a prerequisite for the job. It's all a front, a mirage, a fantasy I maintain to pay the bills. It takes all the money I earn to sustain the façade of a luxurious lifestyle while supporting the only family I have left—my grandmother.

That's what makes tonight imperative. For months, I've bounced from one shitty modeling gig to another, earning barely enough to buy groceries, nevertheless pay rent.

Escorting is my last hope.

Even with the negative stigma, the money is impossible to pass up, especially after the year I endured. Funeral expenses and medical bills are no joke. Don't get me started on the unfathomable cost of my grandmother's rehabilitative nursing home.

Their use of the word *rehabilitative* should be criminal—the place is a dump.

Despite the tightness in my chest, I'm fascinated by the man who stands before me. He's the stereotypical tall, dark, and handsome, but what captivates me most is the intensity in his stormy gray eyes.

Then, he speaks, and I'm even more enthralled.

"Shit. They weren't exaggerating when they said you were stunning." His voice is pure sex, deep and throaty.

Maybe a distraction is exactly what I need—a reckless and broody distraction.

No, don't even consider it.

He extends his hand to assist me into the limo, and my heart takes a dive at the brush of our fingers. His palms are rough and callused. He's more than a suit. He puts in work.

"Thank you." I flash him a flirty smile. "You must be Ethan."

We settle into the backseat, and I make a point of running my gaze over him, hoping my boldness flatters him and hides my nervousness. It's not entirely trumped-up. There's something about him I can't quite put my finger on.

A tempting danger lurks behind his eyes.

He hits me with a cocky smirk. "If I'm not, you're in trouble. Do you make a habit of getting into the back of limos with strange men?" He lifts a brow. It's playful, but there's a hint of disapproval in his words.

"I wouldn't call you a *strange* man." I cock a brow right back at him with enough sass to keep the banter going.

He winks, brushing a thumb over his bottom lip. "Debatable."

A giggle erupts from my chest then abruptly dies.

A wedding band. He's married.

I avert my gaze to hide my shock and disappointment, but it's too late.

He scowls, and the playful mood vanishes so fast, I wither along with it.

But damn, his brooding only amplifies his sexiness. His eyes are smoldering with dominance and a hint of threat.

Why does that not frighten me? Instead, it arouses me.

Bad thoughts.

I take a moment to remind myself I'm an escort. My clients serve as a means of financial support, not as romantic prospects. Ethan isn't my former client, who turned out to be long-term...and unhinged, but that's beside the point.

It has been a while, but I've played this game a handful of times with professional athletes, all of whom could've been married, unbeknownst to me.

But Ethan's blatant display of commitment—that's unfamiliar territory I can't ignore. Right?

I'm offering the Girlfriend Experience to a married man.

Maybe I've become too sensitive for this job since my breakup or bitter after my ex ghosted me when I needed him the most.

The silence in the back of the limo is deafening, and to someone with anxiety, uncomfortable silence is *itchy*. My skin burns from it, and my thoughts play tricks on me.

"Regarding the ring...am I pretending to be your wife tonight?" My tone is subdued, but no matter how hard I try, it doesn't hide my self-consciousness. "I must have missed that in the contract."

"You're a date," he says, engrossed in his phone. "Nothing more."

Ouch. His harshness has my heart rate skyrocketing and my stomach churning.

"Is she... Your wife... Is she dead?"

"Nope. She's very much alive." Not even a glance.

So much for the flirty banter.

The exciting atmosphere of only a few moments ago has soured. My mind is blown, and my doubts race toward dread with every second we get closer to the event.

How am I supposed to walk into this gala hanging from the arm of tall, dark, and dissatisfied with my infamous ex in the same room?

I need to set my emotions aside and salvage this date. It's literally my job and my only source of financial support. I've spent every dime I saved from my former client and can no longer live off my roommate.

I'm twenty-one. It's a gala, and I'm wearing a sexy black dress. This is supposed to be fun. Exciting. I can do this. I *have* to do this.

The limo comes to a halt, marking our arrival. The door swings open, and the bustling sounds of downtown LA shatter the silence.

My nervous excitement takes over.

Ethan steps out of the vehicle and offers his hand to assist me. His fingers envelop mine, and, to my shock, he doesn't release me. My heart stops, only to start up again ten times faster when our eyes meet, and I'm struck by the familiar vulnerability mirrored in his gaze.

I force myself to look away and move my feet.

Well-dressed hockey executives and players make their way on the red carpet, posing for photos with their dates. Some are known faces, although I hardly recognize them outside their uniform and gear.

One person I don't see is my ex, and a momentary sense of relief washes over me.

Then, I remember every player must attend the Children's Charity Gala, and my stomach plummets, along with my newfound courage.

Warm fingers tighten around mine, as if Ethan can read my anxious thoughts. I give him an appreciative smile, and he offers a reassuring wink.

Maybe tonight won't be a disaster.

FIVE
ETHAN

My agent insisted on booking me an escort, arguing it'd be a major *faux pas* to show up in LA without a glamorous woman on my arm. *Everyone does it*, he claimed. *West Coast girls are the hottest in the world.*

He has a flair for the dramatic.

Still, Aurora exceeded all my expectations. She's absolutely stunning.

We entered the event, and all eyes were on us, or I should say, on *her*. In a panic, I steered away from the crowd and directly to our designated table. Once again, she glanced at me with disappointment, her cheeks reddened, after I skipped all the photographers. I'm positive she believes I dislike her.

But no, I'm just a secretive asshole.

In our semi-private booth, waiting for the main course, I struggle to find the words to ease her mind. I haven't been on a date in years, not even with my supposed wife. It has been over six years since I had a meaningful conversation with an attractive woman.

I'm at a loss here, and I'm not accustomed to losing.

Too chickenshit to initiate anything, I sit here, stealing glances at my unbelievable date, while a few hockey players stop by to talk to her. To my surprise, she treats them with familiarity and kindness. She's polite and appropriate and laughs at all their stupid jokes yet doesn't offer them a hint of flirtation beyond her beautiful smile.

They regard me with distrust, and I wonder if I'm dating someone's sister—someone off-limits. But no sane man would allow a woman as alluring as Aurora, sister or not, to date another hockey player. There's no way.

Aurora is the embodiment of any man's desire. She's tall, reaching slightly above my shoulder with heels. Not too slender. Her body is a masterpiece wrapped in black satin that hugs her every curve.

Toned, mile-long legs are highlighted by strappy stilettos, and damn, that ass. Fine enough to convert a celibate priest.

Her tan skin is kissed by the sun. Her hair is a deep chocolate brown, styled in a high ponytail I've imagined wrapping around my fist more than once.

It doesn't help that I haven't had sex in...a long time. A year? Maybe two? Jesus.

I stare at her in a way that borders on creepy, admiring her pouty lips, which curve into a flirtatious smile, and her captivating whiskey eyes, which mirror my favorite drink and reveal all her emotions.

Beyond the physical, her anxious, submissive personality screams to my dominance. She's a rare concoction of mischief, sincerity, and vulnerability I find irresistible.

And she smells like a damn cookie—honey and vanilla. I could eat her right up.

Except she's out of my league and at least a decade younger.

I couldn't hold on to a girl even when I was a pro hockey player. My size. My overbearing attitude. My lack of give-a-fuck.

Not that I tried or gave any effort whatsoever.

I'm not typically drawn to high-maintenance women. They're too much work, offering little *fun* in return. Case in point: my narcissistic wife, who'd rather we didn't have any interaction unless it benefits her public appearance.

From the beginning, I should have known her interest in me was fake. The honeymoon phase ended as quickly as the honeymoon itself, and in retrospect, it was all deception.

Me trying to be someone I wasn't, her pretending to be faithful.

Maybe that's why I'm attracted to Aurora. She's authentic—even when it doesn't suit her.

Initially, I found her candidness irritating. She saw that wedding band, and it was over. Her demeanor changed so fast, it took the wind out of my sails. Her attempt to communicate without passing judgment was commendable, but the disapproval seeping through her tone was impossible to miss.

That irked me. Here I was, putting myself out there, flirting for the first time in years—with an escort, no less—only to be judged for not discarding my wedding band. Believe me, I've contemplated pulling this damned thing off and throwing it away with everything it represents countless times. I'll happily toss it over the Golden Gate Bridge as soon as I secure this coaching position and expose my wife's infidelity.

So, here I am, at a swanky, ten-thousand-dollar-per-plate charity event hosted by the hockey team I'm hoping to coach, gawking at a gorgeous woman who's disappointed to be my date—even though she's paid to pretend otherwise.

Thank fuck nobody here recognizes me. Nor are they aware I'm vying for the head coaching position besides the general manager.

They may not know me, but I'm all too familiar with them. I've made it my mission to learn about every single person involved with the organization—especially the player at the bar, who has caught Aurora's attention from across the room.

Jackson O'Reilly.

You don't have to know hockey to know Jackson O'Reilly. Everyone knows him. He's the team's star player, both on and off the ice. His stats are impressive, unparalleled, and he keeps a low-profile private life. He's a golden boy from a prominent family with no drama, negative publicity, or partying.

He only causes problems on the ice.

Given his restrained lifestyle, it's doubtful the hockey star would take an interest in an escort, despite her remarkable appearance.

So why does her interest in *him* stir up such a powerful wave of jealousy within *me*?

SIX
AURORA

"Don't gawk too long. I hear Jackson O'Reilly is in a committed relationship," says a deep voice close to my ear.

The bitterness in Ethan's words can't be missed, and it startles me from my trance.

Correction. Jackson *was* in a committed relationship. And I *wasn't* gawking. I wasn't.

I shake off the useless emotions and turn toward Ethan. While I was in la-la land, he positioned himself beside me in our private semicircle booth. Our knees are nearly touching. How did I not notice?

"Mr. Blackwood, are you speaking to me again?" I feign amazement, a playful, teasing tone woven into my words.

"The choice was between speaking to you or watching you stare at others while you pick at your food. And while you're quite pleasant to look at, the silence was growing rather tedious."

"My apologies for offending you earlier. I'm glad you're giving me a second chance at potentially offending you again."

We both chuckle, and I struggle to rein in my grin, hiding it with a sip of champagne.

His smirk is a sexy, enticing promise, stating he'll pound me into next week if I let him. Add gray eyes that light up with mirth, and he's dangerous to my libido.

"Now that we've gotten past the first-date awkwardness, why don't you tell me why you're not eating?" He nods toward my preposterously oversized wedge of lettuce and runs his fingers through his dark, wavy hair. "Do I make you uncomfortable?"

"What? No, it's an occupational hazard. I'm fine, honestly." If anything, it's me who makes *him* uncomfortable.

"Why did you order a salad if you didn't want it?"

No date has ever asked why I ordered a salad or why I'm not eating. He's observant and attentive, and I like it. A lot.

"I rarely eat while I'm out with clients. It ruins the whole hot-girl persona."

I'm rewarded with that smirk again. "Are you always this honest?"

Now, it's my turn to smile. "Are you always this difficult?"

He runs his thumb over his bottom lip. "Unfortunately, yes."

We stare at one another, an odd sense of familiarity between us, until he averts his gaze and clears his throat.

He pierces a chunk of steak with his fork, but instead of lifting it to his own mouth, he brings it to mine.

I furrow my brows in confusion.

"Eat." His tone is firm, those intense eyes fixed on mine.

Flustered, I concede, not wanting to disappoint him.

The steak is juicy and delectable, and an embarrassing moan slips free.

In my defense, I rarely get a decent meal.

Heat rushes to my face, and oh my goodness, dimples. He flashes a crooked grin, and a dimple pops on his left side.

Lord help me, I want to bite it.

I lick my lips clean, and his attention drops to my mouth.

"I take it you don't eat steak often."

"No." Meat? On my budget? Best to change the subject. "Honestly, I've never had anyone feed me."

He makes a thoughtful sound from the back of his throat, then cuts another piece of steak and holds it to my lips. I don't hesitate this time, and the satisfied gleam in his eyes does something to me.

I want to please him.

Outside of flirting, he tells me he's a former hockey player from the East Coast. I tell him I'm a serial dater with dreams of working in the fashion industry. He tells me I wear a dress well, and I tell him he wears a smirk well. He tells me he's in his thirties, which I knew from the agency, and I tell him I'm in my twenties. We match each other's banter word for word. He laughs at my attempts at being funny, and neither of us pushes the other for more information.

It's everything I need, and the world around us fades away.

He spends the rest of dinner sharing food from his plate. Feeding me seems to please him, and I enjoy pleasing him. We engage in easy, intimate conversation, and I find myself wishing he wasn't married and I wasn't on the rebound.

Who am I kidding? I'm an escort, and no man wants to date an escort.

Later, when I'm in bed, I'll allow myself to fantasize about a life where I'm free to date someone as attentive and engaging as Ethan Blackwood.

I'm about to decline another bite of chocolate mousse when a familiar, raspy voice seizes my attention. My heart pounds and my pulse skyrockets. Ethan and I turn in unison to find Jackson O'Reilly standing at the head of our table in a perfectly tailored designer suit.

Sandy-blond hair, brilliant green eyes, golden-tanned skin, and effortless sex appeal.

Unfortunately, the impressive outside doesn't match the chaotic inside. Reputation and public persona aside, Jackson is a mess.

I'm too conflicted with emotions to think. My anxious brain stalls out with a measly "Hi."

I haven't seen Jackson in over two months, and every impulse tells me to rush into his arms.

He's right there. Do it.

If I concentrate hard enough, I can sense the phantom weight of his body on mine, smell his heady cologne, hear his never-ending promises...

He was the best I ever had—perhaps the best I'll ever have—and a total dick.

"Hi." Jackson scans my body from head to toe then appraises Ethan, his expression hardening. "Jackson O'Reilly."

Ethan reclines and not-so-casually drapes an arm over the back of the booth behind me. "Ethan Blackwood." His tone is devoid of emotion, his aloof, annoyed vibe back in full force.

My face is on fire. I wouldn't protest if the ground cracked open and swallowed me whole.

Jackson clenches his jaw. "How's your grandmother, Aurora?"

My bruised heart beats violently against my rib cage, and I swallow the dry lump in my throat. "She's doing better, thank you."

I glance at Ethan, mortified at what he must think. He calmly sips his dark-amber liquor, his piercing gaze on Jackson. His protectiveness embraces me, loosening the tightness in my chest.

"Actually, can we talk?" Jackson glares in Ethan's direction. "*Alone.*"

I cringe at his sharp tone. "Jackson..." I have no idea how to refuse him. I want to, but I'm accustomed to appeasing him, and I'm scared he'll make a scene. "We can talk later."

Emotionally, I was prepared to see him from a distance. But this unexpected confrontation leaves me grappling for composure and consumed with unresolved feelings for him.

Waves of panic threaten to pull me under. I thought for sure he'd be over our relationship, even if I secretly wasn't. He was the one who ghosted me, taking a vacation after my grandfather died and my grandmother had a stroke.

And *now* he wants to talk?

Ethan scoffs. "It's fine. I'll head to the bar to give you two a minute."

Jackson sneers, his jealousy transparent. "You do that." He watches Ethan walk away then slides into the booth beside me.

I brace myself for the nightmare that's about to be unleashed.

He shoves Ethan's plate aside with disgust. "You're taking clients? You blow through all the money I gave you already?"

Yeah, on medical bills, a nursing home, and fucking rent.

I don't say that, though. I smell the alcohol on his breath—vodka tonic, double, no lemon.

My hands tremble, and my face heats with embarrassment. "You know I have to work. Please, don't do this here, Jax." My eyes plead with him, my words tinged with fear. "I can't take care of my grandmother without this job."

SEVEN
ETHAN

I LEAN against the bar and sip an Old Fashioned while keeping an eye on Aurora. I remind myself she's only in my life for one night. I have no right to be protective of her.

She responds to Jackson's barely veiled anger with nervousness and fear, and a nagging unease comes over me.

LA's hockey icon isn't the golden boy everyone believes.

The blonde beside me eyes me curiously, traces my gaze, and tosses her hair over her shoulder. "What the fuck is that asshole doing now?"

"Trying to figure that out myself. You know them?"

"You could say that." Her tone is sticky-sweet, and she appraises me as if I'm a piece of meat. *Puck bunny.*

"I'm guessing they used to date?" I take another swig of my drink, feigning nonchalance.

"Yup, and the manipulative man-child doesn't tolerate rejection."

A guy next to her bumps his shoulder into hers. "Hey, no talking about my captain. Those are the rules."

He's on the team, but without making it obvious, I'm

unsure who. I do, however, make a mental note of everything said.

"The rules don't apply when my roommate is involved."

"Your roommate is going to fuck up our season."

She scoffs. "Not my roommate's fault your captain can't stay sober. Have fun carrying him out of here tonight."

From a coaching perspective, there's a wealth of information to process regarding Jackson. It's not unusual for a player to struggle with substance use. I've seen it among my own teammates and players.

Still, Jackson's behavior is immature and unacceptable, bordering on abusive.

I was dead wrong to think Aurora was unworthy of his attention. He's the one who's undeserving of her.

And why doesn't anyone stop him? Has his conduct been swept under the rug because of his performance on the ice?

That's about to end.

Aurora tosses me an anxious, apologetic look. I've noticed she does that—sends glances my way to gauge my mood or seek approval. It makes sense if she's been dealing with an asshole with a drinking problem. Explains why she remains quiet when I'm not actively engaging with her. Why invite trouble? Her life has been unpredictable.

She's also naturally submissive—precisely my type.

Mr. Blackwood. Jesus, my dick twitched when she said that.

I leave my unfinished drink on the bar. With dinner concluded and plates being cleared to prepare for tonight's entertainment, people are milling about in the aisles. It makes it easy to blend in while eavesdropping on Jackson and Aurora's conversation.

"I meant it when I gave you the penthouse," he says. "You could come home. I'll pay for whatever you need."

Home. They lived together.

"I moved out after you didn't return my calls or texts for two weeks. My grandmother was in the hospital. You have no idea what I went through."

"I'm fucking sorry. I'd take it all back if I could, you know that."

His despair is painful to listen to. I nearly empathize with him.

"But you *can't*, and you haven't changed. Now please, Jax, leave me alone."

Aurora's pleading has my patience wearing thin. He's wasting his time begging for a second chance while he's tipsy.

"Why? So you can get paid to fuck someone else?" he snarls.

Typical immature bullshit. His desperation has turned to anger, and I've reached my limit. My dominant instincts take over, urging me to protect her from his toxic behavior.

I step out in front of them. "All right, Jackson, enough."

He squints. His reaction time is slow, and his eyes are glazed.

I reach out to Aurora. "Come here."

A sense of victory comes over me when she obeys, taking my offered hand and sliding out of the seat.

Jackson's left alone at the table. His jaw sets, and his nostrils flare. A shadow passes over his gaze, and I get another glimpse of the rage hiding inside the body of a hockey legend.

He emerges from the booth and towers over Aurora with aggression. She visibly trembles, and I encircle her waist with a protective arm. His dark glare fixates on me, and if looks could kill, I'd be slaughtered.

He's almost my height, but I'm bulkier. He doesn't stand a chance intoxicated. Maybe sober, he could hold his own, but not right now.

"Nice to meet you, *Ethan Blackwood*." His words are meant to sound threatening, but with his slightly slurred speech, it's anything but.

I gesture for Aurora to sit, and then I face him. "We'll see each other again, Jackson. I guarantee it."

He holds my stare. "I'm sure we will."

Without taking my eyes off him, I slide into the booth, and he storms off toward the bar, where a few players are gawking.

Aurora places her hands on her chest. "I'm sorry. I—"

Her voice cracks, and the instinct to care for her comes over me again.

"Don't apologize for him." A bucket of champagne and a pitcher of water now sit in the middle of our table, our dishes cleared away. I pour her a glass of water and set it in front of her. "Drink. Relax. I'm not upset with you, and I want tonight to last."

With a soft, "Thank you," she brings the glass to her kissable lips.

She's all I'd ever need in a woman. Sincere. Appreciative. Obedient. *Needy*.

The lights dim to signal the evening entertainment, and I draw Aurora closer, pulling her between my legs and wrapping my arms around her. "Just breathe. Okay?"

She settles into me, resting her head on my shoulder.

Our connection is palpable, blurring the lines between right and wrong. I want to protect and care for her. I've never wanted that with another person, but I know I want it with her.

Shit, that sounds crazy, but I'm inexplicably drawn to her. She fits perfectly with my jagged edges.

We wait for everyone to take their seats, and I tackle the elephant in the room. "You dated Jackson O'Reilly? That's impressive."

Eyes the color of whiskey gaze back at me. "It's impressive I survived, nothing more."

"How did you meet him?" I run my hands over her bare arms. Jesus, her skin is soft.

She leans into me and sighs. "At a season opener party. I was on a date with another player."

"And let me guess? He saw the most beautiful woman with someone else and had to have her?"

She snorts. "Pretty much."

"Then what? Something happened? He didn't get his way and took off?"

Her ribs expand with a big breath. "My grandfather died, and my grandmother had a stroke."

"Fuck. I'm sorry. That's awful." I tighten my arms around her, resisting the urge to kiss the top of her head. "He couldn't handle it, huh?"

"He couldn't handle not partying. He couldn't handle my sadness. He couldn't handle me getting a job to pay for a nursing home and medical bills."

He couldn't handle growing up.

I can't think of anything else to say except, "His last contract was thirty million, baby. He can afford a nursing home."

"He can...if I let him. But then I'd be trapped."

Her response blows me away. "Smart girl."

"He's not all bad. You just never know which Jackson

you're going to get. Might be the one who shuts down Santa Monica Pier for a date. Or it might be the one who punches a hole in the wall, only to spend all night placing hundreds of sticky notes on every surface saying he's sorry."

I don't miss how she still defends him.

"You're incredible and don't deserve to be treated that way." I give in to temptation and kiss her temple. "I caught my wife fucking a colleague in our home. I have no idea how long it's been going on."

She peers up at me in surprise, her wide eyes sparkling in the dim light.

I run a finger along the delicate curve of her neck. "I still wear the ring because I don't want her to suspect I'm leaving until I'm already gone."

Her brows raise. "Ah, your wife is certifiably insane."

She's sincere, not a hint of lip service. Maybe that's why I find myself opening up to her and foolishly longing to take things further.

I'll never have this chance, this night, again, and I refuse to waste it.

I glance down at her pouty lips. "You're fucking beautiful."

She kisses my neck in response, and my cock thickens, pressing hard against my zipper.

The first band takes the stage, and I can't stop touching her. I pray to everything holy that the darkness conceals us.

But when I scan the room, I catch Jackson's furious gaze, only fueling my dominant and competitive nature.

I smirk and jut my chin. Coaching that spoiled brat will be the most fun I've had in years.

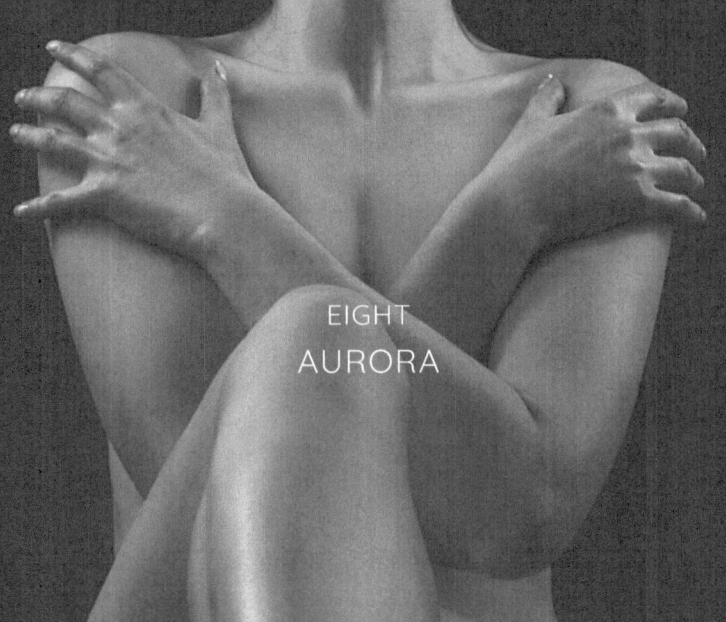

EIGHT
AURORA

The soulful sounds of the cover band fill the room, and I melt into Ethan's protective arms, almost forgetting this is a job. He stood up for me. No one besides my best friend, Emily, has ever defended me against LA's hockey icon. His teammates have all witnessed his emotional abuse, yet not once did they intervene.

It's nice to have someone to open up to. Apart from Emily, who can't stand Jackson, I have nobody to talk to. I used to be close with my grandmother, but she's in no condition to burden with my problems. Most days, the weight of the world is on my shoulders.

My ex hasn't changed. He's still a mess, still drinking. I never meant enough for him to quit or seek help. So why does he suddenly give a shit? Why tonight? Because he saw me with someone else?

I was nothing more than a shiny trophy to a hockey star struggling to hide his secrets. I'm supposed to be a shiny trophy for Ethan as his paid companion for the night. Yet, ironically, I feel a greater sense of care from him than I did from Jackson, at least after the first year.

If Jackson hasn't changed by now, he never will. It's over. It'll never happen again. I'll never let anyone walk all over me. I'll forge my own path, even if it means faking smiles for wealthy men.

Tonight, no faking is required.

"I wish I could kiss you. Then maybe your ex would stop staring." That deep voice sends a shiver down my spine.

I turn my head to find Ethan's face close to mine. The spotlight is on the band, but there's enough light to reveal his handsome features.

His eyes drop to my mouth, and he licks his bottom lip.

My mind goes straight to kissing him, and I can think of nothing else. "Why can't you?"

"Married, remember?"

Reality and disappointment wash over me. "Oh, right."

His muscular arms wrap around me, drawing me further into his chest. "I'm glad Jackson made you forget I was married, at least." There's no mistaking the bitterness in his tone.

"*He* didn't."

His brows furrow. "What did?"

"You." My eyes plead for him to kiss me. Anything.

"Me? Why me?"

He runs his fingers over my bare thigh, his touch the first I've had in months.

I take in Ethan's confused expression. His wife is foolish for letting him go. He's gorgeous—rough around the edges but gorgeous, no less.

My mind dives further into the gutter, and I wonder if that roughness extends to the bedroom. "You truly don't know? Is it wrong for me to tell you? Since I can't show you."

"Tell me or show me, as long as no one else sees." His voice drips with longing, his fingers trailing higher up my thigh.

"I find you incredibly attractive." My face heats. God, that was lame. I lean into the crook of his neck to whisper, and his masculine scent fuels my bravery. "Thinking about kissing you made me lose my thoughts."

I go to pull away, and his fingers wrap around my throat. His grip is possessive and claiming, letting me know he's in control. His hand is massive, nearly enveloping my entire neck.

"I'm pretty sure we're already crossing the line here, Blackwood."

"Hmm...fuck the line, then."

The song ends, and the room goes blissfully dark. Soft lips press to mine, and I suck in a sharp breath.

At first, the kiss is gentle and languid, but once our tongues intertwine, it becomes desperate and greedy. His fingers move to grip my jaw, and he deepens the kiss. He tastes of whiskey and cherries, bold and sweet.

He sinks his teeth into my bottom lip with a guttural groan, sending waves of pleasure through my body.

The next song begins, and the lights illuminate the room.

His eyes search mine, pupils blown with raw desire, his lips red and glistening. "Fuck, I've wanted to do that all night," he says, running his thumb over my cheekbone.

Darkness descends, everything fades away, and his hand on my thigh slides under my skirt. A surge of exhilaration courses through my veins, and my heart thunders. He inches closer to my wet lace panties, and a fiery ache ignites between my legs.

Without thought, my thighs part for him.

"You're not helping me resist you." His deep, gravelly voice is heady.

I weave my fingers through his thick hair. "I don't want you to resist me."

He traces the edge of my panties, teasingly slow. "You want this?"

I bite my bottom lip and nod, unable to speak, his touch alighting every nerve in my body.

He presses his thumb to my clit through the thin fabric. "Words, baby."

"Yes." I grind my ass against his bulging erection.

"Fuck." He slips inside my panties and runs a finger through my arousal. "You're soaked for me."

I release a needy whimper, and he abruptly withdraws, leaving me dumbfounded.

"We need to go, baby girl, before I fuck you right here, and I doubt your ex would appreciate that."

After adjusting himself, he fixes his clothes and bangs out a quick text. Then, I'm in his powerful arms, and he carries me out of our booth, setting me on my feet. He nearly drags me through the room, my five-inch heels clicking a rapid rhythm on the hardwood.

Ethan opens the back door before the chauffeur can even round the front of the limo, and I scramble inside.

He tells the driver to "take a long route," and the door closes behind him.

The privacy glass rises and the music turns up, drowning out the noise of the moving vehicle. It's a pop song, one of my favorites, but all my attention is on the formidable man before me.

After flinging his jacket, he guides me onto his lap, positioning me to straddle him. "Can I take this off?"

I nod, and he lifts my dress over my head with surprising tenderness for a man his size.

"Fuck, you're stunning." He pauses to admire my body, as if I'm the hottest thing he has ever seen. "Goddamn perfection. I want you so fucking bad." He flexes his hips to drive the point home.

Butterflies erupt in my stomach. I reach behind me and unsnap my bra, tossing it aside. My breasts aren't huge by any means. They're adequate for modeling, and no one has ever complained. But the way Ethan stares at me, you'd think I was a *Playboy* centerfold. I've never felt as confident or desired. And his size—he makes me feel tiny and safe.

He palms both breasts with his massive hands and takes my nipple into his mouth like he can't wait another second. He sucks and bites each one until I'm tugging at his hair and grinding against him.

"Ethan," I whimper. *Jesus, give it to me.*

He releases my nipple, grazing his teeth, and desire erupts low in my belly.

"Panties." His tone is commanding, leaving no room for hesitation.

I crouch, slip my panties off, and kick them free while he deals with his pants and puts on a condom.

There's something about sex with a man who's desperate and fully clothed, especially when he's wearing a suit.

Ethan grasps my hips, settling me onto his lap. I take his thick shaft in one hand and cup his nape with the other. I position myself over him and ease down his impressive length. Even though I'm wet from him teasing me, it's still a stretch, and we both groan at the pleasure of him filling me.

He clutches my ass and slams into me. "So fucking tight." My breasts bounce and draw his hungry gaze. He growls, actually growls, and does it again, plunging deeper. "Fuck, you take me so well."

I swear, he's rearranging my organs—in the best of ways. I grip his nape, nails digging into his skin, and bite my lip in an attempt to remain quiet.

He's incredible, every pleasurable inch of him.

Feral, intense eyes find mine. "I don't care if the entire city hears you. I wanna hear you scream for me."

To make sure I understand, he pinches my nipple—hard. My neck arches, and my head drops back. Whimpers become sharp cries when he angles his hips, reaching impossibly deep.

A stinging slap on my ass breaks me from the pleasure-pain haze.

"Ride me, baby." His voice is full of gravel and winded from the rough fuck he has been giving.

I place my hands on his thighs behind me and spread my knees wider, working his shaft. Callused palms caress from my waist to my breasts and back, eliciting a shiver down my spine.

His penetrating gaze fixates on our intertwined bodies, and he watches as his thick cock fucks and stretches my bare pussy. "You're too fucking hot." His fingertips press into my hips, taking claim and leaving his mark. "You feel like heaven and look like sin."

His words are maddening, and his touch drives me to the edge. His mouth and hands are everywhere, dominating and firm. He wraps my ponytail around his fist, biting my neck. Collarbone. Nipples.

Not letting me take control for long, he clutches my ass, rutting into me, harder and harder.

I'm drunk off him, a mindless fuck doll for this man, and I love every second.

"Ethan," I plead. "Don't stop. Please, don't stop."

He circles my clit with his thumb faster and faster. "You keep begging, and I won't last much longer."

My legs tremble, barely holding me up.

He shifts from passionately rough to *Dom*. He grips my neck and yanks me to his chest. His thrusts are deliberate, controlled, deep.

I fist his hair and ride out the storm, whimpering and moaning.

"Come on my cock, baby girl. Give it to me."

My eyes fall shut, and my forehead drops to his shoulder. He pounds relentlessly, and I explode around him, screaming in pleasure. My pussy clenches, and ecstasy shoots through my veins.

He hisses as he draws air through his teeth. "So fucking tight and wet." His arms encircle me possessively, and his thrusts become erratic. He slams into me one last time with a rumbling "Fuck!" and his thick cock jerks deep inside me, prolonging my orgasm.

I return to reality with his hand cupping the back of my head, his fingers intertwined in my hair and his lips on mine. Dominant, yet gentle.

NINE
ETHAN

So that happened.

And I can't find it in myself to regret it. Maybe that makes me a terrible person, but my marriage was dead years ago.

This isn't some revenge plot. I never expected this, nor did I plan to screw around while in LA.

Aurora is a once-in-a-lifetime opportunity.

The woman of all my desires rests on my chest, soft and affectionate, and a part of me wants this moment to last forever—although I know it can't.

I'm still trying to catch my breath and recover from the most incredible post-sex high I can remember. My mind is spinning, blown away by how beautifully she responds to me. Few women truly crave dominance the way she does.

My wife doesn't. She views my behavior as chauvinistic and abhors anything outside of vanilla sex. To put it bluntly, she lacks *any* enthusiasm for sex. At least with me. Who knows what shit she's into with the prick she fucks behind my back.

I can't deny I want to experience this with Aurora again, particularly the part where I'm inside her. She reignited a flame I extinguished long ago.

My thoughts stray to the different ways we could have fun together, and not only in the bedroom. It's not solely about sex—though that was fucking phenomenal. It's about being wanted and desired.

Needed.

I brush her cheek with the back of my knuckles. She's still flushed, her eyes half-lidded, her lips swollen and red.

My dick takes notice, ready for another round. "Where do we go from here, pretty girl?"

She stiffens in my arms before sitting up on my lap. "What do you mean?"

My greedy gaze lowers to her perfect tits, down to her tight stomach, and further to her smooth pussy. I twitch inside her. Yeah, I want more of this. Fuck, I wish I didn't have a meeting early in the morning.

I struggle to brush aside my lust-fueled thoughts and focus on the question at hand. Where do I go from here? Not returning to my estranged wife, that's for damn sure. But how do I tell a twenty-something-year-old escort I met merely hours ago that I want more?

She'll think I'm crazy.

I *am* crazy for thinking this.

"How does this work? To see you, do I schedule with your agency?" I pinch her nipple, and her walls squeeze around my already thickening length. "Fuck, you're unreal."

She whimpers, feminine and erotic. "Yes, you book through the website."

I can't stop from touching her, palming her breasts, grinding against her. I'm hooked. "Okay. And someday, will I have the opportunity to take you on a proper date?"

I don't mind covering the expenses or having my agent cover them. I know Aurora needs the money. But I also know I'll resent her being with other men. Ironic, considering I'm married…for now.

She's silent, perhaps thinking the same thing. Without uttering a word, she rises to her knees, releasing me from her warmth, and slips from my lap. She sits across from me and reaches for her thong, and I stare at her in confusion.

I rake my fingers through my hair. "What is happening? Am I overstepping? Do you only see me as a client?"

She doesn't answer me, snatches her dress off the floor, and drags it over her head. I clench my jaw. I hate being ignored.

Taking her lead, I go to fix my pants, and the sight of my exposed cock has me freezing in place. My heart stops dead, and the blood drains from my face.

Fuck. Fuck. Fuck.

She shakes her head but doesn't make eye contact. "That's not it. I recently ended a terrible relationship. I can't—"

Panicking, I interrupt her. "Please tell me you're on birth control."

Her eyes snap to mine. "What?"

I remove the condom. It's torn. Ice runs through my veins. The gravity of the situation slams into me harder than any hit in the NHL, harder than catching my wife with another man. I've never wanted kids. I *don't* want kids.

I shove the condom in my pocket and tuck my dick away. "The condom broke. Are you on birth control?" I demand, my voice full of fear and irritation.

The *last* fucking thing I need is for my wife to discover I knocked up an escort while I'm divorcing her.

Aurora lifts her chin. "Yes, I'm on birth control, and

before you ask, I got tested before I returned to the agency. I assure you, I'm clean."

"As did I, after I caught my wife cheating. But listen, you're a nice girl—"

She tilts her head back and laughs incredulously. "Ethan, stop." She glances at the map on her phone. Her expression is stern, her shoulders tense. "We're almost at my place. You don't owe me any explanation, and to be honest, I highly doubt we'll see each other again. Let's leave it at that."

"Why are *you* mad?" I throw my arms up in frustration. "I'm married!"

Her eyes, glassy with emotion, narrow into a sharp glare. "Are we back to that? If the ring on your finger wasn't obvious enough, you've made it *well* known on multiple occasions." The limo comes to a halt, and she shoves her bra into her purse. Rechecking her phone, she mutters, "Yet it didn't stop you from fucking me."

My palms burn with the urge to correct her bratty attitude. "You're an escort. Isn't that what you're paid to do?" My voice escalates in anger, driven by the irrational need to justify myself.

And great, now I'm no better than her ex.

She leans in, meeting my anger head-on. "You're right. I *am* an escort. Which you were aware of when you picked me up, married or not. What does that make you? A married man openly out with an escort, who, let me remind you, you asked out on a date. 'A proper date,' as you put it."

I'm stunned, speechless. The mouth on this fucking girl. And here I thought she was submissive.

Grasping the door handle, she pauses. "Just so you know, not all escorts fuck their clients. That's a personal choice made at their discretion. Maybe read your contract more thoroughly next time."

With that final nail in my coffin, she slams the door, leaving me astonished, ashamed, and surprisingly invigorated. I haven't felt this alive in years.

I throw my head back and burst into laughter.

TEN
AURORA

Emily sinks into the patio chair next to me. "Bad night?"

A knowing grin tugs at the corners of her mouth. She has watched this scene play out far too many times, not only with Jackson, but also with escorting.

Still in my feelings, I give her a sidelong glance.

"I saw Jackson with you." She rolls her eyes with exaggeration. "Be glad you left early. His face was spewing more shit than a sewer—talking about how you never broke up with him." She sticks her finger in her open mouth. "Gag. No one wants to be around that asshole when he's drunk."

Pain lances through my chest, and I make a noncommittal sound. I remind myself I'm no longer Jackson's keeper. He wasn't any better when I was with him anyhow.

"But your date was hot. Holy shit." She waggles her brows suggestively.

I've known Emily since middle school. We lived in the same shitty neighborhood in San Fernando Valley. I stayed home after graduation when she moved to LA to pursue something big. I watched with envy as she posted pictures from ritzy nightclubs with celebrities and professional athletes while I worked two waitressing jobs to get by.

She's the one who convinced me to try escorting when my grandparents were struggling. After I left Jackson and had nowhere else to go, she let me live with her. My grandfather had died, and my grandmother was transferred to a state-run facility. I lost everything, all within a month.

Not much has changed. When I returned home tonight, she was still with the hockey team, and I was alone. For obvious reasons, hanging with the guys is no longer my thing—it never was.

I quickly recognized that my envy of Emily was unwarranted. I don't enjoy partying. It's pointless, loud, overstimulating, and I'm...awkward.

I'm a nervous wreck wrapped up in a pretty package.

After I slammed the door on Ethan, I walked eight freaking blocks from our meeting spot to my condo in Redondo Beach. In the dark. In stilettos.

The second I stepped inside, I kicked off my heels, grabbed a bottle of wine, and headed straight to the balcony—my usual sanctuary. I love the ocean. The symphony of crashing waves lulls me into serenity.

The wine is an added bonus.

I'd drunk half the bottle by the time Emily got home, life and the night's frustrations clinging to me like stale, secondhand cigarette smoke.

"Let's see." I wave a hand dramatically and almost knock over the wine bottle on the table. "Between Jackson's public meltdown and my date's ceaseless worry over his *wife*, it's safe to say it wasn't a pleasant evening."

I dread the inevitable negative review Ethan will leave with the agency, and I don't blame him. I regret arguing with him, but something inside me panicked when he asked for a *proper* date. Reality hit me. This is my life. I have to work.

If there's one thing Jackson taught me, it's that there is no knight in shining armor in my story.

And Ethan had the audacity to circle back to the whole "I'm married" bullshit after the way we fucked? Seriously? What a fucking asshole.

Emily purses her lips. "You allow too much headspace for these guys. They're clients, nothing more. Smile, flirt, stroke their egos. Listen to them bitch about their 'oh so terrible wives,' and then collect your paycheck and move on to the next so we can afford this view." She gestures to the midnight sky over dark ocean waves. "Or hook up with one of the other players. Then we can go to dinners and after-parties together."

She puts on that Cheshire cat smile, excited about the prospect of us double-dating athletes we care nothing about.

Unfortunately for me, pretending and socializing is *exhausting*. And let's not forget the absolute nightmare Jackson would become if I dated another player. Could you imagine? It's laughable, not even worth contemplating.

"Em, my date had the nerve to ask me on a 'proper date' when all the while he's quaking in his boots at the thought of his wife catching us." I shake my head in disbelief. "You want me to give up my job before you give up your wife? Get the fuck out of here." Disgusted, I pick up the bottle and take a swig. "Maybe extinguish one fire before igniting another."

She breaks into a fit of laughter. "I swear, men don't think things through. Seriously, though, pass the wine. You have a photoshoot tomorrow. I hope you haven't overeaten."

I gasp. "Damn it! I forgot about the photoshoot!" Probably because they're a waste of time and lead nowhere.

"This is a major talent agency," she chides. "Invite only. It was pure luck I secured us a spot. This could be a new chapter. You wouldn't need to deal with these men anymore —unless you want to fuck around with sad, married dick?"

"Hell no." I wave my hands in front of me to fend off the mere idea. "Ethan was enough, thank you very much."

She stands and stretches her arms over her head. "Good. Chug some water and go to bed."

My heart swells with wine-laced gratitude. "Thanks, Em. I honestly don't know what I'd do without you."

"Thank me by landing this next contract and getting Grams out of that shitty nursing home."

With renewed purpose, I set down the almost empty wine bottle and forget all about Mr. Big Dick Married Guy.

TOMORROW ARRIVES, AND MY COURAGE IS NOWHERE TO be found. I'm nauseated with anxiety and have thrown up twice.

My eyes are adorned with dark, heavy bags, and my stomach is bloated from yesterday's indulgences. Not ideal, considering this is a bikini shoot on the beach with one of the most well-connected photogs in LA.

I shouldn't have devoured that steak...and dessert...and that bottle of wine. Jesus, what was I thinking?

To add to my anxiety, I'm surrounded by slender, flawless blondes. It's intimidating. They strut around with their carefree confidence, and I'm over here spiraling with self-doubt and insecurities. Can we go home now?

"I'll be lucky to land this, Em." My voice trembles with nerves, right along with my fingers.

She drops her magical makeup brush. "Luck favors the

persistent. We've worked hard for this. It's not about luck. Talent and dedication always win."

What talent? What dedication? The only dedication I have is repeatedly showing up at gigs and auditions without a single callback.

She adjusts the coverup under my eyes, tossing me a reassuring smile. "We're going for a natural appeal, because who wears heavy makeup on the beach, right? Your beauty will captivate the camera, I promise."

"Em, I'm not a skinny blonde. You're more likely to be chosen than me. Maybe you should go out there instead."

"Aurora, stop whining. Your unique qualities make you stand out. The industry is evolving, and a diverse representation of beauty is celebrated more than ever. Clients seek models who represent different perspectives and styles. Don't underestimate yourself."

I give her a blank expression. "Did you practice that script?"

She sighs and hands me a mirror.

One thing about Emily: she possesses a silver tongue. She's cunning and charismatic, chewing up wealthy men and spitting them out as if they're nothing but flavorless bubble gum. With her smile, she could beguile the Pope and have him on his knees, worshiping at her feet.

Every introvert needs an extrovert friend, and she's mine. As much as I hate it sometimes, I'd never leave the house if it wasn't for her.

I study my reflection in the mirror. Sharp cheekbones, full, strawberry-pink lips, and dark-lined eyes create a seductive allure.

"Damn, Em. Thank you."

She gives me a proud smile that matches my own. "See? Now get out there and kick ass."

I take a deep breath and exhale my insecurities and self-doubt. My name is called, and my body takes control from the anxious girl hiding inside.

With feigned confidence, I step in front of the camera and turn on the charm. I sink to my knees in the wet sand, spread my thighs, arch my back, and gather my hair above my head. The icy water washes over my bare legs, and my nipples pebble.

It's a rush, a shock to the system, and exhilarating.

Shot after shot, I smile and roll around in the sand and salty ocean. I imagine myself as a sexed-up temptress, seducing a morally gray bad boy I want to fuck me on the beach, spank my ass, and pull my hair.

I lay on my back, rest my arms above my head, and gaze at the camera with lust-filled eyes. Ethan's face flashes in my mind, an image of the first time he saw me naked. Those intense, stormy eyes, his dirty words, dominant thrusts, and satisfied moans fill my naughty thoughts.

The cameraman moves in, directing me through various poses: arch your neck, tilt your chin, bite your lip, hook your thumbs in your bikini bottoms—each pose becoming more and more erotic. We draw a crowd, and for the first time, I feel empowered.

When we finish, the air is chilly. Goosebumps prickle along my body, and my nipples are hard as diamonds. I'm covered in wet sand, my bikini soaked and transparent, and my hair is a messy tangle of dark waves clinging to my damp skin. My shaky legs struggle to support me to the dressing tent.

"That was absolutely amazing!" Emily bounces up and down with excitement. "You were so sexy. Did you see the cameraman? I swear, he had a boner."

ELEVEN
ETHAN

"I WANNA BE upfront to prevent any surprises when I come to coach." I direct my attention to the league's fastest skater, who's moving like a flash of lightning across the ice. "That's your problem right there."

All eyes go to Jackson, and the room falls silent. Management fidgets in their seats and exchange uneasy glances. It's expected. No organization wants to face criticism of their highest-paid player.

I step to the glass surrounding the owner's box and reiterate my point. "Jackson is not the entire team." I gesture to the other players. "To build a successful *team*, we need to grow and incorporate the talents of every player, not rely solely on one individual."

Now it's my turn to sweat and shift nervously on my feet. I await management's response, anticipating some acknowledgment or understanding, but nothing comes.

I'm right about this. I know I am. Jackson's selfish and arrogant behavior toward Aurora prompted me to dive into his career highlights. He treats his teammates similarly. He possesses God-given talent but lacks leadership and respect for others.

Adjusting my suit jacket, I take a slow, deep breath to calm my racing heart. "Jackson is gifted. His abilities are exceptional. But, unfortunately, the team is not. My job as a head coach is to develop a strategy for winning and execute change, no matter how difficult it may be. *That*," I emphasize by pointing at Aurora's ex, "doesn't scare me."

And if the coaching and training staff have ignored Jackson's issues with alcohol, they'll be replaced. I won't allow that on my team, and I'm not afraid to get my hands dirty.

The interview ends, and disappointment hangs heavy in the air. No handshakes, no excitement, only a collective effort to evade eye contact while scrambling from the room with their heads bowed.

Fuck, I can't return to Boston. My wife is the owner's daughter, and the man she's cheating on me with is the general manager.

Everyone knew of their affair—except for me.

An uncomfortable silence marks the elevator ride. I can only hope they're reflecting on my suggestions. On the ground floor, I part ways with all but Robert, the owner.

While texting, he massages the back of his neck. "Let's... uh...Let's go watch practice."

Shit, this doesn't appear promising. I consider other teams in need of a head coach. There's Colorado. It's not as warm as LA, but it's far from Boston. I'll always be welcomed back to New York, where I played for a decade, but no way in hell am I staying that close to my soon-to-be ex. And I left New York for a reason.

Behind the bench, I watch as Jackson takes shot after shot at the goalie, making most of them. He's one of the league's leading breakaway artists, but if he passed the puck, the missed shots might lead to goals. He also fights with his teammates who play defense against him. But I say nothing.

After practice ends and the team gathers around, Robert clears his throat. "Why don't we, ah, introduce you?"

"Yeah?" I ask, taken aback.

"Yeah." A smile plays at the corners of his lips. "Let's do this."

A wave of relief and excitement washes over me, tingling every nerve ending in my body. Adrenaline courses through my veins, and I can't stop smiling.

Only one 6'3" hurdle to get over.

I'm shaking hands with the assistant coach when a helmet thrown against the boards narrowly misses me.

"No fucking way!" Jackson snarls, dropping his gloves to the ice.

If it's a fight he's preparing for, he's not getting one from me. Not on the first day, at least.

The goalie, Killian Rathe, and right-winger Grant Cohen, who stopped by our table to talk to Aurora at dinner, try to calm him. I can't hear their words, but he pushes them away, unable to control his anger. Yet another instance illustrating his lack of leadership.

He's more of a cancerous distraction—a toxic little shit who needs to be disciplined.

I give him a courteous nod. "Jackson. It's nice to see you again."

He sneers and mutters, "Fuck you."

I move on to the next player, not allowing his tantrum to divert attention from the team. He can take a seat on the bench, where he'll be staying if he keeps being a dick.

"Killian, that shutout against Cincinnati was fantastic." I slap the goalie on the helmet and receive a hesitant smile.

"Connor, I missed coaching you at the Special Olympics this year."

A few snickers resonate among the guys. Connor and I met through volunteer work with the Special Olympics program. He wasn't on the team, of course, but we had a lot of fun.

I go down the line, establishing a connection with each player. When it's all said and done, I step out of the arena, and the weight off my chest is tangible. I'm almost free. My plans are coming to fruition, and one person comes to mind.

Aurora.

Despite how things ended, something compels me to share this with her.

I let out an exhale, taking in the LA sun. I can't fucking believe it. I'm getting out of Boston.

And maybe, just maybe, I can see Aurora again.

I'm walking into my hotel room when my phone buzzes with an incoming call from my agent. "Hey, man. Please tell me you have positive news."

Trent's hearty chuckle eases my tension. "You're a rock star! I wasn't sure you could pull it off, but boy, did you ever."

That brings a smile to my face. "Fuck yeah! That good, huh?"

"Good? It's fucking great! Better than great. How does a three-year contract at a guaranteed five million yearly sound?"

His words leave me speechless. My heart flutters, and I can barely string two words together. "Five million?" The shock overwhelms me, and I drop my ass onto the bed. "Per year?"

That's five times my current salary, confirming my suspicions. Not only am I underpaid, but the Huskies were aware of Jackson's issues and needed someone with the balls to manage him.

"Per year. Per fucking year!"

I chuckle at his exuberance. "When do I sign?"

"How about tomorrow? At the arena."

"Perfect, because it's not real until my signature is on that contract."

Trent and I exchange goodbyes, and I text my lawyer, authorizing her to initiate the divorce proceedings. With a new coaching position secured and divorce preparations underway, I only need to find a place to live, pack my belongings, and leave.

Sounds simple—until I have to face my wife.

I sit on the bed, and the silence of the empty room falls upon me—a mirror image of my life. My mother is dead, and my so-called father is in prison. I have no siblings. I am utterly alone. There's no one else to call, no one else to share in the celebration of this moment.

Hockey is my life. I grew up on the streets of New York City—hockey was my only friend, family, and dream. Once I made it, I threw myself into the lifestyle, partying and playing without making a single genuine connection.

Until a dirty hit ended it all.

The fear of being unemployed and alone propelled me into a hasty marriage. I was naïve in believing I had struck the perfect deal—a wealthy wife, a team, and an organization all in one. But it was a façade.

Behind the veneer, I discovered a spoiled, shallow woman who only married me to satisfy her hockey-enthusiast daddy. The man she wants, the man she has been cheating with, is already married. I think she wanted a husband who was willing to ignore her infidelities, but that wasn't me, no matter how hard I tried.

For years, I allowed her perspective to shape my self-worth. I saw myself through her eyes—a nobody from the streets, a washed-up hockey player who became one of the league's lowest-paid coaches. I didn't fit into her Country Club social circles and couldn't care less about upholding a fake marriage. All I did was work.

I was miserable until about twenty-four hours ago.

And now, I'm Aurora's ex's head coach, and he's the star player on my team.

It can't happen.

Technically, I'm not the head coach *yet*.

And I have one more night in LA.

I drag my hand down my face. Jesus, what am I thinking?

I'm thinking about how good she felt in my arms, how eagerly she responded to me, how fucking hot she is.

These things don't happen to me—*will never* happen to me again.

She didn't ask for details about my marriage. She didn't dig into my career, social status, or other identifying factors. She simply enjoyed my company.

I realize that's what she's paid to do. I'm not a complete idiot. Maybe desperate, but not an idiot.

Either way, she won't figure out who I am. After last night, she'll never have anything to do with her ex again. It's not as if she'll be attending his games.

Nobody will know. Right?

I grab two whiskey splits from the minibar and down them, one after the other. Then, setting aside my pride, I text Trent for information on booking Aurora.

He promptly sends me the website and login credentials, accompanied by a smiling purple devil emoji.

After consuming another mini bottle to ease my apprehension, I log in to his account, only to discover she's unavailable for the next month. A fucking month? Is she that popular?

I don't want anyone but her, escort or otherwise. Dejected and bone-crushingly lonely, I end the night tipsy, alone, and angrily jerking myself to fantasies of Aurora riding my cock.

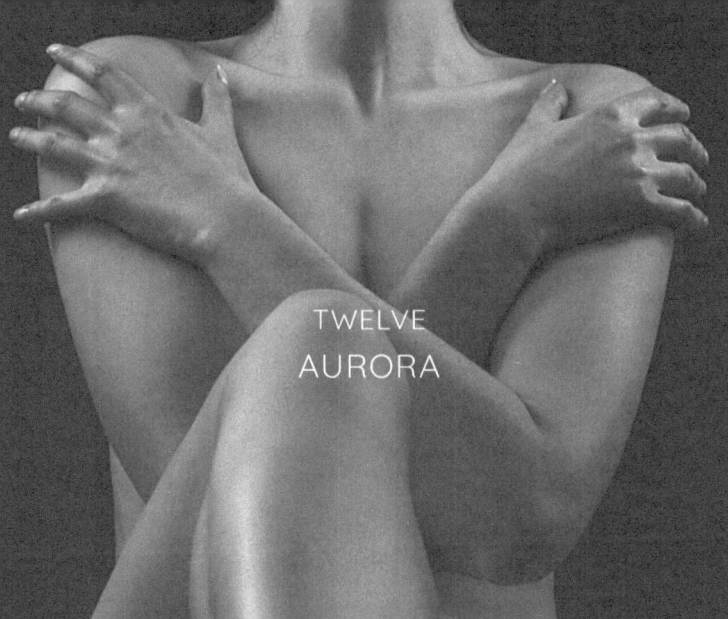

TWELVE
AURORA

The months following the bikini photoshoot are a whirlwind. Not only did I secure a contract for the swimsuit layout, but I also landed an exclusive modeling deal with Worldwide Enterprises, one of *the* top modeling agencies. Even now, I still can't believe it.

Since the morning after the beach shoot, Emily and I have been jet-setting. I've been featured in everything from lingerie to designer clothing. We've been to a different city nearly every week.

Yet, amidst all the success, the first shoot stands as my crowning achievement.

I'm now, and will forever be, a swimsuit cover model—all thanks to one playful photoshoot.

Emily has become my full-time makeup artist, assistant, and closest companion. She's nothing short of irreplaceable. I can't fathom navigating this chaotic journey without her. She's my buffer in social situations and does all the networking, which I loathe.

My dream of providing Grams with the care she deserves came true. She was moved from the state nursing home to a legitimate rehabilitative and assisted living facility in Santa Monica. Her improvement is remarkable. She went from being a zombie to walking short distances and regaining her speech.

And, of course, we're no longer escorting. Or, in Emily's case, dating athletes with the hopes of becoming a wife. Our hectic schedule rarely allows the opportunity to return home, let alone revisit that chapter of our lives.

For the first time in months, we're about to settle down. It's fashion season in New York City, and I'm working with several designers to see who fits before gracing the runway. I love this part—putting all the pieces together and showcasing the finished product. It requires long days and hard work, but in the end, it'll be worth the half-a-million-dollar paycheck.

And I thought escorting paid big.

I yawn, flipping through channels on the flatscreen in our hotel suite. "Where are we headed tomorrow?"

"You've been doing that a lot, forgetting your schedule. Maybe you need to take some time off before you burn out."

I glance over at Emily, her signature stern expression in place. "Doing what?" I set the remote down, too tired to scroll.

"I just said! You keep forgetting what shoots you have coming up. You're always yawning, always tired. I thought you were going to doze off during the shoot yesterday." She crosses her arms and flops back in the leather chair.

"Okay, that photog was slower than a sloth and playing jazz music. Besides, we have to seize every opportunity that comes our way before it disappears." I gesture to our opulent hotel suite provided by the modeling agency, along with our food, driver, and security, not to mention all the clothes.

I fear that, at any moment, someone else could rise to become the new "it girl," and I'll be left in the dust. I'll work my ass off for as long as the offers keep pouring in.

"Not getting enough rest won't maintain your beauty or energy." She purses her perfectly lined lips and raises her brows without a single wrinkle on her forehead.

I love Emily. She's exceptional at what she does, but I often wonder if she resents our new life. I'm too drained to party, and she's always on-point, ready to go clubbing or meet some hot guy who'll sweep her off her feet. When my day ends, I'm too exhausted to do anything except check in on Grams. I pay her forty percent of what I make after paying my agent, which is perhaps the only reason she hasn't returned home.

When I say nothing, she continues. "And your anxiety has gotten worse. You're always sick and not eating. You've lost weight—more than you should."

"Can you blame me? I'm constantly in the spotlight. But, honestly, it's not my anxiety. I'm not anxious." At least, not any more than usual.

"Then what is it? Because you can't keep going like this. Starving yourself, throwing up, sleeping all the time... It's unhealthy."

Giving up the fight, I collapse into the plush couch cushions. Perhaps she's right, and I need a break. "I'm exhausted. That's all."

She leans forward, places her elbows on her knees, and regards me for several long seconds.

I release a deep sigh. "What is it, Em? You want to go home? You miss the guys?"

She never talks about any of them except Jackson. He has become a daily presence in our lives—on social media, where he leaves outlandish comments on my modeling pics.

With dramatic flair, she rolls her eyes. "No, I don't miss them. Why would I? I'm still dealing with your stalker ex."

I've blocked him on everything personal, but my agent isn't comfortable blocking the hockey star on my public accounts. She says his thirsty comments bring me notoriety.

"And I don't want to go home—far from it." She throws her hands up in exasperation. "I want you to care for yourself before you burn out."

"Seriously, I'm fine." Another yawn.

She shakes her head in frustration and stands. "Don't stay up late. You have an early meeting and then a shoot in the fashion district."

Stay up late? I'm already falling asleep.

"Aurora. Aurora. *Aurora*." Emily raises her voice and nudges my shoulder.

"Hmm?" Didn't she say I needed rest? Why is she waking me?

"It's seven in the morning. You need to get up!"

The blanket is ripped from my body, and I bolt upright. I'm ready to ask her why I slept on the couch for nearly *fifteen freaking hours* when a wave of nausea hits me. I rush to the bathroom and fall to my knees in front of the toilet, expelling everything I've eaten in days.

Once my stomach has settled, I rise on shaky legs. I hate throwing up, but unfortunately, it happens with my anxiety, along with panic attacks and, on rare occasions, fainting. Or what I call, *taking a nap from reality*.

I step out of the bathroom, and Emily is there, arms crossed over her chest, eyes glaring.

"This is the fourth day you've been sick."

"I know. I know. I'll see someone. Honestly, though, I'm only sick—" *In the morning.*

We stare at each other, my mouth hanging open and her jaw clenched.

Exhaustion, forgetfulness, nausea. *Ethan. The broken condom.*

Wait. I was on birth control...but was encouraged to stop when I started modeling...and I was throwing up from anxiety before the beach shoot. Did I even take it that night?

No. No. No. No. This isn't happening.

I think back to my last period, struggling to recall the dates. I fail to remember, and terror sets in. I clutch my chest, unable to draw air into my lungs.

"How long?" she asks, reading my mind.

I can't focus, only shake my head. I can't be pregnant. I *can't*. It'll ruin everything.

"I'll get a test."

I skip the panic attack and go straight to dissociating. I'm staring at the pasty-white bathroom wall, absently holding the positive test, when Emily enters.

She lowers herself and sits beside me. "I know you're in shock. I know you think it's the worst thing ever, but it's not. You have options. You also have a meeting with the agency in less than an hour and a shoot right after. We have plenty of time to worry about this later."

No. We don't. We don't have any time for *this*.

I rest my head against the wall. I'm so fucking tired, tired of having the weight of the world on my shoulders.

A tear rolls down my cheek, and I shut my eyes.

"That's it. That's all you get to cry." Her voice softens, and she wraps her arms around me. "We can cry all you want later, okay? I'll even buy you ice cream."

Somehow, I pick myself up from the floor and arrive at

the meeting on time. Felicity, my agent, details my upcoming schedule, and I'm numb. Lifeless.

Over the next few months, I have obligations in New York, Miami, and Houston. On the bright side, I have a week-long respite in LA, during which I can plan for the future and break the news to Grams.

"Earth to Aurora. Did you hear me?"

I raise my head to find Felicity staring at me. "Yeah, sorry. New York, Miami, Houston. Got it."

Her brows pinch. "What's wrong? You don't seem happy. At our last meeting, you were ecstatic about your busy schedule."

Before I can answer, Emily speaks up. "She's exhausted. Perhaps we should scale back a bit. Give her some time to rest?"

My agent gazes at me, and I sense her disappointment. Believe me, I'm just as disappointed, if not devastated.

"I'll hold off on booking you anything additional unless it's something we can't afford to refuse. I'll also send you to La Mar Resort and Spa on Laguna Beach. They'll pamper you, and I'll foot the bill."

"Thank you," I mumble. Pampering won't solve this problem.

On our way to the afternoon shoot, Emily and I sit in the backseat in silence. I don't know what to say. I've screwed up everything—for both of us. For Grams.

She reaches across the seat and takes my hand. "Do you know how far along you might be?"

I shrug. "Google says about nine weeks, based on my last period. Seems accurate."

Her following words are hesitant. "Are you leaning toward keeping the baby? I'll support you no matter what decision you make. But it's going to be hard."

I swallow the lump in my throat. "I'm keeping it, Em. I'll manage. I always do." My voice cracks, and I hold back the tears. I refuse to cry. Having a baby isn't supposed to be sad.

She gives my hand a reassuring squeeze. "We'll make it work. You won't show for another month or more. We'll find a doctor to help balance your schedule and pregnancy. Models get pregnant, and it's not always the end of their career."

Then why does it feel like the end?

"Thank you, Em. I mean it when I say I couldn't do this without you."

Her eyes sparkle, and she smiles. "Babes, we've been through it all together. Remember when we'd hide in the tires on the playground and plan our escape? We'd talk about how we'd make it big?"

A light chuckle escapes my lips. "I'd become a famous singer, and you'd be a top model."

"Even though you have the voice of a tone-deaf donkey, and I haven't grown since middle school."

We both share a heartfelt laugh that briefly lifts the storm cloud hanging over our heads. The air is lighter, and a glimmer of hope sparks.

Until Emily poses a question that churns my stomach.

"When are you telling Jackson? He's going to lose his shit."

I take a deep breath, summoning my strength. "It's not his."

Confusion wrestles across her face, lines furrowing her brow.

"Jackson and I were fighting before he left. We hadn't had sex in over a week, and then he was gone for another two. It's been months. It's not his."

Her eyes grow wide. "The photographer?"

My nose scrunches up. "No, definitely not the photographer." I went on one date in LA with the photog of the bikini shoot, and I couldn't leave fast enough. He talked about himself the entire time and was rude to the waitress. Repulsive. "I know who the father is, and he's not interested in having a child, at least not with me."

She scoffs. "It doesn't matter what he's interested in. He was involved in conceiving this baby and should take responsibility."

"He's married. He claimed to be getting a divorce, but his actions spoke otherwise. I won't tear apart someone's marriage for financial gain, and that's all it'd be."

"Oh, babes. You have to tell him, at least for the financial support. If he's married, he'll pass along some hush money."

I'll never tell her who the baby's father is. She'll hound me about him and might also tell the guys, who'll tell Jackson. I don't need that chaos.

I raise a hand, my decision firm. "I'm unwilling to subject my child to the turmoil of a tug-of-war between parents living separate lives."

And I'm not losing my child to some wealthy couple on the East Coast.

THIRTEEN
ETHAN

THE PAST MONTHS have been an emotional roller coaster, with incredible highs and devastating lows. My departure left my players shocked and confused, and the guilt almost made me reconsider my decision.

Almost.

I had to do what was best for me. My dedication to the sport finally paid off, and I was thrilled to go to LA.

Dealing with my ex-wife was as miserable as expected—a painful reminder of the magnitude of her manipulation and mental warfare. Despite my efforts to part amicably, she made my life hell to the very end.

Moving out was the absolute worst. I packed my belongings as she relentlessly ran her mouth, belittling me and asserting I was nothing without her, that I only had a coaching position because of her. She threatened if I left her, I'd never coach professionally again.

The joke's on her.

When confronted about the affair, she blamed me. She justified her actions by telling me how horrible I was in bed and how I couldn't satisfy her. According to her, I'm a sexual deviant. A *sadist*—which couldn't be further from the truth.

Still, part of me took her words to heart. There was some accuracy in them. We weren't compatible. Her satisfaction requires a man to feed her ego, which wasn't me. I couldn't give her what I wasn't feeling.

Another part of me wanted to retaliate by bragging about how hard Aurora came on my cock, but I kept my mouth shut, knowing it'd jeopardize the divorce.

It was my ex who retaliated, wasting more of my time and money by forcing me to remain in Boston while she contested the divorce. She pulled out all the tricks in the narcissistic handbook. She brought her father to the hearing to embarrass me, cried during negotiations to gain sympathy, and lied through her teeth, claiming I abandoned her while she was off fucking someone else.

She denied, denied, denied until I presented images of her screwing the general manager in our house while I was traveling. She rather underestimated my ability to use the security system or assumed I'd always be under her control. Or she didn't care. Regardless, she finalized the divorce in a day. We both left with what we had. I wanted nothing more.

Now, I'm free from her grip and ready to start my new life in LA. With only a month before the hockey season begins, I'm a bundle of nervous excitement. I hardly slept last night and arrived at the airport hours before I needed to. I couldn't wait to leave Boston.

Eager to pass the time, I stroll around. I can't sit still. I'm too anxious to eat, and bars don't appeal to me.

When nothing interests me, I decide to head to the VIP lounge with a book. I need an escape. I browse through the bookstore, choose a bestseller, and then go to pay.

A familiar face captures my attention, and I come to a halt. I do a double, then a triple-take, my mind struggling to process what I'm seeing.

"Holy. Fuck."

The book slips from my grasp and falls to the floor. With clammy hands, I reach out and grab the *Sports Illustrated Swimsuit* edition.

On the cover is the hottest, most seductive woman I've ever seen, one I've also had the pleasure of having wrapped around my dick.

I gawk at a nearly naked Aurora on the beach under the headline, "White Hot: Special Collector's Edition."

Aurora, the girl on my mind, graces the cover of the *Sports Illustrated Swimsuit* issue.

Her luscious tits are on full display in a soaked and see-through bikini, her nipples pebbled. She's on her knees in the sand with her legs spread, pulling down the sides of her bikini and exposing the top of her bare, smooth mound. Her long, dark hair is wet and messy, as if she was fucked on the beach, and my cock thickens.

The most captivating feature, however, is her lust-filled eyes. They gaze right at me, penetrating my soul. I can't believe I hooked up with this girl in the back of a limo, and it was phenomenal.

Escort Aurora was gorgeous, but swimsuit cover model Aurora is mind-blowingly erotic—like I-wouldn't-mind-blowing-a-load-on-this-cover erotic.

I've been inside this woman, listened to her moan my name and whimper as she came.

No fucking way.

I flip through and find her bio, learning she's twenty-two. Her birthday is August 23rd, meaning she was twenty-one when we slept together. I'm woozy. I knew she was young, but not *that* young. Jesus, this keeps getting worse—or better, depending on your perspective.

I'm drooling over her centerfold when a man browsing the magazine section fixates on Aurora's enticing figure. Possessiveness takes me, and I grab the stack of magazines, preventing him from having one. I glare at him, and in return, he side-eyes me as if I'm deranged.

And maybe I am, because I feel ownership over a cover model who rejected me.

Boy, did I fuck up with her. Or maybe I could've fucked up even better?

Now I'm regretting *not* getting an escort pregnant.

I *am* deranged.

I WANT TO THINK MY TIME WITH AURORA IS WORTHY of bragging rights, but unfortunately, I have no one to brag to except Jackson. With him, it'd be unprofessional to say anything, at least where others could hear.

Although he makes it extremely difficult not to throw it in his smug face.

It's my first day, and of course, I can't resist the temptation when I enter the locker room and see Jackson's cubby proudly showcasing Aurora's magazine photos. One, which I don't have, is a centerfold of her in a transparent crop top, with her back arched to highlight her beautiful breasts and peaked nipples, and unbuttoned Daisy Dukes.

Jesus, she's a wet dream.

"Do you typically display pictures of the women who dump you, O'Reilly?" I ask, my voice tinged with amusement and maybe slight bitterness over him having a photo I lack.

Silence permeates the locker room, and all eyes turn to us.

His face contorts with anger, his muscles tense. "What the fuck did you say?"

I hold my ground, a self-satisfied smile curving my lips. "You heard me." I tilt my chin toward the collage of swimsuit and lingerie pics. "Does that shrine remind you she dumped you?"

He smirks. "I'm displaying pictures of my future wife. Jealous, *Coach*?"

I swell with possessiveness that grows stronger and stronger every time I reminisce about my encounter with Aurora. "Not at all. Why would I be? Those pictures are as close as you'll ever get to her."

We stare at each other, neither one of us backing down.

The door to the locker room opens, and everyone's attention is diverted to an older man who strides in with all the confidence of someone who owns the place.

Though I know he doesn't.

Jackson's attitude shifts. His shoulders become rigid, and a grimace crosses his face. He turns his focus to his cubby and rifles through his bag, seemingly preoccupied.

The other players follow suit, engaging in similar behavior to distance themselves from our unexpected visitor. Their discomfort is palpable, and as a coach, it's my responsibility to ensure a positive and safe environment.

I know that sounds hypocritical after I was goading Jackson, but so be it.

"Can I help you?" I interpose between the man and my captain, who he's walking straight toward.

"I'm here for my son." He disregards my presence, not even acknowledging me.

Fuck that. This is *my* locker room. "Sorry, but family

members are not allowed in the locker room. It's strictly reserved for players and coaches."

His eyes connect with mine, and he raises a condescending brow. "Coach Blackwood, I presume. I'm Police Commissioner O'Reilly. I've always had access to the locker room. Ask anyone." A fake smile spreads across his face, and he gestures around the room.

"I don't need to ask because it stops now. I need the team's full attention. I'm sure you can understand." I match his condescending attitude, crossing my arms over my chest.

"No, I don't understand." A sneer tugs at his upper lip. "I'm here to support my son."

"I can see where your son gets his bullying from, which is another reason you're not to be in this locker room. If I have to ask again, I'm calling security." My frustration mounts, and I sense Jackson shifting behind me.

"Are you serious right now?" It's almost eerie how his features and arrogant tone mirrors his son's.

"Yes, and I'm also revoking whatever other privileges you think you have. Like everyone else, you need to support Jackson from the stands."

He scoffs with disdain. "I have a suite."

"Perfect. Now is the time to go there."

I turn my back on the tyrant and direct my attention to my captain, who, for once, is speechless. His wide eyes follow his father as he leaves and slams the door.

"You shouldn't have done that." His words are rushed, barely above a whisper, his face flushed.

I'm not afraid of Jackson, and I'm certainly not afraid of his father. I didn't make it this far by being a coward. Something is off about this situation, and I'm not about to let it go.

Reaching out, I clasp his tense shoulder.

He bats my hand away. "Don't fucking touch me."

Yeah, something is very wrong.

I drop my hands to my sides. "Here's a piece of advice. Set your boundaries and cut off his access to you until he learns to respect them. You're a big boy now, and if you want that," I gesture to his shrine of Aurora, "you need to grow up and dump the toxic baggage. You can't keep a girl like that by being an asshole, and we both know I'm not talking about her physical appearance."

FOURTEEN
JACKSON

Ethan Blackwood is our head coach and a giant fucking prick. He's controlling and arrogant and on my dick twenty-four-seven. He tells me where to be and when. He tells me what I can and can't put in my body. He has turned the entire organization against me, firing whoever doesn't follow his *rules* where I'm concerned. He fired most of the training staff, including the head doctor, for giving me an IV.

A fucking IV.

For hydration.

So what if I came to practice hungover? I've done it a million times. He's lucky I'm not drunk or high.

I toss my helmet into my cubby. It hits the wall and bounces onto the locker room floor.

"Pick it up," demands the asshole.

I yank my jersey over my head. "Fuck you."

"The staff shouldn't have to clean up after you. You're not a fucking child. You're a grown-ass adult." He steps closer, a vein bulging in his neck. "You wanna play on my team? Pick. It. Up."

I don't. I turn and face him, sick of his fucking dictatorship. One controlling bastard in my life is enough. "I didn't choose to be on *your* team. You weren't the coach when I signed my contract."

"I've read your contract. Nowhere does it say you're free to show up drunk, hungover, or use substances. In fact, there are stipulations against it. So you can pick up that helmet, go home, and get your shit together, or I'll drug test you."

I scoff. "You think I haven't tested positive before?"

"I'm sure you have, and everyone who swept it under the rug has been removed from this team. There's no place for that shit here. I'll submit your positive drug test myself and suspend you without pay. What will Daddy think about that?"

I step into him, fists clenched and my body quaking with fury. "Fuck you."

He doesn't back down. If anything, he stands taller. "Say it again, and you'll sit the bench."

"Do you want this team to lose? Because that's exactly what will happen if I don't play."

He shakes his head, an expression of pity on his face that I absolutely despise.

"Winning isn't everything. Your life and health are more important than a few goals. And if you haven't noticed, this team hasn't made it past the first round of the playoffs since your rookie year. So tell me, Jackson, how are you improving this team? Each year, your performance declines."

Shame and rage ignite. I pick up the helmet and slam it into his chest. "Fuck you and your team."

He doesn't even flinch. He lets the helmet fall to the floor, skewering me with his death glare. "Go home and sleep. Be back here tonight at seven."

"Good luck with that. I won't be here."

"You will."

"And why is that?"

"When you enter the Hall of Fame, this moment will be your speech. You'll share with the crowd about the day you stopped drinking and how that decision transformed your life."

Tears well up, and I grind my molars to stop them. "I don't care about the Hall of Fame."

He glances behind me at the pictures of Aurora. "What about the girl who loves you but doesn't love your addiction? Do you care about her? If not, let me know. I'd love to—"

My chest cracks wide open. "Shut the fuck up. Do not finish that fucking sentence."

"That's what I thought. Seven on the ice, not a minute later."

I regret coming home immediately. Scratch that—this is not a home. It's nothing but an empty shell.

In the doorway, I contemplate whether to stay or leave.

If I stay, I'll be bombarded with memories, and it'll fucking hurt. It might drive me to drink—or worse.

But if I go back to my father's, there's a 99.9 percent probability I'm getting drunk or high. Most likely both.

The thought of checking out of reality is inviting. My heart races, my mouth goes dry, and that familiar, relentless craving claws at my brain.

What about the girl who loves you but doesn't love your addiction? Do you care about her?

Fuck him.

The irritation of Ethan's words drives me forward, into the penthouse and away from the door. This place is a strange dream, a nightmare, and I leave my shoes on.

Aurora should be living here. I gave it to her when I left.

I grab a bottle of water from the fridge and down it as I survey the hollow space.

There's nothing here, not a single trace of her. That can't be right. She lived here for nearly two years. There has to be something of hers here.

I search the cabinets, find an open bag of Jolly Ranchers used for drinks, and pop one into my mouth. The sweetness tricks my brain and quenches my dry throat, and I continue searching.

There's nothing in the kitchen, not her bubbly water or that ridiculous kettle corn she can't live without. I make a mental list of her favorite foods and decide to order them. Why? I don't know. To feel close to her?

I move to the living room, throwing off all the couch cushions. Nothing. It's spotless. The maids have cleaned. I open every drawer and cabinet. I stop and think. Did she have anything here? Only personal items, and they remained in the bedroom and bathroom.

Was she even comfortable here?

She gave me a PlayStation for Christmas, and I check the media room. It's still here. I used it at most twice. Why didn't I use it? I'd tell her I was going to play *COD* with the guys, and I never did. It was an excuse to leave and get high.

She bought me the PlayStation so I'd stay home, and guilt hits me hard in the chest.

More fucking tears.

The pain is unbearable.

I can't be sober for this.

My gaze flashes to the balcony.

Just end it. End all this torment.

I was doing the right thing to protect her.

Another lie. I don't know where the lies end and the

truth begins. At one point, I started using drugs and alcohol to escape, and then I was escaping to use. I couldn't stop.

I *can't* stop.

Another lie. I can. I refuse to. I have no reason to.

What about the girl who loves you but doesn't love your addiction? Do you care about her? If not, let me know.

Like fuck I'll allow him to have her.

I sit on my bed and drop my head into my hands. Where do I go from here?

First, because Ethan Blackwood is a dick, I have practice at seven.

Second, I avoid the places where I get drunk and high. Not difficult, as long as my father doesn't force me to see him. I can always tell him Coach has me on a short leash. *That's* not a lie.

Next, I need to sell this penthouse. I can't stay here, or I will eventually jump from the balcony.

I remove my boots and climb into bed. I'm exhausted but unable to sleep. I take out my phone and search IG for any new pictures of Aurora.

She's currently in New York City. Her public profile has a picture of her behind the scenes with the caption: Getting ready for fashion week *kiss emoji*. She's wearing a black lace bra, a pink feathery miniskirt, and high heels. Her legs are a mile long. Fuck, I miss having them wrapped around my waist.

Her ribs are showing, and the skirt is low enough to see the indentation of her ab muscles and prominent hip bones. She's stunning, as always, but she has lost weight.

The best part of the picture is her bright smile. She appears happy. She deserves it.

It'd never work out between us, even if I was sober and

my father wasn't a snake. We both travel, and I'd be insanely jealous of every guy who saw her this way.

I could work on that, though.

Well, I can get sober. I'm still trying to figure out the jealousy.

I leave her a comment. *I miss that smile. *heart emoji**

She never writes back. I don't blame her, but I'd give anything to talk to her.

"I thought I was here for practice, not a fucking therapy session."

"Shoot the fucking puck, then."

I take another shot at the empty net, nailing the top-right corner.

"Left side," Ethan calls out then resumes asking his stupid fucking questions. "When did you start playing?"

"Fourteen." I hit the left side.

"Ding the bar, I wanna hear it. You play as if you started at four. How'd you make pro in five years?"

I take the shot, dinging the bar, and the sound echoes through the empty arena. "Surfing. I've surfed since I was little."

His brows furrow. "What?"

"Surfing teaches you balance. Skating is about balance. Low and wide. Strong core. It's all the same. Most of the fights I get into, the other player falls first. They lose their balance, and I'm on top."

"Holy fuck. That's impressive." He gestures toward the goal. "Five hole."

This shot is supposed to be between the goalie's legs. Easy enough without a goalie. "When did you retire?" I ask.

"When I was twenty-eight. Hit the top shelf."

Ding. Twenty-eight is too young to retire. "What happened? Why'd you stop?"

"Fractured my neck. They won't let you play after that."

A sadistic smile forms on my face as I aim for the next shot.

"Jesus. Does that make you happy?"

My grin widens. "Happy to hear you have a weakness."

"Why? So you can murder me? Everyone has a weakness."

I *should* murder him. He *knew* he was coming here to coach, *knew* Aurora and I had history, and he fucked her anyway.

And I only have myself to blame.

I shrug. "If you say so."

"Don't act smug. Everybody knows yours."

I straighten to my full height, leaning on my stick. "And what's that?"

He scoffs and raises his brows. "Aurora."

Shaking my head, I return to shooting slap shots against the bar.

"You wanna talk about it?" he asks.

Ding. "Nothing to talk about."

"Why'd you break up?"

Ding. "We didn't."

"Yes, you did. She broke up with you."

Ding. "Keep telling yourself that if it makes you feel better. She never broke up with me."

"You're in denial. You left town. She left you. Same thing."

Ding. "She left my house. Moved out. Blocked me on everything, but she never broke up with me."

He crosses his arms over his chest, his perma-scowl

deepening. "You need to let that shit go. You can't hold on to her forever. She's not yours."

I drop my stick on the ice and clench my fists. The fuck I can't. I'll hold on to her until I'm six feet under. I have no issue with that. "You don't know what the fuck you're talking about. If I'd have stayed, she'd have stayed. She'd have never left me. I was a full-blown addict. She deserved better. I gave her the penthouse. I told her to keep it. I was the problem, and I left." My voice cracks, and I swallow the lump in my throat. "I spent that time getting obliterated on every drug I could get my hands on, hoping to fucking—"

Die.

I rub at the ache in my sternum. "She's better off."

He nods, taking it all in. He no longer regards me with pity or arrogance. "Don't you think it's a little obsessive to be this hung up over a girl?"

"Are you asking for me or you?"

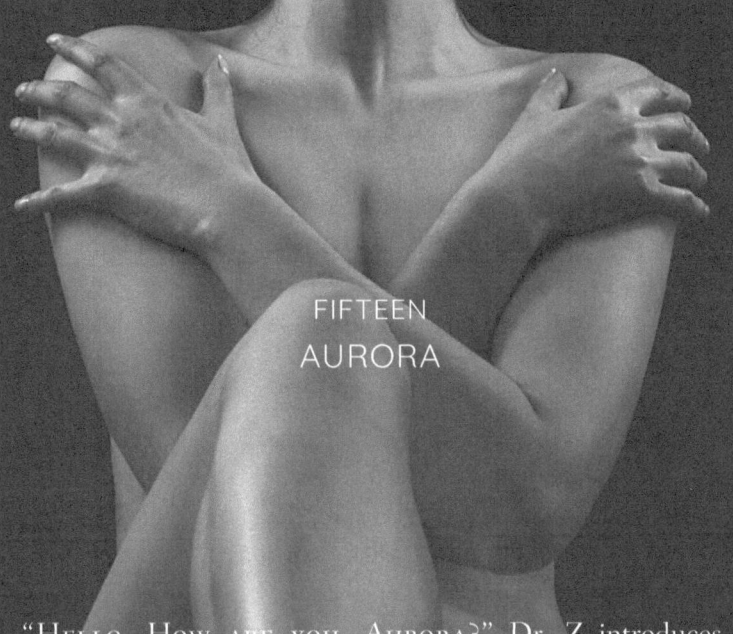

FIFTEEN
AURORA

"Hello. How are you, Aurora?" Dr. Z introduces herself.

She's known as *the* celebrity obstetrician in LA. We've been meeting virtually for the last five weeks, but today is our first in-person appointment.

"I'm pretty good. Still experiencing fatigue and morning sickness, but that's to be expected."

Once I got past the initial shock of my pregnancy and shared the news with my grandmother, my entire mindset shifted. Gram went from depressed to overjoyed at the thought of having a grandbaby to love, and that put everything into perspective. It's as if the baby motivated her to live and overcome her stroke. I haven't seen her with this much energy and life since before my grandfather's diagnosis.

Holding my hand, tears streaming down her face, she said, "A child is always a blessing. You were an unexpected blessing, and I've never regretted raising you, not for a single moment."

I bawled my eyes out, washing away all my shame and guilt.

We're having a baby, and I couldn't be more elated.

Unfortunately, Emily doesn't agree. I don't blame her. This is a tremendous responsibility that changes everything. I love her, and her support means the world to me, but the more I express my excitement, the more suffocating she becomes.

Not just suffocating—irritated and overbearing. We disagree on many aspects of this pregnancy, particularly on how to handle paternity. I've asked her not to tell anyone. I don't want the news to get back to my ex—I'm not ready for that nightmare. That created even more tension between us. I sense she sees this baby as either a paycheck or a burden.

And I'll never let either of those opinions become reality.

That's not to say balancing a modeling career and pregnancy is a cakewalk. I'm nauseated all the time, tired, and already underweight. I'm navigating the best I can.

I've always had a rocky relationship with food, but one thing's for certain: I don't want to deprive my baby of any nutrients that might impact his or her development. The nutritionist has assured me babies require fewer calories than expected. If I eat healthy, take my prenatal vitamins, and get sufficient rest, my baby will develop as nature intends.

My anxiety, however, is still a work in progress.

"All our tests have officially confirmed your pregnancy. Congratulations! Now, all we need is an ultrasound to assess the baby's development."

This is why I'm at this appointment alone. I wanted nothing to spoil this incredible moment. I only wish my grandmother could be here.

Dr. Z flips through my medical chart. The technician fusses with what I assume is the ultrasound machine, and I settle onto the exam bed with a wave of nervous anticipation.

The tech applies the cool gel to my barely noticeable baby bump, and I take slow, measured breaths to calm my nerves.

Everything goes silent, the air seeming to stand still until the sonic lullaby of my baby's heartbeat fills the room. Tears burn my eyes.

An image gradually appears on the screen, and I blink to clear my sight. Tiny facial features, delicate fingers, and the flicker of a heartbeat become visible. My heart swells with love and happiness.

I'll do anything to protect and provide for this child, even if I have to do it alone. All my worries seem petty in comparison.

The sonographer points out different parts of my baby's body and explains the significance of each detail and measurement. "Using 4D technology, we can determine the sex of your baby as early as fourteen weeks," she says. "Would you wanna to know?"

I arch my neck to clear my throat, my voice thick with emotion. "Yes, that'd be amazing. Thank you."

The technician chuckles and points. "No need to thank me. Your little boy is proudly showing off his goods."

A little boy. *My* little boy.

An unexpected wave of longing comes over me. His father should be here.

My tears now hold both joy and sorrow. A part of me regrets not searching for Ethan Blackwood, the former hockey player on the East Coast. I haven't even allowed myself to Google him, too fearful of what I might find.

A perfect life, a perfect wife, a perfect family.

He could have other children.

No guarantee he'd be standing beside me, elated and proud. Quite the contrary—he made it clear he was married and detested the idea of a pregnancy.

Once again, I'm alone in this.

The ultrasound continues, and I scrutinize my baby's tiny facial features, searching for any similarities to Ethan. Will he have his unique, stormy eyes? His strong build?

In my heart, there's a quiet yearning, a hidden wish for our son to resemble his handsome daddy.

I CHECK IN AT THE LAGUNA BEACH RESORT AND SPA, glowing with happiness.

This is one of my favorite places. It's a beautiful fall day, and the sun is shining through the wall of windows overlooking the Pacific Ocean.

I'm on top of the world.

The receptionist gives me a radiant smile. "Is this your first time visiting?"

I hand her my ID. "No, I've been here before." *With my ex.*

Memories flash through my mind before I can stop them, visions of us entangled and happy before it all went to shit. A wave of *something* I'm reluctant to admit rises within me, and I push it down.

It's loneliness. It has been an emotional day.

Feeling vulnerable, I glance away to avoid any further conversation.

Then, as if my thoughts conjured him, I spot a tall,

athletic, sandy-blond figure striding through the lobby as if he owns the place.

A tight fist grips my heart.

No. No. Nope. Absolutely not.

I spin around with such suddenness, it leaves me light-headed. I duck my head while the receptionist prepares the key fob, my pulse pounding violently.

Jackson can't see me pregnant. I'm not prepared for that monster to be unleashed. I doubt I'll ever be.

Maybe he won't recognize me.

Yeah, right.

Each passing moment amplifies the tension like a ticking time bomb.

Please don't notice me. Failing that, please somehow miss my pregnancy.

The receptionist hands me the fob, and I dart toward the safety of the elevator.

From the edge of my vision, I see Jackson sliding onto a bar stool next to a blonde, grabbing my attention.

Why am I gawking? Who cares if he's with another woman?

Before I can avert my gaze, his eyes snap to mine, and his jaw drops. A bolt of fear lances through me, and I will myself to breathe through it. Now is not the time to have a panic attack.

I jab at the elevator button. "Come on. Come on. Come on," I mutter, attracting curious glances.

The doors open, and I dash around a couple holding hands to get inside. I punch the number to my designated floor. More people flood the small space, and I hide behind the crowd, praying to all that's holy for the doors to shut.

All my prayers are useless, and I watch in dismay as a frantic Jackson rushes in.

Just my freaking luck.

He locks sights on me and says, "Excuse me. My girlfriend's in the back," and everyone jumps aside because he's Jackson O'Reilly, revered hockey god.

I scoff at the preposterous nonsense—particularly the part where he dares to call me his girlfriend.

He leans against the mirrored wall beside me, his lopsided, boyish grin warming my insides despite my anxiety and annoyance.

"Running from me, Aurora? Really?" His tone is light and teasing, with no trace of agitation.

He's in his usual designer jeans, loosely laced motorcycle boots, and black Henley, his hair perfectly tousled as always...but he's different.

The change in his demeanor is staggering. His features are brighter. The dark circles under his eyes and the angry scowl are gone, and his devilish gaze holds a spark of life again.

My foolish brain conjures memories of him from the early stages of our relationship, and I know I need to get away or risk being sucked back into his orbit.

Worse than bumping into an irate Jackson is being blinded by a charming Jackson.

But I can't force myself from him. He's so close, close enough for me to feel the hum resonating between us.

He flashes a smug smirk, and his face beams with amusement. "You look good, too."

I roll my eyes, too tongue-tied to formulate words. Fortunately, my floor is announced overhead, and a strong sense of relief washes over me, making me almost giddy.

"Sorry, that's me." A teasing smile plays across my lips, and I break free from his trance, eager to put some physical distance between us.

A large man blocking the front of the elevator turns to let me sneak by. With nowhere to go, he knocks into me. My protective instincts surge, my arm extends to shield my stomach, and I stumble backward...right into Jackson.

Wide eyes meet mine, guilt sears my face, and as predicted, his stunned expression twists into seething anger.

All too familiar with his fits of rage, I scramble forward, bumping into the same person again.

Jackson's arm encircles my shoulders from behind, and he shoves the poor man who barely touched me. "Get the fuck out of the way!"

The guy stammers an apology, and people raise their phones.

That fist around my heart constricts, and terror grips me, my head spinning with dizziness. "Jax, please stop."

Gray walls and greedy faces blur, and my mind races with fearful thoughts.

Jackson assumes this baby is his, and he's furious I've kept this from him. He'll demand a paternity test and scream accusations at me. I can only imagine the horror he'll unleash when I tell him the baby *isn't* his.

It'll go viral.

This is the worst possible outcome.

The air ceases in my lungs, and I drown in panic.

"Jax." My voice is sluggish. *I'm* sluggish.

Dark green eyes stare into mine. His lips are moving, but I can't hear the words.

My thoughts spiral, and my heart hammers. My clammy skin burns, and nausea curdles in my stomach. My legs grow weak, and I grip Jackson's shirt in a desperate bid to stay upright.

The world lurches sideways, and my vision distorts. A

murmur of voices swirls around me, undistinguishable through the fog.

I become weightless and close my heavy eyes.

"Breathe, baby."

A ragged inhale.

The enticing scent of familiar cologne.

A rapid heartbeat against my ear.

Blissful darkness.

SIXTEEN
ETHAN

"WHERE THE FUCK IS O'REILLY?" My booming voice is agitated, and the locker room goes silent. It's our last preseason game, and they've been chattering like a bunch of farm hens while my overpaid captain is MIA.

Jackson may have the personality of a chihuahua, but he's never late, not anymore, especially not for a game. In the past four weeks, he has become annoyingly punctual. His life has been nothing but hockey and our *therapy* sessions.

"Did you check your phone, Coach?" Killian snickers.

"Yeah, I've texted and called him. No answer."

Chuckles and laughs ring around the room.

"No, Facebook or Insta, Coach. Or any sports network."

Fuck. What did Jackson do now? Please tell me he hasn't asked for a trade or some shit.

Frustrated, I take out my phone and make my way back to my office, preparing myself for whatever shitstorm lies ahead.

I open the NHL app and am bombarded with posts about my missing captain.

LA Hockey Star Jackson O'Reilly Shoves Fan for Injuring Girlfriend

Jackson O'Reilly's Girlfriend Injured After Being Crowded by Fans

Jesus, I hate social media. I don't have time to read the articles or watch the videos, but it's likely a random girl, and this whole thing is being blown out of proportion.

This is Jackson. He has mellowed since getting sober, but he's still a hothead. It doesn't take much for him to throw down. My only saving grace is knowing he's not in jail. His father, Police Commissioner Kyle O'Reilly, would never allow it.

He'd never allow anything to hinder Jackson's paycheck.

I benched Jackson during our first preseason game for not passing the puck. I wasn't going to play him to avoid the risk of injuring our most valuable player, but he insisted, and I gave in. He was a machine dominating the ice but ignored my instructions. When I pulled him, his eyes strayed to his father's suite.

After, Kyle barged in on my post-game speech, disgruntled and smelling as if he was doused in bourbon. He hadn't taken two steps past the threshold before I kicked him out.

Only this instance, I followed Kyle out into the hallway, letting him know that if his son didn't adhere to my rules—rules prohibiting drugs, alcohol, and meddling fathers—he'd continue to sit the bench. Since I'm pretty sure the police commissioner is betting on games and needs Jackson to win, those rules have kept him away from my locker room and my star player.

Without Kyle and substances, Jackson is entirely different. He's less temperamental, more receptive to constructive criticism, and overall happier.

He's still the most annoying person I've ever met, never misses an opportunity to bust my balls, and spends far too much time in the penalty box, but he no longer throws helmets at me, and dare I say, we might even be friends—loosely.

And because of our stellar relationship, I think he'd tell me, along with everyone else in the locker room, if he had a girlfriend.

I'm sure he's dealing with the media and his controlling father.

My assistant coach yells for the players to get their shit together. We have five minutes before we need to be out on the ice.

I call Jackson one last time. He doesn't answer. I send him another text, trying not to be a royal dick. It's preseason. He wouldn't have played a full game anyhow.

> Me: Hope everything is all right. Let me know if you're going to make the game.

> Captain Diva: I won't. Sorry. I'm in the ER.

> Me: No worries. You okay?

> Captain Diva: I'm good. Thx for not ragging on me.

> Me: Keep me updated.

I shut the office door behind me. "All right, let's go! Suit up! We've been running new patterns all week. It's time to put them to work. Hoosier, you're in for O'Reilly."

After the game, I'm not surprised to find the commissioner leaning against the wall outside the locker room.

I pass him without so much as a glance in his direction. "You might as well leave. He's not here."

Unfortunately, that prompts him to follow me. "Where is he?"

"Don't know." I wouldn't tell him if I did.

"You're his coach. How do you not know?"

His snide tone gets on my last fucking nerve.

"You're his father. How do you not know? And this isn't high school. I won't be held responsible for your son."

I'm not one to interfere in my players' personal lives, but I refuse to stand by and let this egotistical prick destroy Jackson.

Kyle stops and faces me. He's much older, maybe in his late fifties or early sixties, at most six feet tall and overweight. I'd wipe the floor with him, yet he appraises at me as if I'm nothing more than dirt under his shiny Italian loafers.

"You know I own this city, right?" He spreads his arms wide. "I own this arena. I own this team." He steps closer and stabs a finger in my chest. "Which means I own your ass."

I hold his stare, not giving him the satisfaction of intimidating me. "Get your hands off me and take a hint. Leave Jackson alone. He's much better off without you."

A fake fucking smile creeps across his plastic face. "Enjoy your last season." He raises his chin and walks away.

Ten years ago, I'd have knocked this pompous asshole out. How has Jackson not killed him already?

SEVENTEEN
JACKSON

"We're getting the ultrasound." I cross my arms over my chest, staring down at Aurora. "I'll sit here all night until we do."

She's trying to convince me to leave the emergency room without the recommended procedure. It's not happening.

The same caramel eyes I've dreamed of for months gaze up at me. "Jackson, I had an ultrasound today. Everything was fine. I had a panic attack and felt faint. It doesn't mean anything is wrong with the baby."

Her voice is filled with more patience than I'll ever have, even when she's irritated with me.

"You fainted, not merely felt faint. There's a distinction. And I don't think you're *fine*. The nurse said your blood pressure is high. We're getting the ultrasound. The doctor recommended it, and I'll cover the expenses."

I want this baby to be mine as much as I want my next breath—which, right now, with Aurora, is whole hell of a lot. I realize it's unlikely. She's barely showing, and we haven't been together in five months, but the thought is stuck in my head.

If the baby is mine, Aurora intended to hide it from me, which is understandable, considering how I treated her during our relationship.

Who wants a kid with an addict? Among other things. Like my father.

Yeah, I'd hide a pregnancy too if I were her.

Her brows furrow. "Please stop pacing." There's that gentle tone again, the only one ever able to calm me.

I sit in the chair beside her bed and gather my courage. "Tell me the baby is mine." *Lie to me. Please lie to me.*

A sympathetic frown adorns her beautiful face. "Jax, you know it's not." Fear trembles in her voice, and her hand moves to her belly. "We haven't been together in months."

Her protective gesture irritates me and provokes doubts about her honesty.

My knee bounces, and I crack my knuckles. "What if I got a paternity test?"

She swallows hard. "It can't be. And I know you won't because your father would disown you." Her expression hardens, her tone brimming with bitterness.

My father has been the center of our arguments, in one way or another, throughout our entire relationship. Little does she know, I hate him more than anyone.

"I don't give two flying fucks what he thinks. I don't talk to him."

"Really? About time." Her pleased smile fills me with hope until she says, "But let me reiterate: the baby isn't yours."

I reach in my pocket for a Jolly Rancher, unwrap it, and pop it in my mouth. "Damn. I wouldn't mind getting a supermodel pregnant." I wink.

I've lived a life filled with disappointment. It's easy to make jokes. Part of me doesn't want to believe her. Another part of me doesn't care if the baby is mine or not. Nothing matters as long as she gives me a second chance.

And fuck, I hope she does because being in the same room with her, having her smile at me, is a total mindfuck. My body is energized, adrenaline pumping hard through my veins. My heart is beating against my sternum as if it's trying to escape my chest, as if it knows its home is right in front of us.

"Well, you had your chance. Clearly, I'm already pregnant." She gestures toward her slightly rounded stomach.

She can't be far along. I wouldn't have noticed had she not shielded her belly, which means she's pregnant by some fuck she met while modeling.

That pansy-ass photographer she went on a date with? She could've reunited with him. Fuck! I should've done more than threaten him with the loss of his job. I should've broken his nose—or neck.

The one time I refrain from violence, and see at what happens?

I twirl the candy with my tongue. Before I get too worked up and add someone else to my hit list, I need to verify who the father is.

"Will your baby daddy mind if I stay?" Not that I fucking care. "After all, you are *my* girlfriend."

I refuse to listen to what anyone says. She never broke up with me. No form of those words ever came out of her mouth or via text. Nothing. She ghosted me.

Again, I don't blame her. I was off the rails. Deep down, I realized it was over, and I couldn't bear to go through that sober. Or breathing.

Now that I'm clean, she's all I think about. All I want. All I dream of.

She rolls her eyes in response to my thinly disguised attempt at gathering information and pushing my boundaries. "No father involved, and I'll let you stay if you stop calling me your girlfriend."

Fuck, yeah! My heart leaps. I'm demented for wanting her alone, especially while pregnant, but I need her all to myself.

Plus, that's one less person to consider murdering.

I try to control it, but my grin is downright wolfish. "Perfect. Now tell me about the asshole who did this."

She adverts her gaze and twists the banket, all humor between us fading away.

I take her hand in mine, and a jolt of electricity runs through my fingers, scorching heat dancing along my skin from her touch. "Hey, look at me."

With tears in her eyes and trembling lips, she glances up. My mind jumps to the worst. A spark of rage burns in my chest, and I clench my jaw, struggling to contain my emotions.

"It's okay, baby." I tuck away loose strands of her hair that have fallen from her messy bun and pin them behind her ear. "Did he hurt you?"

All joking aside, if he did, I might kill someone.

No, I know I would. I have no mercy for those who harm women or children—just ask her ex, who now resides in prison. Turns out, Aurora wasn't the only girl he was *unkind* to.

She shakes her head, her voice barely above a whisper. "No."

"Tell me, Aurora. No matter what, I'll always be here for you." I bring her knuckles to my lips and inhale her intoxicating scent. A wave of heady recognition washes over me—jasmine and vanilla, her favorite lotion.

She settles against the starch-white pillows with a deep sigh, and I continue to hold her hand, not daring to move. Anguished eyes meet mine, and I'd do anything to erase it all.

"I'm overwhelmed, Jax."

That goddamn pouty lower lip tears my heart from my chest.

Here, fucking take it. It's yours. Whatever you want.

"This is hard," she cries. "I went to the resort to relax. I've been working my ass off to prepare for this baby. Emily has been supportive, but lately, she's..."

"Emily," I finish for her. "She only cares about two things—herself and money."

"That's not true."

"Fine. I'll add dick to the list, since she's been through the entire team."

Her brows rise. "The *entire* team?"

"Fuck no. I'd rather die. Now, continue." I gesture with my hand.

I don't need Aurora thinking about me with other women. It has never happened and will never happen, but it is an area of insecurity for her.

"*Anyhow.*" She gives me that sass I secretly love. "I have to find a place for me and the baby and tell Emily. On top of that, my agent doesn't know I'm pregnant, and my dream job is probably lost."

A few phone calls. That's all it'd take for me to fix all her problems if she'd let me.

"I'll bring you back to the resort once we're finished and ensure you get all the rest you need." I wipe away her tears with my thumb. "The agency won't release you. You're absolutely beautiful, even pregnant. I'll fucking riot if they do."

I ghost my knuckles over her cheekbone, and she stares into my eyes.

My voice becomes raspy. "I have every one of your magazine photos. I'm an avid collector." I'm unable to stifle my mischievous thoughts, and a sly smirk plays on my lips.

"Jackson," she chides and slaps my arm.

We burst into laughter, and fuck, I've missed this. Her smile lights up her entire face, and I want to get on my knees and beg her to take me back.

She's my best friend.

"Everything will work out. I'll make sure of it." Compared to the rest of my life, *this* is easy. Spoiling her is an honor. But I still need to know my competition. "Now, tell me about the baby's father. Why can't he help you?"

Part of me, driven by jealousy, feels a twisted sense of satisfaction knowing he's not involved. His absence is the second-best option. Another part of me, filled with curiosity and concern, wants to understand the situation. Either way, I need Aurora and her baby in my life. Therefore, he'll have to fuck off.

She presses her lips together, seeming to contemplate whether to tell me. "He's married." Her eyes implore me to remain calm. "He made it clear he didn't want this."

Her gaze shifts downward, as if reminiscing over her time with him. And nope, she will not be thinking about him while she's with me.

"Fuck him."

She cringes at my snarled response.

"You don't need him. You may find it hard to believe, considering how badly I fucked up, but I'd do anything for you. *Anything*. And if not me, any guy on the team would give their right nut to help you."

I'll never let another player near her, but it's the truth and makes her smile. So, we'll pretend I'm not certifiably insane for this girl.

Despite Aurora's resistance, I find peace in our shared moment. *Peace* isn't the appropriate word. I'm ecstatic. We could stay overnight in this hospital, and it'd be the best day of my life.

We sit silently, waiting for the ultrasound, and I can't stop staring at her. When I'm not, I'm learning about her pregnancy.

They brought a machine to monitor the baby's movements and heart rate. I've positioned my chair next to it and checked it a dozen times, obsessing over every detail.

It's going to crush my soul when I have to leave them.

Aurora clears her throat, capturing my attention. "You look good, by the way. Healthier. Happier." Her cheeks flush, and she picks at her nails—a habit of hers.

I grasp her hand to stop her. "Thank you. I've been, ah, seeing someone."

"Oh, shit!" She snatches her hand from mine. "You had a date tonight."

"What? That's not what I meant. I didn't have a date."

She glances away. "The blonde at the resort."

I smirk at her nervousness. She's not immune to me. I've seen it in her eyes. There's vulnerability and something more.

Something I'm too afraid to let myself believe.

"I was meeting a realtor. I had a game tonight. No date." *Or any date. Ever.*

Her mouth pops open with a gasp. "Jackson, go! I'll be fine."

She tosses the blanket aside and swings her legs over the edge of the bed. She goes to detach the monitor from her stomach but freezes when I clasp her bare thighs, pinning her in place.

"Get back in bed." My voice comes out husky, a surge of arousal shooting through me. "I'm not leaving you."

Our eyes lock, and I know I should remove my hands from her, but I *can't*. Not tracing them along her smooth, sun-kissed skin is agonizing. It's unbearable, and I give in to the temptation, letting my fingers graze her thighs.

Fire ignites my veins, and my throat goes dry. She sucks in a sharp breath and presses her legs together. And fuck me, desire sweeps through my stomach, and every fiber of my being urges me to lean in and kiss her.

I can practically taste her.

The door opens before I have the chance, and Aurora jumps away from me. She rushes to arrange herself in bed, and my hands fist, holding on to the feeling of her skin beneath my palms.

A technician enters, pushing what must be the ultrasound machine, and I do my best to adjust the erection pressing against my zipper.

He takes one look at Aurora's flushed face and stills. He picks up a paper, glancing down and then back up at her, recognition flaring in his eyes.

"Aurora Embers?" he asks, a little too dreamy for my taste, and a smirk tugs at the corner of his lip.

Damn, I'm not used to her being recognized or having men envisioning her naked on the beach when they see her.

She casts a nervous glance my way and nods.

His smile widens. "Tonight's my lucky night."

Like fuck it is. My spine straightens, irritation bubbling

in my chest. I've never been good at controlling my emotions regarding Aurora, especially jealousy.

I pat my jeans for a Jolly Rancher—fuck, I'm out.

I take a slow, steady breath.

I've lost her once, and if I want a chance with her again, I need to channel these feelings inside of me.

Another deep breath.

If these months have taught me anything, it's that life without her is far worse than any insecurity.

I huff, crossing my arms over my chest. This affirmations shit isn't working. I still hate this motherfucker.

They engage in pleasant conversation while he prepares the ultrasound. I try to concentrate on the procedure, clenching my jaw whenever he makes her laugh.

I lean in, placing my elbows on my knees, and watch intently as Aurora lifts the hospital gown, keeping her lower half discreetly covered. Her belly is adorable, and I want to put my hands all over it.

My knee bounces with anticipation.

The technician reaches to tuck the sheet into her underwear, and my patience snaps.

My reaction slips out, and I jolt to stop him. "Dude, seriously?"

He raises his arms in surrender, and Aurora glares at me.

"What? He doesn't need to be touching you."

She cocks her head in warning.

"Okay, I'll be good," I relent, but fuck, this guy needs to learn some boundaries.

After squirting some clear jelly on her stomach, he continues, moving the wand over her lower abdomen. With brows pinched, she takes several trembling breaths, and worry flutters in my chest.

Then, the sound of the baby's heartbeat erupts in the room, and she peers over at me with a huge grin and glassy eyes. Her sheer happiness steals the air from my lungs, and I stare at her in awe.

She wholeheartedly loves this baby, and it's fucking beautiful.

The technician moves the probe over Aurora's belly, and I'm captivated by a grainy, black-and-white image. My entire body heats. Indescribable emotions take hold of me, and tears sting my eyes. Time stands still while I grasp the significance of what I'm seeing—a baby.

Holy fuck. A baby inside the woman I love.

"Do you know what you're having?" he asks.

She beams a proud smile. "Yes, a boy."

My heart stops. I wouldn't care either way, but an image of a little boy takes shape in my mind. Stick in hand. Skates on his feet. Because, of course, he'll be a hockey player.

A hockey god.

I grip Aurora's hand. Eagerness grows with every detail that comes into view. Every movement, every flutter of the baby's heartbeat, intensifies my desperation to care for them, to provide for them, to protect them.

Something breaks in my brain. I'm truly obsessed.

I want her more than ever—more than anything. I'm willing to do whatever it takes to earn the privilege of being part of their lives.

EIGHTEEN
AURORA

I AWAKEN to the sound of waves crashing against the cliffs. The scent of salt fills the air, and the morning sun warms my face. I sit up in bed, mesmerized by the view. Azure waters stretch endlessly, merging with clear skies on the horizon.

The day is going to be lovely, and I'll savor every minute.

"It's you and me, baby." I place my hand on my growing belly. "What do you want to do today? Yoga, massage, swimming, maybe a mani-pedi?"

Our fleeting moment of solitude is interrupted by a quiet knock. I scramble out of bed, grab a white, fluffy robe, and wrap it around me. I peer through the peephole and open the door for the hotel staff.

"Hi! I'm Sam, your concierge. Good morning!" He wears a resort uniform and a bright smile.

Behind him stands a much, *much* larger man not in uniform.

In Sam's grip is a food cart, and I gaze at the coffee in longing. "I think you have the wrong room."

His grin never falters. "Nope. This was all ordered by Mr. O'Reilly."

Of course it was.

I step back, and Sam rolls the cart past me. The other man follows, towering over us both.

The concierge uncovers the platters and arranges everything out on the balcony. "We have fruit, eggs, waffles, yogurt, granola—you name it, it's here." He chuckles warmly and pushes through the sheer curtains in the doorway. "Call the front desk after you eat, and we'll move you to the penthouse."

My eyes snap to his in confusion. "The penthouse? Why?" I gesture toward the ocean, unable to form more of an argument.

"Oh, don't worry about that!" He beams and claps his hands. "The view upstairs is far more breathtaking. You won't be disappointed, I guarantee it. Housekeeping is stocking the kitchen as we speak."

"But I'm already in a suite."

I didn't even make it to my room yesterday before Jackson insisted on taking me to the hospital, and when we returned, I found myself in a spa-level suite, no doubt Jackson's doing.

"Mr. O'Reilly wants you to have access to the private elevator. He's worried about a recurrence of the previous day."

I grimace, thinking about the viral incident. "Okay," I reluctantly agree.

I'm a whirlwind of emotions—grateful for Jackson's thoughtfulness but wary of accepting his help. If I give him an inch, he'll take a country mile.

I face the man lingering in the entranceway, his massive stature dominating the space. He's the size of a football player, a linebacker. With burly arms crossed over his chest, he keeps a vigilant eye on Sam. He's dressed all in black, and glimpses of tattoos peek out from his collar and along his coiled forearms where his shirt is rolled. His blond hair is shaved on the sides and styled longer on top.

"And who are you?" I ask.

Midnight-blue eyes meet mine. "Ricky, ma'am. Mr. O'Reilly hired me as your bodyguard." His voice is deep, with a hint of Southern twang.

"My what?" I sputter. "I don't need a bodyguard. I'm only going to the spa."

I can't comprehend someone following me around all day. That sounds ridiculous and anxiety-inducing. I'll feel obliged to socialize, and it'll exhaust me.

Not to mention ruin the solitude I was hoping for.

He gives me a curt nod. "It's simply precaution, ma'am. I promise to stay out of your way."

"Now, don't worry about a thing," Sam gestures to the spread of food, his upbeat demeanor contagious. "Eat."

Both men exit the suite, and I wonder if Ricky is standing outside my door. I make a mental note to text Jackson and tell him I won't need a bodyguard. He's being overprotective.

The aroma of freshly brewed dark roast and warm pastries wafts through the air, tempting my senses and making my stomach growl. I sit and go straight for the carafe of coffee. The first orgasmic sip of creamy heaven hits my soul, and I groan out loud.

In the center of all this delicious overabundance is a beautiful arrangement of pale-pink roses. Nestled within the bouquet is an envelope. I know who it's from and know I shouldn't open it, but I'm a glutton for punishment.

· · ·

I think about you every hour of every day. I'd do anything to get you back. You're my best friend. I miss your smile, your laughter, your love, everything.

I'll wait as long as it takes for you to forgive me.
Please let me spoil you. You deserve it.
I love you always.

Yup, I should not have read that.

My head and heart battle, and a dull ache settles in the pit of my stomach. Jackson's words evoke painful memories and emotions I'm too vulnerable to process.

I don't doubt he regrets everything, but I can't ignore the past. I can't ignore his drinking, his jealousy, or his temper. They say time heals, but some things, you never forget, and his alcohol-fueled rages live rent-free in my head.

Even worse are the nights he never came home.

Yesterday at the hospital was nothing like old times. After I agreed to the ultrasound, he wasn't pushy or demanding. He wasn't angry or irritated with me. He accepted my predicament without lashing out, and I'd be lying if I said I didn't adore his excitement over the baby.

I'm pregnant and alone, and I'm not ashamed to admit I'm lonely and scared. I'm desperate to share this happiness with someone, and when he gazed at the baby with stars in his eyes, my heart nearly gave in right then and there.

He sat beside me, holding my hand, and I wanted him. Fiercely.

I longed for his powerful arms around me and his promises to ease my troubled mind—if only I trusted him.

But I know Jackson. When he wants something, he moves fast. He obsesses, he love-bombs, and when he has what he wants, he becomes controlling and possessive.

He's my weakness, and I can't let my loneliness lead me to heartache, not when I have more than myself to think about.

NINETEEN
ETHAN

We're on a private jet en route to our first game. All around me, the team is a buzz of excitement, bordering on obnoxious. Their mouths haven't quit yapping, and it has nothing to do with the start of the hockey season.

It has something to do with my pain-in-the-ass captain, who hasn't stopped grinning. It's infuriating.

"How's the *girlfriend*?" Grant asks, and a few of the guys snicker.

My attention is piqued, and I eavesdrop from a row ahead.

"Much better," Jackson says, a smile clear in his voice. "Doctor said everything is fine with her and the baby."

Baby? He has a girlfriend *and* a baby? Holy shit. I was way off.

"They think she's stressed," he continues. "They'll monitor her blood pressure, and she's staying at the resort while I'm gone."

"Are you sure that's safe?" Hoosier chimes in. "After all those videos went viral? People will know she's your girlfriend."

Someone scoffs. "She's not his girlfriend."

"Doesn't fucking matter," Jackson barks. "I hired a bodyguard to watch over her and spoke with the manager this morning. She's been moved to my penthouse. It has a private elevator and staff."

"Leave him alone." Grant chuckles. "We all know Jackson is still hung up on Aurora."

I'm lost. Jackson isn't in a relationship with the mother of his child because of lingering feelings for Aurora? He hasn't mentioned her in over a month. He has been dedicated to hockey and getting clean.

But this is Aurora we're talking about, bikini supermodel with the heart of an angel. Who could forget her? Not me, and apparently not Jackson.

"The one who got away," another player sings wistfully.

"Enough, assholes. Aurora is pregnant by some dickhead and needs a lot of support right now."

His words hit me like a bullet to the chest. My world stops. My vision blurs. The chilling grip of shock knots my insides, the air frozen in my lungs.

Aurora is pregnant.

The girl I slept with months ago.

My body moves in slow motion, my limbs numb. With trembling fingers, I reach for my phone and search for the videos that captured Jackson's moment of elevator fury. My heart ceases to beat until I find what I'm looking for, what I already know I'll see.

Sure enough, it's an unconscious Aurora falling into Jackson's arms.

I scrub the video and watch it over again, blinking at the sight of her slightly rounded stomach.

Everything in me screams *mine*.

My girl. My child. The realization is so intense, pure adrenaline surges through my veins.

Pieces of a puzzle I didn't even know existed snap into place. *Of course,* it'd be a threat to Aurora that'd have Jackson losing his shit. How did I not think of that?

"Dude, are you sure it's not yours?" Grant asks.

I find myself both hoping it *is* and *isn't* his.

"Positive. I threatened to get a paternity test. She said the father is married and wants nothing to do with them." Jackson's disgusted tone only twists the knife deeper into my gut.

Oh. My. Fucking. God.

My dreams and nightmares have collided. The baby is mine. It has to be. I got Aurora pregnant, the one woman my team captain is in love with. Obsessed.

Can this get any more fucked up? At least my divorce is final, and nobody here knows I was married. Not even Jackson seems to question if I'm the father.

"His fucking loss," Grant says.

"For damn sure," Killian agrees.

A wave of guilt washes over me. I'm *that* guy. I may not have explicitly said I didn't want a baby, but during my panic, my behavior made it painfully clear. I judged her, acted superior, and used my marriage as a feeble excuse for my actions. And to make matters worse, I kept her in the dark about my plans to become the head coach of her ex's team.

"That's what I told her." Jackson is grinning again. And why wouldn't he be? Everything he wanted fell into his arms, quite literally. "I saw the baby at the hospital. A little boy. It was fucking incredible."

A little boy. Tears burn my eyes, and I bite my lip to stop from crying or raging.

"She's thrilled but working her ass off. I offered for her to move into my place because Emily is giving her trouble. You know how she can be."

"Jealous and self-absorbed," Killian answers, bitterness lacing his tone. "And she'll cause problems between you and Aurora. She's done it before."

"Exactly, and I plan on spoiling the shit out of them."

"Dude, that's fucking awesome," Grant says. "I'm happy for you."

You know what's not *fucking awesome*? Learning, in the back of an airplane, from the man in love with the woman carrying your child, that you have a son on the way.

Pursuing Aurora will cause Jackson to despise me and shatter the integrity of the team I've poured endless hours into building. Yet, I can't ignore the fact I have a responsibility. I won't give up my child.

Eventually, she'll find out I'm Jackson's coach. What then?

I can handle them being together. After all, I'm accustomed to burying my emotions in work. But the idea of not being a part of my child's life is unbearable.

I never wanted kids, but now that I know I am, I can't let it go.

Bang!

Bang!

Bang!

"Jackson! Open up!" I shout through the door, my words coming out slurred, no matter how hard I try to avoid appearing drunk.

I admit, I had more than a few drinks at the hotel bar. I

only intended to have one, enough to take the edge off while I processed the predicament I got myself into.

Then I thought about Aurora, overwhelmed with work and her roommate, and one whiskey became two. I thought about how she was supporting her grandmother and our child—a child I could easily afford—and the guilt pushed me to order a third.

The situation sank deeper.

The mother of my child is relying on another man—a man who met my son before me. She was hospitalized and had nobody but her ex to lean on. That shameful realization led me to one more.

I lost count, thinking about Jackson, who, surprisingly, has grown on me. I kind of like the kid. His attitude reminds me of the chip I once had on my shoulder. And even though he's in love with the woman I desire, I still don't hate him. He's too fucking charming to hate.

Except in this particular moment, when he refuses to... "Answer the damn door!" I pound my fist harder.

Defeated and unsteady, I rest my forehead on the hard surface, rejoicing in the swirling darkness.

My thoughts turn chaotic. Deep whiskey eyes and a mischievous smile. The whimper of my name, a weight off my chest. A free fall.

I fell hard.

No, I'm falling—*actually* falling.

I attempt to catch myself, but my heavy arms aren't quick enough, and I crash face-first. My world spins, and I decide staying on the floor is better than trying to stand. So I don't.

"What in the actual fuck are you doing?"

I know that voice. Reality pierces through the haze, and I realize I'm in the room of the person who possesses the phone number I need. The problem is, I'm sprawled on the carpet, and standing is a monumental task when the floor is a tilt-a-whirl.

I groan and roll onto my back.

Jackson chuckles. "Wow, Coach. Can you even stand?"

Summoning all my strength, I push myself into a sitting position and cradle my head in my hands. "I need Aurora's number." My words are a drunken scramble.

"What are you saying? Jesus, it's two in the morning."

I lean against the wall and slowly articulate my thoughts. "I need. Aurora's. Phone number."

It doesn't take him long to figure it out. After all these months, why else would I want to call her?

His expression contorts with rage, and his fists clench. "Are you fucking serious?" He shakes his head. "No. Absolutely not. You didn't want her then and don't deserve her now."

"I was married—"

He looms over me. "So, what? You're single and think you have a right to her? She's not a second option!"

Somehow, I muster the last of my sobriety to face his anger—self-preservation and all. "I'm sorry. I was in a bad place."

"And what? You're in a good place now?" He scoffs. "You're shitfaced and can hardly hold your head up. Real fucking mature, *Coach*. Weren't you the one who told me to stop trying to solve my issues with alcohol?"

He mocks my title and guidance, and I realize I've only worsened the situation.

"Yeah, I have a problem facing my problems." I sound like a tool, but at least it's the truth. "But I just found out I'm having a baby with a woman who has every right to hate me." I swallow the bile rising in my throat. "Oh, and you love her, so there's that."

He sits on the edge of the bed and drops his head into his hands. "How the fuck did this happen?"

"Condom broke," I mutter.

"Shut the fuck up. It was a rhetorical question. God, I wish you were sober so I could beat the shit out of you."

I regret being here, but I'm desperate. I pull myself to my feet, holding the table for balance. "I don't want her. I want to be involved."

"Fuck off. I saw you and her, remember? If that were true, my feelings for her wouldn't concern you—they *don't* concern you."

Well, damn.

I stumble to the mini-fridge, grab a bottle of water, and chug it, attempting to clear the fog of alcohol from my head.

But my mind has a singular focus. "Can I please have her number?"

"Are you a fucking idiot?" He holds my blank stare. "The answer is no. You're intoxicated. You'll do something impulsive, such as call her at two in the morning. She deserves better, and she's resting." His gaze drops to his phone, inadvertently raising my hopes.

"You've changed from that person who ignored and demeaned her."

"Are you trying to piss me off?" He flashes his screen too quickly for me to comprehend. "And here I was, about to show you a picture of your kid."

I snatch the phone, trip over my feet, and nearly fall on my face. Again.

Seated across from him, I stare at the grainy photo of my son, and tears fill my eyes. I now understand Jackson's irritating smile.

The ultrasound pic doesn't reveal more than the baby's closed eyelids, button nose, and pouty lips, but it's a small glimpse into my future, making everything incredibly real.

Holy fuck, I'm having a son.

I swallow the lump in my throat and return his phone. "Can you text it to me?"

His knee bounces. "Yeah, now, get out of my room." Not glancing my way, he gestures toward the door.

"Jackson—" What could I possibly say to ease his heartache? "I'm sorry."

He glares at me, his jaw clenched so tight, the muscle furrows. "I won't let you have her."

"I never thought you would."

TWENTY
AURORA

I EMERGE FROM THE BEDROOM, smiling. "Good morning, Ricky. Ready for prenatal yoga?"

It's impossible not to be happy here. Sam, the concierge, calls every evening to arrange meals, activities, and any other requests for the next day. The penthouse is unbelievable. The infinity pool overlooks the ocean, and the plush king-size bed is to die for—like sleeping on a cloud.

The kitchen has all my favorite foods and beverages—coffee, bubbly water, fresh fruits and vegetables, hummus, Greek yogurt, kettle corn, cheeses, pasta, and bread. You know, all the essential carbs.

Jackson must have specified what to bring. He always teased me about my picky eating habits. That boy is a garbage disposal. He can eat anything and everything without aversion or consequence. Not me. If I even taste a tiny sliver of pickle or olive, I'm throwing up and avoiding food for days. Don't get me started on slimy foods—eggs sunny-side up, clams, oysters, mayo—I gag thinking about it.

Ricky stands beside the elevator door, the same as

yesterday. I offered him a chair, but he declined. When I texted Jackson about not needing a bodyguard, he insisted, stating that Ricky is well-compensated to ensure my safety. Now I feel a little less guilty having him follow me around.

"Good morning, ma'am." He gives a sharp nod. "Wherever you want to go."

I toss my gym bag over my shoulder. "How old are you?"

Midnight-blue eyes focus on my belly, and a frown creases his brow. "Twenty-nine, ma'am. Should you be carrying that?"

"Should you call me 'ma'am' when I'm much younger than you?"

The corner of his lips twitch. "Suppose not."

"Then we have a deal." I hand him my bag. "You can carry my bag and follow me as long as you stop calling me ma'am. I'm not ready to be thirty."

He shakes his head in amusement and leads the way into the elevator.

Driven by excitement and a hint of guilt, I invited Emily to stay tonight. Being alone at the penthouse solidified my decision to move into our own place—baby and me. While here, I plan to break the news to her. She's not only my assistant, she's also the only friend I have. I hope she understands, and we can fix this tension between us, but I doubt that'll happen.

The viral elevator videos haven't helped. I've been brushing off her incessant texts about Jackson, and I didn't tell her I was staying in a place he's paying for. She'll figure it out as soon as she walks through the door. There's no way she'll believe Felicity afforded me this luxury, and Emily will demand the full rundown of our current relationship, which I'm unsure of myself.

In case I needed anything, Jackson had me unblock him before he left for the start of the season. Now, we text back and forth, and every time my phone lights up, a wave of anticipation hits me. Butterflies flutter in my stomach, and I have to fight a smile. I blame my stupid, *stupid* heart.

He called before flying out yesterday. Initially, it was awkward, and neither of us knew what to say. He broke the silence by asking how my day went and how I felt. He listened as I blabbered on about the baby, morning sickness, food cravings, and going to prenatal yoga.

A few hours later, a *Morning Sickness Emergency Kit* arrived, containing everything from ginger pops to essential oils to wellness tea. After was a delivery of organic cacao dark chocolate bars, free of heavy metals—something I hadn't realized was a concern. Next was books and a plush pregnancy pillow.

Again, it's impossible not to be elated when you're being spoiled.

Except when every package is signed *Love, Jax* and you're confused and reminded of your painful breakup.

When we were first together, we fell hard and fast. I was certain I loved him before his anger and drinking overshadowed all else. Deep in my heart, I know I'll love him forever, just not enough.

The illusion of unconditional love shatters when your abuser shares the same face as the one you love.

Jackson is an entirely different person when he uses, and there'll always be a lingering fear of what will happen when he faces a situation that challenges his sobriety. Will he relapse? Will he lose his temper? He's sober now, but for how long?

Yet none of these concerns stop the thrill of finding a missed call from him after yoga. It doesn't stop me from thinking about him in the shower, and it doesn't stop me from returning his call, as his text asked.

Settling into the oversized couch, I dial his number, and he answers on the first ring.

"Hey, babe."

His voice is somber, and my stomach takes a dive.

"Hey. Is everything okay?"

"Are you at the penthouse? I have something to tell you."

My heart hammers. All I can think is: *He's about to confess to cheating.* What else could it be? It's the one thing we haven't talked about yet.

"Yeah?" Uncertain, I draw out the word.

"Listen to me, okay? I love you. I want to be together, no matter what. Nothing will—"

Impatient, I cut him off. "Jackson, spare me the song and dance. If this is about you cheating on me, forget it."

The idea of him and another woman kills me. Cheating has always been my worst insecurity. Given his lifestyle, how could it not be? Women throw themselves at him.

It was a significant reason we broke up. He must have been with someone else when he couldn't return my calls. He's probably with someone now.

And why do I keep torturing myself? We're friends. Nothing more.

"Aurora, stop. I've never cheated on you. Ever."

"Then...what is it?"

He blows out a heavy exhale. "Ethan Blackwood is our head coach."

I bolt upright into a sitting position. "What?"

"Ethan is my coach. Take a deep breath, okay?"

My thoughts drift through a thick fog of panic, my voice weak. "Why?"

"Fuck," he curses. "I wish I was there. I don't wanna tell you this, believe me, babe. But he found out about the baby."

I gasp for air, black spots dancing at the edges of my vision, and blood rushes in my ears. "How?"

"He overheard me and the guys talking about you and the ultrasound. I'm so fucking sorry."

Tears roll down my face, and my chest tightens at the thought of facing Ethan. I've come to terms with being a single mother. I'd much prefer it over losing my son or a custody battle.

"I'm sorry, Aurora," Jackson repeats. "He approached me last night, shitfaced and asking for your phone number."

"Did you give it to him?"

"No. I wanted to talk to you first and didn't want him drunk dialing you."

"What does he want?" My voice trembles and cracks. "Does he want the baby?"

"He said he wants to be involved."

"He's married."

"He's not." His tone is harsher and more abrupt. "He's divorced."

We're silent for a moment, lost in thought. I recall how Jackson began this conversation, by telling me he wanted to be together, *no matter what,* and now the bite in his tone...

"Wait. Are you worried I want him?"

"Yeah," he says, heavy with dejection.

"I don't know him. It was one night. More than my worry about raising this child alone, I fear what Ethan might do." I sniffle, unable to stop from crying. "What if he wants custody, Jax? What if he decides to take him from me?"

"I'll never let that happen, and Ethan won't do anything

irrational. He's...a good guy." It sounds as if Jackson is gritting his teeth when he says that last bit.

I snort through the tears. "Did that hurt you to say?"

"Fucking awful. I almost choked."

We both laugh, lightening the mood.

"I hate being away from you already," he mutters and sighs. "Ethan being the father changes nothing for me. I want you and the baby in my life. I'm not pressuring you, but I don't want to lose you."

My head is a jumbled mess, but one thing stands out. "I can't believe you're calm right now. You're keeping me from falling apart."

This is undoubtedly difficult for Jackson. Ethan is his *coach*. He'll have to see him almost daily, and the fact that he's not losing his shit is a testament to how much he has changed.

His voice deepens. "I've wanted you back, but I needed to sort myself out first. Kyle's no longer breathing down my neck, and I owe Ethan for that. He's, uh, the person who helped me get clean."

"Wow, that's... " I falter, my mind blown. "I don't wanna screw things up between you two."

"You won't. He'll get over it." There's that hint of jealousy.

"Jax," I scold and dry my tears with the back of my hand.

"What, babe? He already knows about us."

"About what?" My tone elevates.

"Pretty much everything."

Again, I'm speechless. Jax rarely confides in anyone, me included.

"How are you feeling?" he asks, thankfully changing the subject.

I crisscross my legs on the couch, relaxing into the cushion. "I'm fantastic. It's hard not to be. This place is truly amazing. I wish I could stay forever."

"That's interesting."

"What?"

"You can. Stay forever."

"Pardon?"

"I own that penthouse. When I said I was meeting a realtor, it was to finalize the contract."

"You own this penthouse? The one I'm in right now?" I don't know why I'm whispering. I'm astonished, I guess.

"Yes, babe." He chuckles. "I own that penthouse, and you can stay as long as you desire," he purrs, his voice smooth and flirtatious.

"Holy shit." Then, I remember myself and add some sarcasm. "It's a shame I have to leave in a week."

He huffs. "I'll be home in two days, and we'll talk more. Watch my game tonight. I'll score for you."

There's a trace of disappointment in his tone but also determination, making me wonder what he has up his sleeve.

Doesn't matter, though. I'm leaving for New York. Nothing is stopping me from succeeding—not when I have a baby to support.

If I still have a job, that is.

"I'll do my best. Oh, by the way, Emily is coming over later. Is that all right?" I guess I have to ask, since it's *his* penthouse.

"Of course. It's your place too," he says, a cocky grin clear in his voice.

"Jackson..." I draw out his name in warning. "I never agreed to stay here."

"Have to go, babe. Love you. I'll text you Ethan's number, and you can decide what to do."

The call ends before I have the chance to argue—typical Jackson.

TWENTY-ONE
ETHAN

Someone is striking my skull with a sledgehammer.

I groan and roll over, only to be assaulted by the nasty taste of bile and bottom-shelf whiskey. Jesus, fuck, why does everything hurt?

Cracking my eyes open, I'm blinded by intense sunlight. What time is it? Better yet, what the hell happened?

I lift my aching head to realize—thank fuck—I'm in my bed, fully dressed, and my phone is lying under my face. Did I fall asleep while on the phone? Highly unlikely, since I have no one to talk to.

Fragments of last night's drunken fuckery flood my mind, leaving me panicked and nauseated. Oh, shit. I'm an idiot. I told Jackson about being the baby's father. The entire team must know by now.

I grab my phone to check the time and do a double-take at the blurry screen. I sit up so fast, my head spins. Not only do I find my background image is an ultrasound picture of a baby—*my baby*—but I also find several unexpected texts.

> Hi. It's Aurora.
>
> Jackson gave me your number. I heard you had a rough night. Call whenever you're free.
>
> Or don't. That's okay too.

Before I can stop myself, I'm texting back with shaking hands.

> Me: No, it's absolutely not okay.

Three dots pop up then vanish, only to reappear. I save her number to my contacts, and a strange sense of male pride swells in my chest. I have the phone number for bikini model Aurora Embers.

Oh, yeah, and I got her pregnant.

What a fucking way to wake up.

My dick has never made me prouder.

I place the phone on the bathroom counter, keeping a vigilant eye on the screen while I brush my teeth. The dots disappear, and I second-guess myself. I shouldn't have written that. I should've called. A respectable gentleman would have called after he got a woman pregnant.

I'm far from a respectable gentleman—look at how I *got* her pregnant.

Countless thoughts race through my mind until I finally see her response.

> Aurora: I don't want to fight with you. I know this is a shock. I've had a few months to let it sink in. I understand you didn't want this. It was a mistake, and I won't force you into anything. I'm not about to disrupt your life. I won't ask you for a single thing. You can pretend it never happened.

Ouch.

I reread her words, trying to grasp their meaning. I read them again, still conflicted. Does she truly want nothing to do with me, or is she saying what she believes I want to hear? She almost sounds afraid. But why?

> Me: You disrupted my life the moment I laid eyes on you.
>
> Me: It's not a mistake if I'd do it again.
>
> Me: I can't pretend it didn't happen when I think about it daily.

I may have taken things too far, but she and our baby have consumed my every thought since I found out she was pregnant. How could they not? And why should I hold back?

Jackson. That's why.

But fuck, I don't want to.

> Aurora: What do you want?
>
> Me: You. My baby. Tell me what you need and when I can see you.
>
> Aurora: I don't need anything. Next week, I fly to NYC, and I'll be there for a month.
>
> Me: No.

> Aurora: No?

> Me: You were in the hospital. No work. Tell me what you need, and I'll get it.

> Aurora: That's funny. What am I supposed to do when I'm no longer pregnant? I'm not quitting my career.

> Me: If Jackson isn't taking care of you, then I will.

> Aurora: Jackson and I aren't together. He doesn't take care of me.

> Me: Even better.

> Aurora: Don't be difficult, Blackwood.

God, I love her. I need to choose my words wisely. She's independent and will resist me every step of the way, but there's no chance she's traveling the country with my baby.

Besides, I want to see her, and I need to know where she is.

I owe her an apology. I can't imagine she'd turn down an apology.

> Me: Where are you right now? What's the address? Can I send you something for being such an asshole?

> Aurora: You'll have to ask Jackson. It's his penthouse.

> Me: Of course it is. Will my son be living there too?

> Aurora: Not that it matters, but I plan to find a place soon.

> Me: Where?

> Aurora: Santa Monica. My grandmother lives there.

Simply texting with her brings a ridiculous smile to my face. Even when she's fucking with me, it's exhilarating, and I find any reason to message her.

> Me: When is your next doctor's appointment?

> Aurora: November 5th.

> Me: I want to be there.

> Aurora: Okay.

> Me: How are you feeling?

> Aurora: Can't complain. Some morning sickness, and I nap too much.

> Me: Never too much.

> Me: Rest as much as you need.

> Me: I have to go coach your boyfriend. Can I call you later?

> Aurora: He's not my boyfriend, but sure.

I picture her rolling her eyes and smile. All my worries have vanished, exactly as they did when I was with her. And the thought of *how* she made me forget all my problems has my cock thickening.

Jesus, we're only texting. Calm down.

I undress and step into the hot water, letting last night's events wash away. I can't take them back and wouldn't even if I could. It got the job done.

My eyes close, and vivid images of Aurora dance in my mind, intensifying the throbbing sensation of my already aroused state.

Palming myself, I leisurely stroke my shaft while fantasizing about her riding my cock in the limo. Her full, round tits. Her nipples between my teeth. The sound of her whimpering. Her hair clenched in my fist.

I envision grasping her ass and pounding into her perfect, tight cunt and increase my pace. The way she gripped me; I'd never felt anything so fucking good. My legs tremble, and my balls tingle when I remember how she creamed my cock while moaning my name.

My forehead falls to the tile.

This time, when I picture coming inside her, it's raw, with no fear of consequence.

I explode against the shower wall and imagine slamming deep, filling her with my cum, ensuring the results are exactly as they are today—with my baby in her belly.

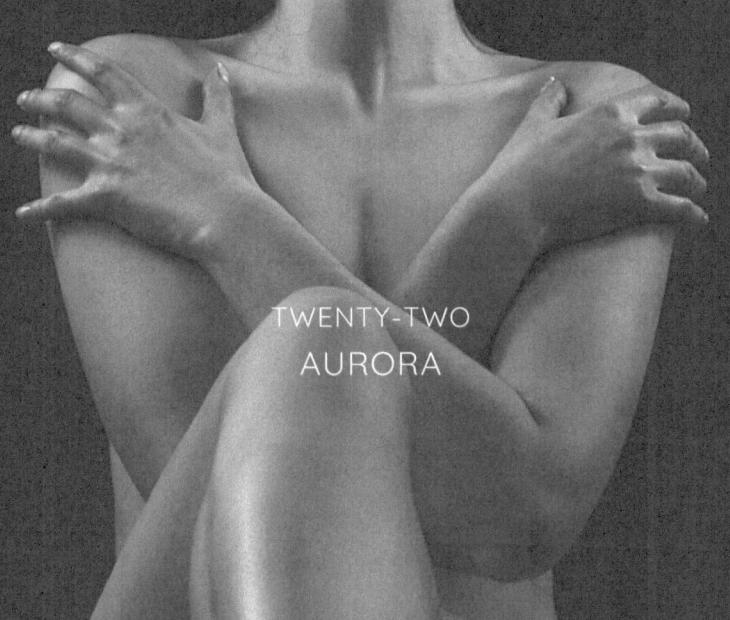

TWENTY-TWO
AURORA

Emily's jaw clenches. "You're moving in with Jackson?"

"No. I'm not moving in with him, Em. I want my own place in Santa Monica to be close to Grams."

She glares at me from the other end of the sectional. "Why are you staying at his place, then?"

"He wanted to ensure I was safe and look at this penthouse." I offer her a placating smile. "It's unbelievable."

She crosses her legs, her dainty high heel slipping off. We didn't even make it to the pool. "Exactly. Isn't that a bit suspicious? Or did you plan to meet him here?"

"No," I draw out the word. "He was here meeting someone, and we bumped into each other. Besides, didn't you want me to tell him and the guys?"

She throws her arms up. "To receive support! Not shack up with him!"

I lean in, placing my hand on my chest. "I'm not moving in with him."

We're not working through things. We've been arguing since she walked in. No matter what I say, she remains focused on me moving in with Jackson. She let me move in with her when I had nowhere else to go, and I feel guilty she's losing half the rent. But our shared condo has no space for a baby, and eventually, she'll return to dating and partying. That's not my life anymore.

Fighting with her is pointless. I'm shutting down and haven't even told her about Ethan.

It doesn't help that Jackson's first game of the season is getting intense, and I'm eager to watch. I'm trying to split my attention between the two, but Emily's nagging voice is irritating me more and more.

"Is this what you want? To be back under his control?"

What I want is to tune her out and watch the freaking game.

She hates him. I get it. She has every reason to, which is why I've disregarded her relentless criticism.

But right now...

The other team scores, and the camera zooms in on the chaotic scene. I spot Jackson's jersey amidst the skirmish on the ice, and my breath catches.

Emily's voice cuts through the air—something about Jackson attempting to buy my forgiveness. I ignore her, focusing on the fight in front of me. I've explained my perspective, and further discussion will only heighten my frustration.

The announcers' excitement rumbles through the speakers, vividly describing the scrum.

"Ladies and gentlemen, we've got some intense action on the ice tonight! A fierce altercation has broken out between two players, and things are heating up!"

"You're spot on, Mitch. The tension is palpable. O'Reilly and Irving are engaged in a full-on brawl, throwing punches left and right."

"It's a heavyweight bout out there! Jackson O'Reilly

lands a solid hit to the jaw of Vince Irving, and now, they're both grappling, trying to gain the upper hand."

"O'Reilly isn't backing down. Oh, and he delivers a powerful punch!"

"The referees are doing their best to intervene, but these players are fired up! Trading blows, and that'll be time in the penalty box."

"Absolutely, Mitch. These guys must have some serious beef, and they're taking it out on the ice tonight."

Butterflies flutter in my stomach. I admire Jackson's passion for the game, but watching it is another thing entirely. Every punch exchanged on the screen sends a tangible jolt through me, as if the impact reverberates through my own body. It doesn't matter how many times I've witnessed it. I hate seeing him hurt.

"Are you even listening to me? Or are you too focused on Jackson being a moron?"

Her interruption pulls me away from the fight, but I dismiss her comment, knowing nothing I say will make a difference.

"Watch the game, Em. Focus on another player, please."

She shakes her head. "Do you want this around the baby? A man who's violent?"

I understand she's concerned for me and the baby. I tell myself she only wants what's best for me. Yet, deep down, I know that isn't the whole truth. More and more, it seems as though Jackson was right. He poses a threat to her.

She wanted me to find someone to support this baby financially.

But not someone who'd swoop in and care for me, who'd take me and all that I offer away from her.

Or maybe that's Jackson's influence speaking.

The camera pans away, and a commercial interrupts the on-screen action as Emily drones on.

"He's psychotic. You know that, right?"

A burning irritation simmers within me. Does she not realize her pessimistic attitude only fuels my determination to protect him? "It's just a hockey fight. Can you please stop?"

This behavior from Jackson isn't his norm, at least on the ice. He can't score from the penalty box. Something must have triggered him.

She only persists, using my own words against me. "It's *just* flowers. It's *just* his penthouse while you're on vacation. You're *just* talking. Do you hear yourself? You sound the same as when you were dating, always making excuses for his behavior. *He was drunk. He was angry. He was stressed over the season.*"

Her accusations ring true, and that irritation boils over. My stomach is in knots. I want to enjoy my night, my time off, my life. Is that so wrong?

"Em, I understand your concern. I do. I'm not rekindling anything with Jackson. We're friends, that's all."

I try to sound confident, but I can't deny the flicker of uncertainty in my voice. I know Jackson wants more, and he'll do everything in his power to get what he wants. Emily knows that too.

"Jackson will never be friends. To him, you're still together. And don't expect him to change because you're pregnant. If anything, he'll become more controlling. It wouldn't surprise me if he bought this penthouse to lure you back in."

What if he did? For once, I have enough money to support myself and my family. It'd be difficult if I lost my modeling contracts, but I'd manage. I don't need to depend on Emily, Jackson, or even Ethan. I can make my own decisions *and* mistakes. I'll do what is best for me and my child. I'm not rushing into things with Jackson, but if I ever needed to leave him, I can. I didn't always have that option before.

Play resumes, and the camera focuses on Jackson in the penalty box. His nose and eyebrow are bloodied. The medical staff tends to his wounds, but his gaze is fixated on the ice and the ticking clock.

"I'll let you watch the game." Emily's mumbling barely registers.

I nod, my attention on the screen as I wait for Jackson to make his next move. The atmosphere in the arena is utter chaos, and I'm filled with nervous excitement.

The penalty counter runs down, and he bursts from the box with fierce determination.

Grant passes the puck his way, and I hold my breath. In an unbelievable display of skill, Jackson maneuvers through the opposing defense, twisting, dodging, and spraying ice in front of the goalie. Adrenaline courses through my veins, matching the escalating roar of the crowd, and then, with a flick of his wrist, the puck soars into the net's top-right corner.

"Holy shit!" I jump from the couch, my arms shooting up in celebration.

The camera zooms in, and Jackson raises his hands, forming the shape of a heart over his chest. His mouth is open, screaming "Fuck, yeah," and his face is pure elation.

A rush of affection washes over me. I turn to Emily, unable to hide my grin. "Did you see that?"

But she's not sitting next to me, nor is she in the room. Once again, I'm left alone to revel in my excitement.

Disappointment settles in my chest. I thought we'd

work through this. I thought she'd support my decisions, even if she didn't like them. I thought she'd be happy for me, happy to spend time somewhere beautiful, happy I'm moving forward with my life.

A twinge of sadness comes over me. If I decide to share a future with Jackson, I'll lose Emily. What about Ethan? The fear of her reaction and judgment is why I couldn't confide in her about him.

Either way, I'm moving out. I'm moving on.

Perhaps this widening gap between us reflects the shifting tides in my life. If confiding in someone makes you fearful, what type of friendship do you have? This whole time, I thought Jackson's reaction was the one I needed to be afraid of. I'm not so sure anymore.

TWENTY-THREE
JACKSON

"You're a fucking idiot. You know that? And so we're clear, *that's* a rhetorical question." Ethan is spitting mad, furious I was nearly ejected from the game.

"Yes, Coach." My sincere tone cuts through the hushed locker room, all attention on us.

If it was any other time, I'd have responded, *"Calm down, Coach. Don't blow that bulging vein in your forehead. I won the game, didn't I?"* I'd have escalated things and got in his face for calling me an idiot.

But for once, I don't want to argue.

"I heard what he said. I would've done the same," Killian says in my defense.

I lift my chin in acknowledgment. "Thanks, Kill."

My right hand throbs with pain, and I struggle to unlace my skates. Now that the adrenaline has worn off, I fear I've broken something. It wouldn't be my first "boxer's fracture." That happened by punching a wall after Aurora politely smiled at a flirtatious guy. *That* was me being an idiot. This time, I'm directing my aggression where it belongs.

Ethan throws his arms up. "Do you want to explain

what almost cost us the game?" He scans the room. "And someone get him a fucking x-ray!"

I loosen my ties, deliberating on what to share. The locker room remains silent, and I realize every player will eventually find out. You can't hide anything from this team.

Lifting my head, I glare at Ethan. Just because I'm calm doesn't mean I won't lose my temper if he mocks me about Aurora. "He said he'd *pile-drive my baby mama like he did that goal*." I take a slow, deep breath to quell my agitation. "He questioned if the child is mine, claiming every player in the league has *come on her tits* or some fucking shit."

My nostrils flare, and my chest heaves. Although Irving's comments were directed toward Aurora's centerfold pictures, he inadvertently hit me where it hurts. Few people know the baby isn't mine, but fuck, I wish he was.

And when the truth is revealed, I expect nonstop harassment on the ice. In hockey, when you're challenged, you'd better fight back. If you don't, you'll be the target of every player.

Tonight's altercation was to make it clear I won't tolerate any disrespect out of their mouths, not when it comes to Aurora.

Ethan presses his lips together and nods. He steps closer and clasps my shoulder. I don't love it when he does that, but it doesn't trigger the same jarring reaction as it once did.

"Before you let baseless insults provoke you, get a paternity test. The truth might have you laughing at their stupid shit instead of throwing fists."

Confused, I tilt my head and furrow my brows. What's he suggesting? Is he telling me he's not the father, that I have a chance here? Did he and Aurora have a conversation I'm unaware of?

He lowers his voice, even though nothing is missed in

this locker room. "Perhaps she's afraid of your history or Kyle. Lies don't send people into a rage. It's the truth that hurts. Your reaction is only going to spur more harassment."

My heart rate elevates, and I wonder what he's playing at. Is he letting me take the fall for this? Letting me claim his child? If he wants, I'll disregard him as the father and return to my plan of spoiling Aurora and the baby.

That's the plan, regardless. Only now, I have to contend with him—the one respectable man in my life, except for maybe Grant and Kill.

I gaze down at my skates, smiling. To the other players, it may appear as if I'm contemplating the idea of the child being mine because Aurora lied to me. If that were the case, I'd be fucking ecstatic. So, I allow myself to believe it, allow it to swell in my chest and light up my veins.

Raucous conversation fills the room, and we move on as if nothing happened. The trainer brings an ice pack and removes my skates while I sip a protein shake, and Ethan gives the postgame speech.

When he finishes, he reminds everyone we're a team on and off the ice—we don't talk shit, and we don't involve the media. I can't help but wonder if his words carry a deeper meaning, one that speaks to the two of us.

With a day between games, there's no time to travel home. Right after I get an x-ray, showing no significant injury, only inflammation from aggravating my previous fractures, we leave to catch a flight to Colorado.

Before boarding, I shoot a text to Aurora.

> Me: Flying out. I can't wait to talk to you tonight *kiss emoji*

> My life: Great goal! Ice that hand *pink heart emoji*

She watched my game—a goofy smile spreads across my lips. I'm utterly infatuated with her.

No, I'm thoroughly obsessed. I can't get her and the baby out of my head.

I enter the cabin of the plane and find an open seat next to Ethan. I wouldn't usually choose to sit beside him, but curiosity has gotten the best of me.

He eyes me with suspicion and shields his phone. "What are you doing?"

"What are *you* doing?"

"Looking at houses for my future wife," he says, echoing my previous taunts but ignoring my actual question.

"You can fuck all the way off. Tell me what you're really doing."

"She mentioned wanting a place in Santa Monica. I thought I'd beat her to it, you know?" He shrugs and feigns nonchalance, and it's damn obvious.

But I'm prepared to play his game. I can trump whatever he comes up with, other than the baby, for now.

"I already have a penthouse on the beach. Don't waste your money."

"Yeah, she told me." His smirk ignites my jealousy, and he knows it. "By the way, what's the address? I want to send her a few things."

I have a feeling he's not only purposefully aggravating me but also vying for Aurora's attention. Why wouldn't he?

"Don't bother. I already give her everything."

"That's fine. She'll be in New York soon. I'll send her gifts there."

He dismisses me, returning to his house hunting, and a growl of frustration slips from deep in my chest.

"What's the matter?" He chuckles. "Not up for some friendly competition?"

"No, it's not about you." Not a complete lie. "I'm pissed she's leaving again."

He lowers the phone and faces me. "Speaking of which, did you know she'll be in New York City for a month?"

"What?" I choke.

A month? I just got her back. With time away, she may reconsider our *friendship*. She may consider this asshole a better choice.

"That's what she told me, anyhow."

The hint of uncertainty in his words bolsters my confidence and lessens my panic—some.

"She's preparing for Winter Fashion Week." I discovered this by stalking her IG, but he doesn't need to know that. "I didn't expect her to continue her grueling schedule, considering the baby."

"What's our plan then?"

"*Our* plan?" I ask, brows raised. "I doubt either of us can change her mind. Believe me, I've been there. She insists on being independent."

He cocks his head to the side. "Did you support her independence? Or did you ignore her needs and throw a tantrum?" His accusation hits home. "See, you think she works for money. She works for *security*."

What's the difference? I have no clue, and that irritates me. "Have I ever told you how much I hate you?"

He narrows his eyes. "I'm being serious."

"So am I." I shake off my discomfort and gesture with my hand. "But let's move on. What are you talking about?"

"You have this huge platform. You're practically a celebrity in LA. Did you use your status to create opportunities for her? Have you even posted a single picture of her on your social media? Or did you hide her and worsen her insecurities?"

"I don't run my social media." I have one private account, and that's for stalking Aurora.

He gives me his *"Do you think I'm an idiot?"* expression.

"Fine. I didn't want my father to know I was serious about her."

Unimpressed, he proceeds to stare at me.

I clench my jaw and sigh. "I didn't want to draw attention to her. I wanted to keep her to myself. Her career is my worst nightmare. Fuck, is that what you needed to hear?"

It's as if he has the narrative to our relationship, and I've been the clueless character unable to see the product of my actions. I'm only scratching the surface of my mistakes, and here I thought I was doing well by working on my anger and addiction.

In reality, I've only reached the bare minimum of boyfriend material.

"Just making sure we're on the same page. Aurora's an overthinker. She worries, especially about caring for her grandmother and now a baby. She's independent out of necessity. She doesn't trust *either* of us and can't take the risk of failure. Do you know what it's like to be hungry or homeless? Or responsible for another human being?"

All I can do is sulk at how blind I've been and resent him for pointing out my shortcomings.

"That's what I thought," he continues. "Now, let's brainstorm ways to support her. I want to see her and my kid, not have them travel the fucking country."

I focus on his last sentence, unable to shake the suspicion he has an ulterior motive. "Why are you doing this?"

He lowers his voice. "Everyone assumes you're the father. No one thinks it's me. They associate Aurora with you. If people find out I'm the father, we all lose. I'll lose the respect of my team, you'll face constant harassment on the ice, and people will talk shit about her getting pregnant while escorting."

My cheeks burn with anger. "I don't give a fuck what people say."

"You might not, but she will, especially if she's worried about her career. I'm trying to help you here. Set your ego aside for a minute and think about it. If Aurora is dating you, it's a win-win situation. She's a supermodel with a pro-athlete boyfriend. No agency is letting her go, pregnant or otherwise. Everyone will want a piece of her."

"How's that a good thing?"

"Seriously? Are you that insecure? It's basic supply and demand. She'll get paid more and work less. Jesus, never fire your agent." He shakes his head and sighs. "Ideally, she'll stay in LA and spend time with *us*."

I sit silently for what feels like an eternity, my mind swirling with everything he suggests. Being with Aurora has always been my endgame, but I approached it all wrong. While Ethan is manipulative, and the prospect of her gaining more popularity is a tough pill to swallow, I see the logic in his argument.

Yet, I haven't put together one piece of the puzzle.

"What's in this for you? You keep saying 'us' as if you're not stepping aside."

He scoffs. "Hate to break it to you, but I'm not. She loves you—sober you," he adds. "I doubt she'll let me near her anytime soon, but I still need her in LA to see my child. Plus, I get to annoy the fuck out of you."

He grins, and I can tell by his smug expression he's playing the long game. Little does he know, I've already taken up that position.

"I'll send my bodyguard with her to New York and

update my publicist." I circle back to our prior conversation. "But we still have to convince *her* to go along with your plan."

"I'm calling her tonight." He relaxes in his seat with an air of superiority. "I'll let you know how it goes."

My brows furrow. "You talked to her earlier?"

"We've been texting." He half-ass shrugs, aware he's getting under my skin and wearing away at my last fucking nerve.

Still, I need to know. "What did she say?"

"You're ridiculously jealous. You make this too easy."

He laughs, and I have the sudden urge to punch him in the throat.

"Calm down, killer. We're on the same team here. She told me she's going to New York, she's not quitting her job, you don't support her financially, and she's searching for a place in Santa Monica. She says she feels fine and agreed to let me attend the next doctor's appointment."

My frown deepens, and my knee bounces. "Why'd she say I don't support her?"

Gray eyes lock with mine, radiating defiance. "Because I told her if you wouldn't, I would."

I'd care for her without hesitation if she let me. He knows that. Why is he warning me? So I don't fuck up? That's a no-brainer.

Unless he offered to support her and she shot him down, which is why he's scheming.

A self-satisfied smile graces my lips. "You won't be able to buy her affection."

"Oh, I know, and neither can you. That puts us on an even playing field. Aurora doesn't want shit from me, which only makes me want to give it to her more."

"Dude, hate to break it to you," I mimic in his same

annoying tone, "but it sounds like she's not interested. I don't fuck with puck bunnies but maybe shoot your shot there. I hear they come cheap and easy."

The sharper my sarcastic jabs, the more amused he becomes. He's impossible to fluster or intimidate.

"No thanks. Aurora is hotter than any puck bunny I've ever seen." A cocky, shit-eating grin lights up his face. "Besides, I can't imagine the sex is any better."

That's a punch to the gut, and I huff. "I fucking hate you. I *really* fucking hate you."

That only makes him laugh harder.

TWENTY-FOUR
ETHAN

I PACE the hotel room and rake my fingers through my hair, waiting for Aurora to answer my call. All day, I've been thinking about this, going over my words again and again.

But when she picks up, my mind goes blank, and I freeze.

"Hi."

That simple word in her soft voice lights up my entire body, bringing my heart and brain back to life.

"Hi." She remains silent, and I add some humor to ease the palpable tension. "I'm sorry I got you pregnant."

She laughs, and the knot in my stomach loosens.

"It's not so bad. Quite a shock at first, but I'm excited about it now."

There's distance in her voice, and I hate it.

"Tell me everything. How did you find out? Let's start there."

"We were in New York, doing a photoshoot for a clothing line. I was exhausted and almost fell asleep on set." She chuckles. "Then, several mornings in a row, I was sick, and here we are, fourteen weeks pregnant."

I can't imagine her in New York, going through this whirlwind of emotions, while I was thousands of miles away. A pang of guilt hits me. I should have been there—I should be there now, or at least doing *something*.

"Jackson tells me you're having trouble with your roommate. Is everything okay?"

"No." She releases a heavy sigh. "Emily refuses to speak to me."

"Why?"

"Because I'm friends with Jax," she says, too curt for my taste.

"Just friends?" I tease.

"As of this moment, yes."

As of this moment. So there's a possibility, and I'm pushing her right into his arms. Great.

"Are you considering being with him?"

"Like I told Jackson, my only concern is this baby, not dating."

I can see her rolling her eyes, annoyed with my prying.

"Okay, I respect that." I draw a breath and blow it out slowly. "I wasn't lying when I said I think about you. I want to be a part of this baby's life—and yours. My behavior in the limo was appalling, and I apologize. I was only thinking of myself."

"I don't blame you for anything. I have no hard feelings toward you. I just don't know you. I worry about the future," her voice shakes, "such as shared custody. You know?"

I hadn't even considered custody issues. Now I understand why she wanted nothing to do with me and seemed afraid. She's worried I'll take her to court, take the baby.

She didn't hunt me down or use this pregnancy to extort money from me. She could have, and I would've given it to her, and that tells me everything I need to know.

"Don't worry about that. It's the furthest thing from my mind, I promise. We'll work this out together." I take another deep inhale, gathering my courage. "I do have something important to discuss, though."

"Okay…" She drags out the word.

"And that's how we portray this pregnancy in the public eye."

The line goes quiet, and I sense her aggravation.

"I'm not gonna trash your reputation. I already told you that."

Her tone has a bite, and it's the last thing I want, but unfortunately, this situation is escalating quickly. Between Jackson's freak-out over the elevator mishap and his recent fight, the media will circle like a pack of vultures soon enough.

"Can we FaceTime and have an honest conversation?"

"Umm, I'm in bed with no makeup on."

I scoff. "I'm sure you're gorgeous, no matter what."

I sit on the couch and switch the call. Her face comes on the screen, and I bite my lip to stop from outright groaning. Somehow, I forgot how young and beautiful she is.

She's sitting against a white, fluffy pillow that engulfs her. Her alluring eyes instantly captivate me, drawing me in with their shy gaze. Sexy, dark waves frame her face and shoulders. Her lips, pouty and inviting, complete the seductive package, and fuck me, this wasn't a good idea.

"Wow, okay." My cheeks and ears grow warm. "You're even better in bed." Wait? What? "That's not what I meant." Jesus, I'm a teenager fumbling over my words.

We share a laugh, and I'm glad she still has her bubbly sense of humor.

"Let me rephrase that. You're perfect, regardless of makeup."

She offers me a gentle smile. "You also look great." She appraises me, and it reminds me of the first time we met—the way she noticed me, the way she flirted with me. "You seem happier," she says.

"Thank you. I am happier, a lot happier." *Mainly because of you.*

She bites her lip and drops her gaze, and the camera angle shifts as she relaxes. She's wearing an oversized white T-shirt, nothing underneath, and I'm left speechless.

Stunned stupid, I stare.

The sight of her peaked nipples has desire stirring low in my gut, but it's her swollen belly that really does it for me.

I did that.

Thank fuck she can't see me reach down and adjust my pants. Face-to-face, I'd never keep my emotions in check. If she ends up with my captain, I'll need to stay away. She's too tempting.

"What did you want to discuss?"

What were we discussing? Oh, yeah, my idiotic idea to allow Jackson to claim her publicly.

This decision is best for everyone involved, including the team, I tell myself. Repeatedly.

"Please hear me out before hanging up on me, okay?"

She maintains an annoyed expression while I outline my plan.

By the end, her glare is icy, her jaw tight. "You want me to fake date Jackson for the publicity? Let him pretend to be the father of *your* baby?"

I wince. "Not dating exactly. Although I believe it's the best solution for everyone."

"Do you not want to be involved? I've given you that

option." Her lips tremble, and her eyes turn glassy. "I have enough stress in my life. I'm not interested in playing your games." A tear escapes, and she quickly brushes it away.

I wish I could be with her, comfort her, and make everything disappear.

But that's not possible.

"Aurora, I want to be involved. I *plan* to be involved. But I don't fit the narrative of your public lives. People assume Jackson is the father. Other players are already harassing him over the elevator incident. If they find out this baby is mine, it'll get worse—much worse, especially in the locker room. And the negative publicity will jeopardize all our careers."

She lays a hand on her stomach, her voice cracking when she says, "You're ashamed of this...of me."

My blood boils, and my heart breaks simultaneously. "Fuck, no. Don't twist this around. If anything, I don't deserve *you*. You're young and beautiful, and this whole situation is surreal to me. Supporting you financially is the easiest way for me to help, but you won't allow me to do that. I'm trying to make the best of this situation, and maybe that means me stepping aside—not that I want to."

Silence falls between us. I hang my head and push my fingers through my hair in frustration. "I didn't even think of this plan until Jackson's fight."

"You care about Jax." It's not a question or an accusation, simply her observation.

"He's changed. I've had a few unfortunate run-ins with his father, so I can empathize with what he's been through. That doesn't mean I don't think he has work to do, but he clearly loves you. Lucky fucker."

The last part slips out of my mouth, and she smiles.

"Say I agree to this plan of yours. What happens if he relapses? And you know Jax isn't capable of fake dating, right?"

There's no straightforward solution to this. Jackson is already attached, and if he wants her half as bad as I do, he won't fuck it up.

If he does, it's ultimately better for me. I have a three-year contract with the team, and this infatuation of his needs to run its course. I can wait him out.

"He's going to pursue you either way. That train left the station long ago. And, as far as I know, he quit drinking. I fired the staff who ignored his addiction and hired a sports doctor with experience in substance use. If he relapses, I swear, I'll drag him from whatever hole he crawled into and knock some sense into him."

Her eyes soften, and her face lights up. "You did all that?"

"Along with revoking his father's privileges to our locker room and training facility, yeah."

"Wow," she nearly whispers. "Thank you."

The adoration in her gaze takes my breath away. She's thanking me for doing what's right. I did it for Jackson and the team, unintentionally giving Aurora her boyfriend back. Yay me.

I roll my shoulders, releasing the tension in my neck. "I promise I won't stand by and let him mistreat you. If he does, you break up with him. People break up." A smug smile plays on my lips.

She shakes her head. "I don't get you. You make comments such as that, tell me you think about me and don't consider this a mistake, but you're pushing me toward someone else."

There's that brutal honesty I both love and hate.

"You're a decade younger than me." I shrug, the playfulness lost. "I'm too jaded. A committed relationship isn't in the cards for me. But you and Jackson"—I picture them together, the supermodel and the superstar—"make a hell of a lot more sense. And if, by some miracle, you choose me... can you at least wait until the end of the season?" I jest, but I'm more than somewhat serious.

I caught my ex cheating and still finished the hockey season before planning my divorce, enduring months of daily business meetings with the prick she was fucking behind my back.

A player missing a game differs from a coach blundering everyone's year. I need to stay focused.

Even with all that said, I know I'm fooling myself. If she wants me, I won't resist. She'll be my entire world.

Which is why I need to distance myself.

"I guess you're unhappy with my March due date?" She beams, and relief washes over me.

"Not ideal, but preferable to playoffs. I'd have to disown you then." I return her smile, then joke, "Maybe we need to add a fourth person to this love triangle. That way, someone can be with you during the season?"

Her answer is immediate. "Oh, don't worry. I have Ricky." And the way she sings his name triggers something within me.

"Who's that?" Unable to hide my jealousy, my tone comes out harder than intended.

She cocks her head and bites her bottom lip. "None of your business, Blackwood."

That playful teasing and mischievous gaze gets me every fucking time.

"Aurora," I warn, unsure if I'm more irritated by this

Ricky bastard or her flirtatious manner. Shit, I'm irritated by another man. "Who is he?"

"Just my bodyguard," she says too sweetly.

"Consider him fired."

"You don't get to make decisions. You're not my boyfriend, remember?"

Oh, we'll see about that.

TWENTY-FIVE
AURORA

Perched on the edge of the infinity pool, I dip my toes into the sparkling water. The afternoon is as perfect as ever, with sunbeams dancing on the rippling surface and the melody of the waves whispering through the cool air.

It's not sunny inside my head, however.

I'm overwhelmed. I woke up this morning with texts from Ethan, Jackson, and my agent—nothing from Emily. We fly out in three days. I don't know if I'll have an assistant or friend to accompany me.

My agent wants me to call her. I'm sure she knows I'm pregnant by now, given the videos circulating. I can't continue to avoid her, avoid the heartache of losing my dream.

I let out a long, dramatic exhale. I thought about Ethan's suggestion until my brain hurt. A relationship with hockey star Jackson O'Reilly would undoubtedly benefit my career. My mental health is yet to be determined.

Jax called last night, excited to talk. I didn't mention Ethan's plan. There's no *fake* dating for Jackson. I have to accept the idea of *us* before I bring it to his attention. And he didn't ask about my call with Ethan, content with talking about nothing, which was a pleasant distraction, because I can't get Ethan's conflicting words out of my head.

"You're young and beautiful. A committed relationship isn't in the cards." Whatever. His choice. Not that I want anything romantic with him, but that stung.

Emerging from the water, I walk to the ledge and rest against the glass barrier. I inhale the salty air and gaze out at the ocean, finding peace in the rhythm of the waves colliding with the cliffs.

I understand the rationality behind Ethan's plan. I'm okay with it, as long as we go at my pace and Jackson knows everything is over if he returns to drinking.

Fake or not, it's over.

What distresses me the most is feeling as if I'm nothing more than an escort again, at least in Ethan's eyes. He wants me to date a man for publicity, to save myself from negative gossip. It's essentially the same as escorting, simply a different currency.

Maybe that's all I'll ever be to Ethan—a woman who benefits from dating high-profile men.

But this is Jackson, my first love. He'll dive in headfirst, or I should say, heart first. When he wants something, nothing can stop him. This penthouse. The bodyguard. I'll be spoiled, with little financial concerns.

Another positive is that we're attracted to each other—I mean, Jackson is fucking hot, there's no denying that. The giant red flag is his volatile behavior, and I won't know if I've made a colossal mistake until it's too late.

"Wow."

Startled, I spin around.

Jackson's gaze drags over me slowly, a crooked smile curving his lips. "I could get used to this view."

I'm in a white bikini. He's dressed in black ripped jeans, a black T-shirt, and his beloved unlaced black motorcycle boots. My dark hair is up in a messy bun while his sandy hair is flawlessly tousled. We couldn't be any more opposite.

It's also highly annoying he's effortlessly attractive, even with the abrasion on his cheek and the bruising along his eyebrow—maybe more so.

"You're early." I can't hide the excitement in my tone, and once again, everything in me wants to jump into his arms. "I was getting lonely here."

A wide grin brightens his green eyes. "I was in a hurry to get home."

He takes a tentative step forward, his gaze fixed on my slightly rounded stomach. He extends his hand as if to touch me but hesitates.

"You can touch." I grab his wrist and place his palm on my baby bump.

His hand almost encompasses my entire belly.

"I think you're a little bigger than last time I saw you." His callused palm caresses my stomach. "Damn, that's weird."

"Sorry," I mumble and step back, my heart heavy with disappointment.

He shakes his head, brow furrowed in a scowl and returns his hand. "I didn't mean that in a bad way. Not at all. When do I get to feel him move?"

A nervous giggle comes over me. "Not for a while—a month or more."

Even this innocent touch fuels a forbidden longing. I try to tell myself it's only loneliness. But then, he slides his hand to the small of my back and pulls me in for a hug, and all my problems scatter.

His musky cologne fills my senses, and my eyes squeeze

shut as my head falls to his chest and my arms wrap around his waist.

This is it, right here. What I've been missing since the day he left.

My throat constricts, and tears prickle behind my eyelids.

He feels like home.

"I missed you so fucking much." His tone mirrors my same torment.

His heart beats rapidly, resonating with mine.

Tilting my head back, I meet his glassy gaze. "It's only been a few days."

He clenches his jaw, furrowing the muscle. "You know what I mean."

That husky voice sends chills down my spine, and my nipples harden.

"You're not being very friendly."

He leans in, his eyes fixated on my lips, the anticipation palpable. "What if I don't want to be friends?"

Butterflies explode in my stomach, and my heart beats fiercely within my ribcage. "Apparently, we're already dating."

"Are we now?" He flashes that wolfish grin, and his hand clasps the back of my neck. "Does that mean I get to kiss you whenever I want?"

His mouth inches closer, and my mind is in disarray.

"This is reckless," I whisper against his lips.

"This is inevitable," he counters, his voice deep and raspy.

And before I know it, our lips are pressed together. Desire outweighs caution, and I can't resist him.

The rough stubble on his jaw scratches my skin, and my fingers clutch his shirt.

It's gentle and languid until his teeth graze my bottom lip. A surge of arousal hits me low in the belly, and I'm opening for him. Our tongues intertwine, and he devours me. His taste explodes in my mouth, sweet like candy, like red Jolly Ranchers.

"Fuck." He presses his forehead to mine. "I want you. No, fuck that—I need you."

"Jax—"

He cuts me off with another scorching kiss. His fingers move to fist my hair, his erection digs into my hip, and there's no question where this is leading.

But before we can even begin to unravel this, a haughty voice I hoped never to hear again interrupts.

"Well, well, well..."

I jolt, and Jackson tenses. We release each other, and the tender moment we shared vanishes instantly.

Jackson's father approaches, decorated in a disheveled police uniform, his shirt partially untucked and open at the collar, his face lax. He's drunk.

You become an expert at identifying even the most minute signs of intoxication when your loved one has an addiction, and Kyle appears thoroughly sloshed.

His small, beady eyes lock on to mine, and the revulsion emanating from him is unmistakable. He's here because of me, because of my pregnancy, and he doesn't approve.

I reach for Jackson out of fear of his father and in hopes of holding tight to this new person he has become. Part of me expects him to brush me off and grow cold, as he has in the past when confronted with Kyle's wrath.

Instead, he encircles me in his arms and holds me close. "How the fuck did you get in here?"

The anger in his voice vibrates in his chest, and I flinch at his harsh tone.

"The gentleman at the door was kind enough to let me in." Kyle's words slur and run together. "This is where you've been? Holed up with this whore?"

My eyes burn with tears. His cruel remarks are nothing new but still painful and humiliating.

I won't stay here with Kyle, and I won't be with Jackson, fake or not, if his father is part of his life. Been there, done that. With Kyle around, it's only a matter of time before Jax relapses.

"I'm not doing this." I break free of Jackson's hold.

I face the doors into the penthouse, ready to escape, but Kyle steps in front of me, blocking my exit.

Jackson quickly returns me to his embrace, his muscular arms enveloping me. "What the fuck do you want?"

Kyle tilts his head, feigning concern. "Is it not okay to visit my son and his pregnant prostitute?"

Tears well in my eyes, and mortification stings my cheeks.

Jax points to the doors, his body shaking with rage. "Get the fuck out!"

Kyle reaches around me and shoves Jackson's shoulder. "Boy, you don't scare me. You think you're a man now that you got some bitch pregnant? Good job, Aurora. You got your big payday."

Jax doesn't budge. He's taller than Kyle by several inches and way more powerful. I hate violence, but for once, I wish Jackson would defend himself.

His father's words and behavior are gut-wrenching, but on top of that, his stale cherry cigar smell turns my stomach. I tuck my face into Jackson's shirt, trying to breathe through the wave of nausea. I need to leave before I throw up, but I'm paralyzed by anxiety and fear.

Jax cups my head, holding me tight to his chest, and

rubs my back. "Shut the fuck up and get out, or I'll have security remove you."

Kyle laughs manically, wafting his rotten stench, and my stomach lurches.

"I'm going to be sick, Jax." My head swims, and my words sound distant and sluggish.

"Aww, *Jax*. She's going to be sick," Kyle mocks.

Jackson dips his head. "Ricky stepped outside. Go with him. I'll handle this."

I separate from him, and as soon as we're apart, Kyle's gaze lowers to my baby bump, and his lip curls into a snide smirk.

Even though the ground beneath me whirls, I hug myself and put one foot in front of the other.

Behind Kyle, Ricky's massive body charges toward us, and I focus on his fierce, dark-blue eyes. I take two steps before my vision blurs. Time slows to a halt. A sudden wave of heat washes over me, leaving me lightheaded, and my knees give way.

Black spots shroud my periphery.

Fingers circle my wrist, and at first, I think Ricky has reached out to steady me. But the grip tightens at the joint, and pain radiates through my forearm and hand. My body jolts sideways, and I cry out.

Chaos explodes around me, the sounds of a brawl assaulting my ears. My wrist is freed, and I stumble. My wobbly legs scramble to remain upright, but it's useless. The ground rushes toward me, and my arms shoot out in vain.

I slam into the concrete, and everything fades away.

TWENTY-SIX
ETHAN

"You get her publicly. Spend the day together. Go on dates—*fuck*, for all I care—but she's living with me." I pace the room, gesturing animatedly with my hands.

Jackson ignores me, not giving a shit about my ranting. He hasn't glanced in my direction twice since I arrived at the hospital, keeping his focus on Aurora and the baby monitor. His knowledge of all this baby stuff is another thing that irks me.

The hour-long ride was brutal. Seeing her for the first time in months was equally as hard. I wanted to delay this moment. I knew being around her would only intensify my longing, and I thought if I kept my distance, I could repress my feelings for her.

Now, regret is tearing me apart. She's my responsibility, and her safety should've been a priority.

"Stop talking about me as if I'm not *right here*. I'm not living with you. I don't know you."

Her voice is strained. She's worried about the baby, and the maternity unit is taking its sweet-ass time with the ultrasound.

Jackson lifts his head, his hair in disarray from raking his finger through it. "Dude, fuck off. I wouldn't have called you if I knew you'd be a dick."

I stop pacing to face him, arms crossed over my chest. "Aurora and *my* baby need a stable home. Period. End of discussion. No more roommate problems, no more estranged family, no more fans and paparazzi."

He narrows his bloodshot eyes. "The baby might be yours, but she's not. Don't forget that."

"She's not yours either. Don't get ahead of yourself." I suck in a breath to calm my irritability and bring it down a notch. He and I fighting won't help Aurora. "I couldn't care less about your relationship, but it's clear she's not safe living with you."

Seeing her has my mind playing tricks on me. I envision a gated property in Santa Monica and Aurora with me every night—an absolute dream. The specifics and technicalities are cloudy, but I'll figure them out along the way.

Jackson scoffs, and my dreams come crashing down around me.

"How will you provide a stable home when you spend twenty hours a day preparing for your championship season?"

My frustration boils over, and my temper flares. "I can't concentrate on the season if I'm constantly dealing with you two!"

Am I talking about Aurora and the baby, or Aurora and Jackson? All three? I haven't even a clue. I never expected any of this.

"*That's* what this is about." Aurora's voice cracks, and her lips tremble. "Don't worry about me. I'm not your responsibility nor your shameful burden to deal with."

Her words are daggers, and I quickly realize the magnitude of my fuck-up. I need a muzzle when I'm panicked.

"I was assaulted," she cries. "I haven't seen my baby—*your baby*—and all you care about is your fucking hockey season?"

"No, that's not what I meant," I say through gritted teeth, but it's too late.

Her anger and hurt are palpable, and I watch helplessly as Jackson climbs into the bed with her. He kisses away her tears, and I'm frozen, a spectator to their undeniable bond.

He's rightfully tormented by what happened, apologizing profusely and promising to cut all ties with Kyle. I half expect him to get down on one knee, profess his undying love, and propose.

He touches, kisses, and holds her with the intimacy of a boyfriend while I remain on the fringes, the interloper. Envy gnaws at me, but this is what I wanted, and I only have myself to blame.

My head screams at me to walk away. Watching him with her is torture. I'm not and will never be the shining star Jackson is. The only thing I have, perhaps the only thing I'll ever have, is hockey, and pursuing her will fuck that up.

But my heart anchors me here, telling me that leaving is a mistake. *We made a baby.* No matter how surreal it is, it's happening. I have to make this work. I can't let my temper cloud my judgment and push her away.

Determined, I give them privacy and walk out the door. "Where's the ultrasound?" I ask a passing nurse, who raises her brows at my demanding tone.

Agitation crawls under my skin in response to Aurora's distress. I'm surprised Jackson hasn't blown a fucking gasket already. I expected him to be outraged and over the top while I kept my cool. Apparently, today, we're switching positions, and I get to be the moody asshole.

Unfortunately, this is all Aurora knows of me.

"Sir, the maternity unit is sending someone as soon as they can. Can I bring you something to drink while you wait?"

Although her offer is condescending, I accept, asking for three water bottles, and return to the room.

"He hates me," Aurora sobs.

My feet come to a stop at the threshold.

"No, he doesn't. Far from it. He's trying to avoid letting you in." There's silence and then the rustling of the bedding before Jackson says, "Sleep, babe. You're exhausted. I'll be here."

I tip my head back, inhale deeply, allowing my lungs to expand, and exhale slowly.

She thinks I hate her. Jesus, fuck. Can this get any worse?

And why isn't he seizing this opportunity to outmaneuver me? It'd be much easier if I could despise him.

Quietly entering, I take the chair Jackson was sitting in earlier and hand him a bottle of water before studying the baby monitor. I have no idea what I'm seeing, but the moving lines seem encouraging.

Careful not to disturb Aurora, he leans over. "The right side shows the baby's heart rate, and the left shows his movement."

"And everything is good?"

"Yeah. He moves a lot." A proud smile spreads across his lips.

And what else can I do but return it?

An hour later, the ultrasound machine arrives, wheeled in by a technician who balks when he sees our trio.

He glances between Jackson and me then grins at a groggy Aurora. "Hello, sweetheart! We meet again."

There's enough saccharine in his tone that Jackson and I share a glance of annoyance. It'd take a massive set of balls to get through the two of us. It's almost laughable.

Realization hits me hard in the chest. I compared myself to Jackson. I'm not only irritable, I'm fucking jealous—of him, of any other guy.

I've never been jealous and possessive over a woman. I'm entirely out of my element.

No wonder I can't keep my shit together.

The technician positions the machine close to the bed and asks, "The report states you fell." He eyes Jackson and me with suspicion. "Did you take any hits to the stomach, darling?"

That's two strikes with the endearments, and I'm itching to snap. I need Jackson to step up his game so I don't get into more trouble with Aurora.

"I...I don't know." She glances at Jackson for help. "I fainted before I hit the ground. I'm not sure. I have scrapes on my arms and knees, nothing on my stomach."

Jackson tugs at his hair. "Not that I saw, but she landed pretty hard."

Aurora twists the bedding, and I take her hand in mine. My pulse races when she doesn't pull away, allowing me to bring her knuckles to my lips. I make the mistake of breathing her in. She's as sweet as I remember, and my eyes fall shut.

Holding her hand, I pay close attention to the assessment, learning she's fifteen weeks pregnant. She hasn't felt the baby move, and she has been having dizzy spells. Jackson mentions her high blood pressure and stress, which only adds to my unresolved guilt.

I never wanted kids, but I also never expected to be incompetent at taking care of what's mine.

The ultrasound tech finishes the setup and reaches for the blanket, presumably to expose Aurora's stomach.

Before he can, Jackson finally steps in. "Nice try, handsy, but no." He adjusts Aurora's bedding and gown to reveal her rounded belly.

Internally, I groan at the pleasurable sight of her sporting my baby bump. Seeing her pregnant with my child stirs something primal inside me, and the craving to touch her gnaws at my insides.

It's my baby. I should be able to caress and kiss her stomach whenever I want.

The tech glides the gel-covered wand across her abdomen, delicately maneuvering until the stillness of the room is shattered by the rhythmic melody of our baby's heartbeat. My throat tightens, a painful knot of unshed tears and unspoken words.

Aurora releases a shaky sigh, happiness and relief tracing a path down her cheek, and I lean over to brush away the tear. "It's going to be all right, I promise."

I'd give her anything right now. I'm such a sucker for this girl. If it wasn't for Jackson, *I'd* be on my knees, begging and proposing.

Okay, maybe not.

Ah, shit, probably.

A tiny figure appears on the screen, and the reality of becoming a father blows me away. Fuck, this is mine. I can hardly believe what I'm staring at, marveling at the small, moving being.

Jackson gives Aurora the biggest grin I've ever seen grace his face. "I love him already," he says, further solidifying his attachment.

How could I possibly deprive him of this? It'd ruin him. The kid has nothing but Aurora and hockey.

Does it have to be him or me?

I watch my child's tiny, flickering heartbeat, silently vowing that regardless of the chaos, I will withstand any fallout to provide Aurora and our unborn child the love and protection they deserve.

Even if that includes Jackson.

TWENTY-SEVEN
JACKSON

THE LAST TWENTY-FOUR hours have been a real test of my patience. Aurora was in the hospital for observation overnight while Ethan and I returned to LA.

Leaving her was rough, but it gave him and me time to discuss the future and what's best for Aurora and the baby. Neither of us wants to complicate things further, and Ethan assures me he's not trying to replace me, and for some odd reason, I believe him.

This morning, she was released after doctors determined her fainting was caused by anxiety. Again.

Her wrist is only bruised or sprained, and no concussion symptoms were noted. Her obstetrician will monitor her high blood pressure, also potentially brought on by stress. But thankfully, the baby showed no signs of distress and appears to be developing like a champ.

My father received a dislocated shoulder and some bruising when Ricky tackled him to the concrete. If I hadn't been terrified over Aurora, Kyle's screams would've been music to my ears. I offered Ricky a bonus, but he declined, taking blame for allowing the drunk asshole into the penthouse.

We both agreed *no one* is allowed up without prior authorization. Aurora's safety is our top priority.

Kyle might be the police commissioner of the nation's second-most-populated city, but he's more corrupt than any prisoner from Alcatraz or Ryker's.

A special place in Hell awaits him, and if he ever lays a hand on Aurora again, I'll deliver him there myself.

I purchased the penthouse mainly to keep him away from her—if she granted me another chance. I never even mentioned the property. How he figured out we were here is anyone's guess. I wouldn't be surprised if he had someone watching me.

Aurora loves the beach and everything the resort offers. When we were together, it was one of her favorite places to stay, and when the place expanded, I overbid for the cliffside penthouse to ensure it was hers.

Fate brought Aurora to the club the first night we met, and it couldn't have been anything other than fate that brought her to Laguna the exact moment I was finalizing the contract. She's my destiny, and I won't allow anyone to ruin my second chance.

Which is why I agreed to split Aurora's time with Ethan. I'll spend the afternoon with her, and he'll meet her tonight and take her house hunting in the morning.

At least, that's the plan for now. I've got a few tricks up my sleeve.

For today, I reserved a cabana on the beach and arranged for a picnic. The weather is perfect—it's a warm fall day, and the California sun is shining.

I can't stop staring at her lying on the blanket beside me

in nothing but a black bikini, showing off her cute baby bump.

Turning to me, she gestures to a group of spectators. "We're garnering attention."

I spot two photographers among the crowd, snapping pictures. "You want to go in?"

"No, but we could give them a show." She flashes that mischievous smile. "You know, because we're fake dating and all."

I come up onto my elbows. "There's nothing fake about us."

"You didn't want a public relationship last time we were together, remember?"

"I want it all. I don't give a fuck about the publicity."

"Are you sure about that, O'Reilly?" she challenges, getting to her hands and knees.

My heart races. I can barely breathe at the sight of her, let alone think. "Is this a test?"

Before I'm able to make sense of what's happening, she's crawling between my legs while biting her bottom lip, giving me a tantalizing view of her perfect tits.

I lay my head down on my crossed arms, trying like hell not to gawk at her half-naked body and pebbled nipples. But when she reaches my abdomen and begins trailing kisses, fuck, does my cock take notice.

Her sinful caramel eyes lock on mine, and I'm a goner. I don't know if she wants a relationship, public or not, but it's impossible not to get my hopes—or dick—up.

Agonizingly slow, she kisses up my stomach and chest. I draw in staggered breaths, unable to refrain from shifting my hips, my erection pulsing along with my heartbeat. It's pure torture.

Her knees straddle my waist, and she gazes down at me. "Do you want me to stop?"

"Fuck no."

Leaning in, she presses her pouty lips to mine, and I can't take anymore. I wrap my arms around her, weave my fingers into her hair, and deepen the kiss.

Our tongues intertwine, and we're no longer pretending for the paparazzi. Our kiss becomes urgent and needy, punctuated by soft moans.

She captures my bottom lip between her teeth then whispers, "I've missed your mouth."

"Let me show you what else this mouth can do."

She moves from my lips to bite and suck my neck, and I sense her smile against my skin. "I remember."

I release a low groan and flex my hips. My aching erection grinds against her thinly covered pussy, and I'm reminded of our surroundings and the colossal tent I'm pitching.

"Baby, we have to stop. These shorts aren't gonna hide what you're doing to me, and I doubt anyone wants to see that."

What the fuck am I saying? I should let her do whatever she wants. Fuck the cameras.

She keeps going, and when she hits that spot under my ear, goosebumps erupt on my skin.

Yet, nothing compares to the rush of pure adrenaline when she says, "I do. I want it."

Sitting up with her straddling me, I hastily stand. She encircles my neck with her arms and my waist with her legs. I support her with an arm under her ass and make a beeline for the resort, offering the cameras a middle finger.

Aurora can't stop laughing and giggling. "Jackson, the blankets!"

"Fuck the blankets."

The staff will pick up the blankets and whatever else we left.

I fumble with the key card in my pocket, cursing myself for not having this picnic on the balcony.

Once I manage to open the door and call the elevator, I adjust her in my arms, palming her ass cheeks. "You better not be teasing me, babe. I swear, my dick will die of sadness."

The lift is taking forever, and I consider the seven flights of stairs. But with her wrapped around my waist, her warm center pressed to my length, I doubt my cock could handle the friction.

"I'm not teasing you." She bites my earlobe and drags her nails over my neck. "I could always kiss it and make it better."

"Aurora, stop, or I'll fuck you right here. Then no one will question if we're together." I dig my fingertips into her thick ass and thrust my erection along her core to emphasize my point.

As soon as the elevator doors open, I've got her against the mirrored wall, my lips on hers. Our kiss is full of desperation, our moans filling the quiet space, and I rock my hips to relieve some of the throbbing ache.

All I can think about is being inside her, claiming her.

I miss the way she whimpers my name, the feel of her body beneath mine, the taste of her on my tongue...

"Grab the railing, babe. I need you in my mouth."

She places her hands on the bar behind her, and I slip to my knees, holding her tight in my grip, her legs over my shoulders. With my thumb, I hook the fabric of her bathing suit aside, revealing the most perfect pussy I've ever had.

I waste no time and dive in. I run my tongue along her

wet slit, and her sweetness erupts in my mouth, eliciting a groan from deep within my chest.

"Fuck, I've missed you." *Lick.* "I could live on this alone." *Suck.* "Die right here." *Lick.*

I devour her, sucking and teasing her clit while her hips writhe and her whimpers become needy. The sounds of her pleading moans and my mouth working her slick sex are interrupted by the ding of the elevator before it comes to a stop.

After fixing her bikini, I set her on her feet and grab her chin, bringing her in for a rough kiss and letting her taste herself on my tongue. We break apart, both of us winded, her cheeks flushed and pupils dilated.

The doors open into the penthouse, and I can't hold back any longer. I'm taking her on the first available surface.

Thank fuck, Ricky isn't here.

I push her up against the wall, my forearms trapping her in place. Her hands roam over my abs and chest, and our heavy breaths mingle, filling the silence.

"I love you." My words come out husky, my body aching with a craving I know only she can satisfy.

Her gaze meets mine, hesitant and vulnerable. "Have you been with anyone else? While we were apart?"

My answer is immediate. "No. Never."

She searches my eyes, and I'm tempted to tell her the truth, but that will undoubtedly kill the mood.

"I don't even have a condom on me, but if you don't believe me, I just had my yearly physical."

"I was tested...for the baby."

"I trust you. Please, trust me on this. I'd never intentionally hurt you or the baby."

"Okay," she whispers and gives my lips a peck.

She spins and loosens the ties of her bikini. The pieces fall to the floor, and I shove off my shorts.

I take in the sight of her luscious naked body, and my cock twitches. She's the epitome of erotic, with suntanned skin, graceful curves, and those butt dimples that drive me fucking insane.

Every fiber of my being is frantic, greedy for her. She leans on her forearms, and I grip her hips, pulling her closer. I glide my hands over her swollen belly to palm her breasts and pinch her nipples.

She arches her back and whines, "Jax."

"Damn, I love when you say my name like that." I trail kisses along the curve of her neck and grind the head of my cock through her drenched slit.

I let out a low, guttural groan and press into her hot, wet cunt.

Her head tips back in a shuddered gasp.

"Fuck, baby." I thrust home, and her pussy squeezes around me.

Our bodies come together, and my emotions rush to the surface, lust and physical need turning into something different entirely.

It has been months since I've felt her this deeply, and I've been starving for her.

My forehead falls to her shoulder, tears prickle my eyelids, and my arms crush her to my chest.

Everything hits me at once, and I know if we separate again, I won't survive. I almost didn't this time.

I lift my head, inhaling her jasmine and vanilla scent into my lungs. "Stay with me. I'd rather die than hurt you again. Please stay with me."

She had to foresee this. I'm too attached to engage in something fake or superficial.

Reaching back, her fingers tangle in my hair, and she rocks her hips, seeking friction. "This is your chance, Jax. You know my limits. Now, please, fuck me."

By *limits,* she means no cheating, no drugs, and no alcohol.

Easy. Done.

"Fuck, yeah." I grasp her waist and pound into her, her ass rippling with each slap of my hips. "Fuck, I love you, and I love fucking you."

Pleasure builds with each stroke, coiling tight in my stomach. There's no way I'm going to last, having been pining for her with nothing but my hand and fantasies of her.

My balls are throbbing, my legs are twitchy, and my head is hazy with ecstasy. "You feel too fucking good. I'm not gonna last long in your perfect pussy, baby."

Her fingers in my hair shift to my neck, and her nails bite into my skin. She widens her stance and rises onto her tiptoes, further arching her back, and meets me thrust for thrust. "Fuck me, O'Reilly. Make me yours."

I slam my hand into the wall and growl, "You are mine." I angle my hips and sink deep, aiming for the spot I know will have her flooding my dick soon enough. "Always."

"Don't stop." Her breath hitches, and she bites her bottom lip.

I find her clit and circle it with my fingers. "Come for me, baby. Soak my fucking cock."

"Jax," she whimpers so sweetly.

It goes straight to my balls. Her low moans turn into unrestrained screams, and her tight-as-fuck pussy grips me.

"God, fuck, baby."

My eyes fixate on our conjoined bodies, and the sight of

my rock-hard shaft glistening with her cum sends me over the edge.

I'm about to withdraw and unload on her ass when I realize...*I don't have to.*

"Oh, fuck. I'm gonna come inside you." My words are barely above a whisper, nothing but a throaty moan, and I lose my breath, coming harder than I can remember.

So hard my abdominal muscles clench, and I suck air through gritted teeth, my cock jerking with bursts of hot cum that fill her pulsating cunt.

I can't stop fucking her. Our combined releases drips down her thighs, and a new addiction unlocks in my obsessed brain. "Goddamn, I love that. I'm gonna spend my life filling this pussy."

We devote the rest of our day to exploring each other's bodies and making up for what we missed. When we leave Laguna, I'm more exhausted than I am after most games and happier than I've been in a long time.

TWENTY-EIGHT
AURORA

The elevator ride to Ethan's apartment is uncomfortably silent. I've sensed Ricky's gaze on me, but each time I glance in his direction, it quickly darts away. I'm sure he finds this arrangement odd and thinks I'm a slut, although he'd never say it.

The doors open, and we step off to Ethan's floor.

Ricky clears his throat. "You want me to stay with you?"

He drove me here after dropping Jax off at his downtown penthouse. We're running late. My ex—not ex anymore, I guess—wasn't ready to let go. I'm nervous about being alone with Ethan, but I'd rather be anywhere other than where Jackson and I made most of our memories, good and bad.

I shake my head. "No, it's okay. You don't have to do that."

Ricky's brows are furrowed, his dark-blue eyes filled with concern, an expression he has held since the Kyle incident. "I don't mind."

Ethan might, though. He wants to spend time together and get to know one another before the baby comes. It's a good idea, but my stomach is in knots. He still intimidates me. He's older and exudes this dominance that leaves me feeling both inferior and safe. It makes no sense.

I give Ricky a soft smile. "I'm fine. Honestly."

He stops in front of Ethan's door, hoists my bag over his massive shoulder, and takes my injured wrist in his hand, inspecting the bruising.

"They do an x-ray?"

"No, because of the baby."

He releases a heavy sigh. "Right."

Despite his daunting size, tattoos, and ability to snap me in two without breaking a sweat, Ricky is surprisingly gentle.

"I'm sorry. Had I known he was a complete piece of shit, I would've never let him in."

"It's okay. You didn't know, and it doesn't hurt."

He raises my arm and assesses the scrapes around my elbow. "I'm gonna get you to stop saying that. You're not always fine or okay. You're too nice."

I pull away, eager to escape this conversation.

I'm not the person I was before Hurricane Jackson, when I was a naïve pushover, and Emily did most of the talking for me. But even though I've learned to stick up for myself out of necessity, it's still a struggle.

"Honestly, it wasn't your fault. Kyle is an asshole."

He makes a noise deep in his throat but, thankfully, doesn't push the issue any further.

I rap on the apartment door, and Ethan answers almost immediately, having cleared our way with the doorman, and my body freezes. I want to go home. To Jackson.

Ricky places a hand on the small of my back, guiding me forward, and I focus on breathing slow and steady. He drops my bag and introduces himself, and I look anywhere but at the man who turned my world upside down.

Ethan's barely lived-in apartment is modern and well-appointed, with monochromatic, clean lines and high-end furnishings. The most captivating feature is the floor-to-ceiling windows, which offer a panoramic view of downtown LA. It's similar to Jackson's nearby penthouse, though nowhere near as large. Still, it's equally impressive.

Before he leaves, Ricky tells me to text him if I need him, and I nod, unable to speak. The door closes, and I'm left with Mr. Big Dick Married Guy, except he's no longer married.

"Yeah, I'm not fond of him." Ethan's deep voice, filled with hostility, grabs my attention.

"Are you fond of anyone?" It slips from my mouth, but it's an honest question.

He bites his lip and doesn't answer, and I return to admiring his space.

"Sorry I haven't got an oceanfront penthouse like your boyfriend." There's that bitterness again.

I cross the open living area to the kitchen, where he's leaning against the counter, watching me.

"Oh, yes, because this downtown high-rise is truly awful. Is that a view of the Staples Center? How horrendous. How do you live with yourself?"

My tone drips with sarcasm, and his lips spread into a rare smile that reaches his eyes and shows off that dimple.

Fucking dimples.

"I see you still have that attitude."

Ignoring his smart-ass comment, I glance around. "This isn't what I expected. It doesn't look like you."

He tilts his head. "Oh yeah? And what do I look like?"

The corner of his mouth tips up, and he runs his thumb over

his bottom lip, as if trying to stop himself from smiling again.

In a white T-shirt and faded jeans with tousled hair and an unkempt beard, he's as handsome as I remember, if not more. The laid-back style suits him.

Unlike this staged and untouched apartment.

I lean against the counter across from him, appraising his brooding demeanor. "Rough, impatient, and in need of sleep."

I'm teasing but not exaggerating. Ethan's hair is messy and overgrown, revealing adorable curls, and he has a scruffy beard, only adding to his rugged appeal.

He's harsh and magnetic, and I'm drawn to him, but I also want to run out the door.

His gaze falls on my slightly swollen stomach, and he pushes away from the counter. He lifts me by the waist and plops me onto the granite island as if I am weightless.

My mouth pops open, and my heart goes wild.

"You'd be right," he says, resting his hands on the surface next to my hips, boxing me in. "We need to talk."

"Okay." I stretch the word and twist the fabric of my sundress. Nothing good ever begins with "We need to talk."

"First, I'm sorry for upsetting you at the hospital. I have a knack for speaking before thinking, as you know."

I bristle. "But it's still what you think."

He arches a brow. "And what do you make of my thoughts?"

All my fears come tumbling out in a rush of words. "I think you still perceive me as the escort you got pregnant, a burden you're trying to pass on to someone else, which is fine. I told you that. But you're too good of a guy to walk away entirely."

His jaw clenches and grinds. He grips the granite, and

his muscular arms flex, the veins in his hands and forearms protruding. I breathe deeply to steady myself, only to inhale his heady, masculine scent.

Jesus, why does he have to be damn irresistible?

His furrowed brow begs for me to smooth out the lines, and don't even get me started on the vein porn. I want to trace every single one.

Instead, I allow my gaze to wander from his powerful hands to his ripped forearms, bulging biceps, thick neck, kissable lips, and intense eyes that watch me with a hint of amusement.

He swallows, and his Adam's apple bobs—why is that hot?

"None of that is true. I want you, and not only in a physical sense. I want that hungry gleam in your eyes." He flashes a smug smirk. "The one you had while eye-fucking me."

"I was *not* eye-fucking you."

"You're a terrible liar, baby girl." He places a lingering kiss on our baby bump. "I don't intend to walk away. I intend to take it all. I *want* it all. Even your brutal honesty." He cocks his head. "Though I'm tempted to punish that smart mouth of yours." His smirk grows devilish before his expression becomes serious. "My feelings for you scare the shit out of me. I've been through hell and back and managed to survive. But you...you have the power to ruin me. After you, I might not recover."

He's not making this easy on me.

I should leave. But I don't, and my fingers travel up his neck, disappearing into his wavy hair. His head drops, surrendering to my touch, and his broad shoulders rise and fall with every breath.

How is this my life? With two men I can't resist.

Callused palms glide up my thighs, and my heart skips a beat or three.

My mouth goes dry, and I swallow my nerves. "Your hair is longer. I—"

"What the fuck is this?" His gruff words cut me off. He straightens and lifts my dress to scrutinize the red and purple fingerprint marks Jackson left behind. "Who did this?"

"It's not what you think...at least, I don't think. It wasn't done intentionally...or it was, but not in a bad way. You know?" I'm rambling again, and I need to shut up.

"Is that why you're nervous? Because you came here after fucking him?" He spits the words, sharp with betrayal.

My stomach swoops. This man is giving me whiplash.

"No. *You* make me nervous, and you said you didn't care if I was *fucking him*," I spit right back.

He fists my dress and yanks me to the edge of the counter until my body is flush with his and my legs are around his waist. "I know what I fucking said."

I clutch his shirt for balance and suck in a sharp gasp. "What are you doing?"

His fingers encircle my throat, and his eyes darken. "I think you owe me."

TWENTY-NINE
AURORA

I try to pull away, needing space to collect my thoughts.

But Ethan's grip on my throat tightens, and he growls, "Don't move."

His hold isn't punishing. I can breathe easily and break free if I wanted—maybe. But his powerful claim over my body is louder than any words could express, and I find I don't want to—quite the opposite. My body *wants* to submit to him.

It's my mind that rebels.

He reaches between our bodies and slips his thumb under the gusset of my lace thong.

My face flushes with heat. "Ethan—" I'm speechless, embarrassed, and aroused.

He glides his finger through my already wet slit. "You let him come in you?"

Before I utter a word, he pushes two fingers inside me.

"Answer me," he demands.

I swallow the lump in my throat, my voice weak. I swear, I lose all sense when this man touches me. "Yes."

He curls his fingers and circles my swollen clit with his thumb. My thighs tense, and I bite my bottom lip.

"What's wrong, baby girl?" he teases.

The carnal sound of him working my sex only fuels my desire, and I rock my hips.

"Too sensitive."

He slows his pace. "And why is that?"

"Ethan," I whine. "We should talk."

Didn't he say we needed to talk? How did this escalate from *I have feelings for you* to him tormenting me in less than sixty seconds?

And what about Jackson? I can't deal with his jealousy. He'll be furious and hurt.

Conflicted, I grab Ethan's wrist.

His expression hardens. "Unless you plan on clawing me while I make you come, remove your hand."

His voice is low and deep and frightening.

And why am I so aroused?

I snatch my hand away. "But…"

"Good girl. Shut off that overworked brain of yours. I'll handle him."

He presses his lips to mine, his beard tickling my skin, and I open for him without resisting. Our tongues intertwine, and he continues to fuck me with his fingers.

I whimper and writhe. I need to come *badly*, but it's just out of reach, blocked by anxious thoughts.

"Let me have control." His hand around my throat shifts, and his thumb caresses my jawline. "I've got you."

I want that, more than anything, to let someone else take control, to trust someone enough to stop overthinking.

And I want *him*, as wrong as it might be. I want Ethan.

So, I do. I allow my mind to go blank, freeing all shame and doubt. "Okay."

"That's my good girl."

Jesus, those words.

He removes his fingers from me and draws them across my bottom lip. "Open."

Although my clit is throbbing for release, I obey. I suck his fingers into my mouth and run my tongue over them.

He watches me with fire in his eyes. "You enjoying his cum?"

My lips part. I stare at him, stunned. How am I supposed to answer that?

"Don't worry." His intense gaze burns into mine, his voice all gravelly. "I'm going to fuck the taste of him right out of your mouth."

He releases my throat to remove his shirt, and I instantly miss the possessive hold.

With impatience, he hooks the sides of my panties and rips them down my legs, the friction burning my thighs.

My white Chuck Taylors are still on, and he lifts my feet to his stomach. I stifle a giggle. There's something about this formidable man—with his large hands curled around my small ankles as he pries my panties over my immature sneakers—that makes me smile.

I bet he never saw this coming, never saw himself with a twenty-two-year-old who wears sundresses and Converse instead of seductive lingerie and six-inch heels.

But he doesn't miss a beat. He drops my feet and panties, going for his pants. The whoosh and snap of his belt is an aphrodisiac, and I recline, spreading my legs for him.

His stormy gray eyes fixate on my center. "I should punish you and not let you come, but damn, I want that pretty pussy milking my cock."

He palms his thick erection, notches at my entrance,

and fills me in a single, demanding thrust. My back arches, and a lusty moan slips from my throat.

"Fuck, you feel even better than I remember." His soft tone contrasts entirely with the swift pounding of his hips.

No matter what he says, this is a punishment. He's ripping the pleasure from my body and ensuring I feel him for days—only him.

Ecstasy prickles along my skin like wildfire, and I grip the counter.

"Come on my cock, baby girl." He slams into me, hitting fucking deep, and circles my clit.

I tighten my legs around his waist, Converse digging into his back to prevent him from stopping. My mind splinters into a million pieces, and I shatter with a strangled scream.

"Fucking hell," he grits through clenched teeth. "I'm not ready to come yet. Jesus, fuck."

He doesn't slow his powerful thrusts until my moans quiet and my body relaxes.

My brain is still foggy when he pulls out, lifts me from the island, and sets me on wobbly legs.

He fists his shaft. "Get on your knees."

Eager to submit, I drop.

He steps closer and widens his stance. Thumbing his length, he grabs my hair and tugs my head back. "Open."

I do, without hesitation, and that possessive grip returns to my throat.

He slides his cock along my tongue, stretching my lips, and demands, "Clean him off me," in that gruff tone that sends a shiver down my spine.

I take him into my mouth, savoring the erotic blend of flavors that explode on my taste buds and elicit a moan.

"You like that, don't you? You like being my dirty girl?"

His fist wraps in my hair, and I whimper, the restraint shooting straight to my clit.

There must be something wrong with me, because I love his brand of dominance, love being at his mercy.

He gives me no time to adjust to him, thrusting deep, and I gag.

His dick jolts, and he sucks air through his teeth, hissing. "Take my cock." *Thrust.* "Show me who you fucking belong to." *Thrust.*

He holds me in place and fucks my mouth, one hand fisting my hair and the other clasping my throat. His movements are forceful yet controlled, his dark gaze locked on mine the entire time.

"Nobody else, Aurora. You understand me? Or I'll choke you with my cock."

Does he mean him? Jackson? Him and Jackson...

Thrust.

He gives me a sample of his threats, and I try to suppress my gag reflex, the muscles of my throat working against him.

Tears leak out, and I concentrate on breathing through my nose.

"God, you're fucking good."

His pace increases, and I press him to the roof of my mouth, circling my tongue. He releases a guttural groan, and I taste his precum.

Cupping the back of my head, he flexes his hips, and right when I think I can't take anymore and my nails are digging into his thighs, his cock jerks.

"Ah...fuck." He rumbles a deep moan.

I meet his intense gaze, his eyes half-lidded, his jaw

clenched. I swallow his cum until he's satisfied and brushing his fingers through my hair.

"Good girl," he pants. "Come here." He lifts me into his arms. "Let's go to bed."

Then, he kisses my forehead as if he didn't just alter my fucking soul.

THIRTY
ETHAN

I wake to Aurora snuggling against me, her head on my chest, our legs intertwined, and her arm wrapped tight around me, as if she's afraid I'll slip away. Her stomach is pressed to my side, and I can't resist caressing our growing baby.

Thoughts of the future arise, and I consider the repercussions of something that resembles a relationship.

A commitment harms Jackson. If he loses her, he'll slide back into old habits, not to mention the backlash from the media or the potential loss of my coaching career. And I honestly doubt she'll leave him.

Walking away is out of the question. I'm not giving up my son. Shared custody is possible, but it'd be difficult with my schedule. We'd have to maintain a close relationship for her to accommodate my lifestyle.

Which brings me full circle, because there's no way I could have Aurora near and not want her. I can't picture my life without her. The thought of it sends a sharp pang of regret through my chest.

Our sexual chemistry is unparalleled, but it goes beyond that. She fills a void within me no one else has.

My hand rests on her swollen belly, and a fierce longing to claim her comes over me. I knew I needed to stay away, but now, it's too late. I want this.

I want her in my bed every night. I want to wake with her in my arms and watch her grow with our baby.

But that's not possible.

Aurora's waking groan calms my chaotic thoughts.

"Is it time to get up already?"

I chuckle at her sleepy protests and kiss her forehead. "Depends on how long you need to get ready. If you hurry, I'll take you for breakfast."

She's not at all quick to get ready, and I have to deflect all her advances in the shower, which requires superhuman strength and ninja skills. Her teasing is top-notch, along with her wet, sun-kissed body.

I thought she'd appreciate a day together that didn't revolve around sex. You know, one where we *actually* talk.

But she can't keep her hands off me.

"Stop, brat, so I can take you to breakfast like a gentleman."

She sticks her bottom lip out and strokes my traitorous erection. "I'd rather have breakfast in the shower."

I grin but knock her hand away. "I bet that pout works on your boyfriend, but it won't work on me." I slap her ass, one hundred percent regretting it when her skin reddens and my cock twitches. "Now, be good."

She rolls her eyes, and I spank her again, secretly falling in love with this dynamic.

By the time she gets out of the shower, I'm dressed in jeans and a button-up and working on my first cup of coffee. I'm on my second cup when she exits my bedroom in a pair of leggings, an oversized team hoodie, her high-top Converse, and her hair in loose waves. She's ridiculously adorable.

Dread curdles in my stomach, and I glance away. I have no business dating someone this young and pretty. Eventually, she'll figure that out too.

We walk two blocks to a diner without notice from the paparazzi. Still, I keep my hands in my pockets.

Not holding her hand or touching her feels wrong, and I question how long I can continue this charade.

The hostess asks if we want a booth or a table, and I select a booth in the back. Aurora gives me a disappointed glance, and I remind myself not to treat her like a secret—although she is.

We only have forty-five minutes before we need to leave for Santa Monica. After I check my watch repeatedly and mention our time crunch, she gives me another frown, and I realize my overbearing attitude won't be as well received outside the bedroom.

She orders an egg white omelet with spinach and a bowl of fruit, and again, my mouth doesn't get the memo to shut up.

"That's all you're eating? Please tell me you eat more than that."

"I have a nutritionist. It's better if I eat small portions every four hours." She gives me a soft smile. "I promise I'm not starving your son."

Your son. Fuck, I love that.

I take out my phone to set a reminder of her eating schedule when I get a taunting message from Jackson.

> Captain Diva: How's my girl this morning? She recovering from our strenuous day together?

I bet he was itching to tell me they were fucking and going mad, wondering if we were doing the same. I text him back with a smug grin.

> Me: Strenuous? She seemed energized to me. But don't worry, she rested in my bed after.
>
> Captain Diva: About to be my bed permanently. See you soon, asshole.
>
> Me: You better learn how to share, or I might keep her.
>
> Captain Diva: Eat a fat dick.
>
> Me: So not yours then?

Our back-and-forth banter has me chuckling, but then I glimpse Aurora's slumped shoulders and pinched brows, and confusion overtakes my amusement.

I place my phone down. "What's wrong?"

She shakes her head, suddenly fascinated by the traffic outside the restaurant.

"Aurora, this isn't going to work if we don't communicate."

Narrowed whiskey eyes meet mine. "And what are we working on?"

"Being parents, being together. Whatever this is." I gesture between us.

"And what is this? A secret, right? At the end of the day, I go home to Jackson, and you do whatever...or *whoever*."

Oh, shit, baby girl is jealous. My chest fills with male pride, and I want to laugh out loud. That's a first for me, and I find I quite enjoy her jealousy.

I'd enjoy it even more if I could put her over my knee and fix that attitude.

One step at a time.

"I'm not doing *whoever*. We're viewing houses today to figure out what *this* is."

She presses her lips together. "Whatever."

That smart fucking mouth. An image of her choking on my cock last night flashes in my mind, and I sigh.

"Are you upset I'm using my phone?"

"Please stop."

Her voice trembles, and I grind my molars, reminding myself she's twenty-two. Jackson was likely her only serious boyfriend, and he was unreliable and dishonest.

Still, I'm not letting her get away with ignoring me.

"I'll stop when you tell me what's wrong."

"It's the pregnancy," she grumbles.

Although I don't fully believe her, I call the waiter over and ask for a glass of orange juice.

When it comes, I slide it to her. "Drink. Do you have low blood sugar? When was the last time you ate?"

"Thank you." She takes the glass, bringing it to her lips. "Yesterday afternoon."

Yesterday afternoon? Didn't she say she had to eat every four hours? I should have fed her something other than my cock last night.

She sips delicately and inhales deeply, and my worry intensifies. Maybe she's not tearful because she believes I'm talking to someone else. Maybe she's sick.

My tone elevates, and my heart races at the thought of her passing out on me. "Are you dizzy?"

She shakes her head, staring at her lap.

Fuck it. I abandon all caution and relent to the overwhelming urge to care for her.

After ensuring we're not being watched, I move about the semicircle booth and sit beside her.

Her brows furrow. "What are you doing?"

"Stop overthinking and let me take care of you."

I wrap my arm around her and draw her to my chest. I kiss her temple, and she rests her head on my shoulder. She smells of my spicy bodywash and her sweet self, and I groan internally.

"If, for some insane reason, you're worried I'm messaging other women, you can stop. I was texting and joking with Jackson. There's no woman in my life but you. I can't imagine there being anyone other than you."

"I have no right to those feelings."

My heart skips, and my palms turn sweaty. I glance down, and she's clinging to my shirt the way she was clinging to my body this morning.

Desiring me on a physical level is one thing, but her having deeper *feelings* for me? Absurd. Unfathomable. Not possible.

So why is my breath quickening?

"Look at me, Aurora."

Impatient, I tilt her head back. She opens her glassy eyes, and fuck me, I'm blown away by the vulnerability shining through.

"One: I knew what I was getting into when I invited you over. As did Jackson. He wouldn't have let you spend the night with me if he didn't. *I* wouldn't have let you spend the night with me. Two: Give me your trust. I'll protect it. I promise, you'll never have to worry about that with me."

She gives me a doubtful, pointed stare as if to say, *You were married when we met.*

"That was with you, and my marriage was over, which brings me to number three: You're a twenty-two-year-old gorgeous cover model, and I'm a thirty-five-year-old washed-up hockey player. If anyone doesn't have a right here, it's me."

A scowl comes over her beautiful face. "Those aren't your words. Someone told you that, which doesn't make them true."

I swear, she's clawing her way into my heart.

"Doesn't matter. You're still far above me."

She slides her hand beneath my shirt and teases me by running her fingers along the waistband of my jeans. "I've seen every part of you, and there's not a single inch I don't love."

Squeezing her cheeks and puckering her lips, I give her a hard, smacking kiss. "Stop, pretty girl, or I'll put you on my lap right here in this restaurant."

She gives me that mischievous smile. "I won't mind."

And I can't refuse. I tangle my fingers in her thick hair and devour her until we're both breathless.

I'm doing a shit job of keeping this private.

"How many places are we touring today?" Aurora asks as we ride through downtown LA.

She has yet to question why Ricky is driving or why we're in Jackson's custom Land Rover, which I'm pretty sure is armored. Where I come from, an armored vehicle means trouble. Where he comes from, it might be a standard of living.

I'm not complaining. There's a privacy partition I'm quite enjoying, since Aurora hasn't stopped teasing me.

Ignoring her question, I try to distract her. "Are you always this affectionate, baby girl?"

My words are meant to be playful, but she takes them all wrong, pulling away and apologizing.

I scoop her up and return her to my lap. "Did I say I didn't like it?"

With her back against my chest, she relaxes into me. "I don't know what you like."

I slip my hand under her hoodie and palm our baby. My dick twitches, and I will it to calm the fuck down. I lean in, unable to resist her mouth for even a minute. "Oh, I think you know exactly what I like."

She parts her lips, and I weave my fingers through her hair and deepen the kiss. The car comes to a halt, and I fight not to smile.

I live for this.

The back door opens, and she tries to break free. I hold her in place, my hand clasping her throat and my tongue dueling with hers.

Not until the door slams and the seat dips next to us do I release her.

Cheeks flushed, her head snaps in the opposite direction, and her mouth pops open. "Jackson," she gasps.

"You're a fucking asshole," he snarls, his chest heaving. "You're lucky she's between us."

He glares at me, and I can't help but chuckle. Although my captain isn't afraid to throw down, he's nothing but a moody, tattooed puppy.

I lift her from my lap. "Hug your boyfriend, baby. I don't want him fracturing another hand."

She moves toward him, but he hesitates, anger still lurking in his eyes.

For a flickering moment, I worry he'll refuse her. I consider the potential benefits for myself but dismiss the thought, guilt overwhelming all else.

He recovers and draws her into his arms, and relief floods through me. I may revel in annoying him, but I'm not here to crush him.

I work on my phone to respect their privacy, but I can't help but overhear their conversation.

"What are you doing here?" she asks him with genuine happiness.

"You want me to leave?"

"No, of course not."

"Good, because I'm taking you to see our new house." The excitement in his voice is impossible to ignore.

"Our house? What do you mean?"

Jackson playfully shrugs, and she peers at me for the answer. I shrug and run my thumb over my bottom lip to hide my smirk.

Jesus, my cheeks are aching from all this smiling.

She gives him that pout of hers. "Tell me, Jax."

I have no doubt he'll spoil her relentlessly, either out of fear she'll leave again or gratitude at having her back. He already does, whether she knows it or not. A luxury cliffside penthouse on one beach and a gated compound on another?

Excessive for someone who spends most of his life on the ice.

No wonder she doesn't understand me. My emotional availability is less than ideal. Having her in my bed is my way of saying *I adore you*. It'd never happen with any other woman.

Yet this kid buys her mansions—we're not the same.

This time, however, he holds it in. "No more questions. You'll have to wait. Now, how's my baby?"

He caresses her stomach, and strangely, I don't feel territorial or possessive.

"We're fine."

She kisses him, and once again, jealousy doesn't overwhelm me.

Maybe it's because Jackson and I have grown close these past few months—as close as one can be to Jackson, besides Aurora. Or maybe it's because I've always been aware of his attachment to her.

Or perhaps it's *her*—the girl with endless affection and the power to bring a man to his knees.

"Did he at least feed you?" he asks, loud enough for me to know it's directed at me.

"Of course I did. By the way, she barely eats."

Aurora scowls at me, but Jackson glances over, surprisingly amicable.

"She's a picky eater. Only eats about ten things. I can give you a list." He taps her nose. "You better be eating. You're carrying a future hockey god in there, at least if you keep me around," he says, throwing another jab my way.

"And I almost liked you for a second."

Is this what living together will be like? He and I banter back and forth while we tease Aurora? Doesn't seem so bad.

There's a brief silence before Jackson resumes his lovesick behavior, and I reconsider my previous assessment.

He trails kisses along her neck. "I missed you."

She giggles. "You tell me that every day."

"Because it's true. I hate being without you."

Can someone please rip out my eardrums?

Still, I remain captivated by them. It's as if they have

their own language. They stare at each other and have entire conversations with their eyes.

She lowers her voice. "Are you mad?"

"Do I get to be with you?"

"Do you want to be?"

"Am I breathing?" He tucks a loose strand of hair behind her ear. "I have a lot to make up for. If this is what you want, I'll survive. As long as you're with me."

Satisfied with his answer, I return my attention to my phone when he says, "I still plan on stealing you away, but for now, I'll put up with him."

With Jackson, there's no telling if he's joking or not. But, same as him, I have no choice but to deal with it.

THIRTY-ONE
JACKSON

"We agreed to buy a place I could afford. You know my budget doesn't stretch this far." Aurora stands in the courtyard of the Santa Monica beach house, her arms crossed over her chest. She's adorable when trying to be assertive, especially bundled up in the giant hoodie she stole from me.

Little does she know, I've already purchased this home, and she's going to love it.

"Babe, we are splitting. Between the three of us," I gesture between me, her, and Ethan, the third wheel in our fucked-up dynamic.

When Ethan insisted Aurora and the baby live with him, alarms went off in my head. The thought of her agreeing filled me with panic, fearing I'd eventually fade out of the picture.

Her desire to give the baby a stable home with his father is understandable, but shit with Kyle has me feeling mental. He played a significant role in me losing her. Add Ethan, and I'm teetering on the edge of a psychotic break.

"There are four of us if you count the baby. I'll cover the

expenses for my child." Ethan poses similarly to Aurora, arms folded as a protective shield.

I don't know why he's defensive. He's got it made. He's a permanent fixture in Aurora's life for the next eighteen years.

At the hospital, a plan to outmaneuver him formed in my mind. If I own the beach house, add her name to the deed, and ensure she loves it, she'll stay. She definitely won't refuse if Ethan agrees.

He'll have the baby, and I'll have the house until I persuade her to marry me. That way, this asshole can't force me out of our situationship.

Bonus points if I can get the next kid—which I will.

I scoff. "No, that'd give you two shares. You wouldn't be here if I hadn't fucked up. I'll cover the baby's costs."

Pissing Ethan off is my new favorite hobby. I mean, he started it—first, by putting his dick—and baby—in her when he knew she was mine, and second, by taunting me with that kiss.

I may have fostered the misconception that Aurora would only accept a place she could manage financially. Not a complete fabrication. However, he believes a larger financial split is required because this is Aurora's dream home. Again, not entirely untrue.

Thus, I'm necessary and can't be forced out of my own home.

I've truly outdone myself this time. I even have a lawyer who'll finagle the contract.

"Don't even think about taking credit for my child. It was my fuck-up." He turns to Aurora, a hand over his heart. "A very, *very* good fuck-up." Then, he levels his stern coach expression at me. "It's on me. I had that expired condom in my wallet for over six years."

Aurora's cheeks flush, and her caramel eyes widen. "Are you serious, Ethan? Why?"

He grins, all smug, and I want to wipe it off with my fist.

What if he did this on purpose? I would. If she wasn't already pregnant, I'd be poking holes in every condom I own. After this baby, I'll have to keep him away from her.

Maybe I can convince him to get a vasectomy. He's, what, fifty?

"What do you mean, why? Obviously, in case some hot model flung herself at me."

"Which clearly hadn't happened in at least six years." I match his smirk with an arched brow.

All I need is for him to prove me wrong, for him to mention sleeping with someone else. Aurora will forget he even exists. Come on...

"Please don't answer that. I don't want to know." Aurora's hands dart up, covering her ears and ruining my chance of knocking him down a notch.

Ethan directs his piercing gaze my way. "This brings up another topic. Why is she insecure about other women?"

How the fuck did this get flipped on me? I'd rather cut off my dick than cheat on her.

"Why are you looking at me?" My blood boils at the accusation. I don't need Ethan planting seeds of doubt in Aurora's mind. I do that well enough on my own, thank you very much. "Maybe it's because you regrettably fucked her while still married."

His body stiffens, and he advances on me, fists clenched and fury blazing in his eyes. "The only regret I have is dealing with you. Repeat that, and a broken hand will be the least of your fucking worries."

He's a tad taller and bulkier than me, but I've been brawling my whole life, thanks to Kyle. It's muscle memory, and I won't feel a thing if enraged. Ethan's size doesn't intimidate me. The only thing I fear is losing Aurora.

"Then don't insinuate I cheated on her. It never fucking happened."

This is an ongoing theme in my and Aurora's relationship, and she has every reason to be insecure. For one, there's the stigma of being a hockey player. Add my addiction, and that puts me in places with people I shouldn't have been. Then there's Kyle, who never met a stripper or prostitute he didn't fuck.

To worsen the situation, I ended our relationship by not returning home and ignoring her calls and texts.

I've yet to grow balls big enough to make that confession, but no women were involved unless you count the nurses I was surrounded by. And I was in absolutely no condition to be thinking about sex. Even if I could, I wouldn't.

"Stop." Aurora wedges herself between us, a palm on each of our chests. "For fuck's sake, you two. Is this my future? Can we see the place now? Please."

She turns toward the seven-thousand-square-foot beachfront estate, leaving Ethan and I grumbling behind.

"I fucking hate you."

He grins, because of course he does.

Once we return to the car, Aurora withdraws into a familiar shell.

She said she loved the house. Her eyes lit up over the nursery and the beachside pool.

It's everything I knew she'd want. So why is she not excited?

Ethan and I share a worried glance. He must sense her brooding as well.

He raises her chin to meet his gaze. "Do you need to eat, baby? It's been about four hours." He runs his palm over her neck and his fingers into her hair.

"I'll eat when I get home."

She tries to pull away, but he tightens his grip.

"Tell me what's wrong, and don't deny it. That's a waste of time."

Sad, caramel eyes bore into his, her whisper almost inaudible. "It's too much."

He shakes his head. "Nothing is too much for you." His words echo my thoughts exactly.

"I can't live somewhere I can't afford, especially with the baby."

Instantly, I'm on edge. "Babe—"

Ethan shoots me his signature deep scowl. "I got this."

Instead of pushing the issue, I pay close attention to how he handles her. I've never been great at responding to her anxieties, and he deals with twenty of us idiots daily without murdering anyone.

He also coached for the Special Olympics and an underprivileged peewee team in Harlem, where he grew up. Fucking *Harlem*.

I may have used my stalker tendencies to find dirt on him. Unfortunately, I found only killer defensive skills and a mean penalty record.

He tucks an unruly wave behind her ear. "Tell me what you need. Do you need your name on the deed? Ownership?"

"I don't know." Her fingers wring the hem of her hoodie. "I have other things to pay for."

I've witnessed a few of her panic attacks, and she appears to be heading in that direction.

My eyes shift to the arm where she needed stitches after I shattered a bottle against a wall, aiming for a bastard interested in her. Visions of her gasping for air, blood pouring from the wound, flash through my mind, and my stomach churns.

She should've never been there.

"You're overwhelmed." Ethan's deep voice breaks through my spiraling thoughts. "You can't trust anyone because everyone has failed you. I understand that. Believe me, I do. But you have to trust me." He places a hand on her abdomen. "This child is mine too. I want to see you. I want to see the baby. And I know Jackson wants that too. Can we at least try to live together before you dismiss the idea?"

"I can't live off someone."

My heart hurts knowing I'm the reason she's this way.

In the beginning, I paid for her time and trust. I forced her to depend on me, and when *I* failed and she naturally wanted distance, I threw it in her face. Intoxicated, I'd told her I must not be paying her enough.

She should've told me to shove it up my ass. No amount of money is worth staying with a drunk asshole. But she never did.

"Someone made you feel that way. Right? And what did you tell me? It doesn't make it true. I love the idea of you needing me. I'd love to take care of you. I love it when you cling to me. You don't even know how much it means to me." He takes a deep breath and blows it out slowly. "But I get the feeling, no matter what I say, you're going to put boundaries between us."

A tear slides down her cheek, and he brushes it away.

"You both have hockey. You're both successful. I'm only

getting started, and if I quit now, I'll always be the gold-digging whore Jackson's father calls me, or—"

"Aurora," I growl.

But her anguished eyes silence me.

"No. You repeated similar words. It doesn't matter if you were drunk or if you're sorry. I still feel it." She places her palm on Ethan's chest. "I still feel like the escort you dreaded getting pregnant or the woman you're ashamed of." She takes a ragged inhale. "I can't do this."

She covers her face with her hands, and my heart shatters. Words cannot express how much I regret hurting her. I only wish I knew how to fix it.

"Look at me." Ethan lifts her chin. "Nothing I say will erase the past or convince you you're worthy of the life we want to give you. What do you need? A photoshoot where you're crawling all over me on the beach? A ring on your finger? Will that help? Think about it."

Aurora shakes her head, which sucks, since I coincidentally have a ring.

"Say what you need instead of pushing us away." After pausing to search her eyes, he says, "Tell him. I won't let anything happen."

THIRTY-TWO
JACKSON

Ice runs through my veins, and my panic skyrockets, fearing Aurora wants to be with Ethan—*only* Ethan.

She winces. "I need to work. I need to go to New York. Maybe elsewhere."

They're not the least desirable words, but close. She's leaving me, and I doubt I'll get her back. It's a repeat of our breakup. Only this time, she's pregnant and traveling across the country, and I'm sober, feeling everything.

Fuck that.

"No. No way." I shake my head. "You can't be serious. You're not going to New York or Miami for weeks to months? What about the baby?"

Her brows furrow, and her caramel eyes plead for my understanding. "We'll make it work."

"With our schedule? When the fuck will I see you?"

I want to be with her. Every day. Every night. Why can't she understand that?

She reaches out to me but hesitates and lays her hand on the seat between us. "We can fly to meet each other."

Her trepidation only irritates me further.

My knee bounces, and I clench my jaw. "For how long? I just got you back."

Three days. I've had three whole days with her.

"I don't know, but I need this, Jax. I need something of my own."

The walls are closing in. My body is vibrating. It's as if I have a scream stuck inside me, and if I don't let it out, I'll explode.

So, I do. I scream at her. And I hate myself for it.

"You have us! Why is that not enough for you?" My voice is harsh and reverberates through the confined space.

Ethan meets my anger head-on, a threat in his glare. "Were you listening at all?"

But I'm too far gone to deal with his shit. "You can fuck off!"

Aurora flinches at my sharp tone, and Ethan puts his arm around her. Ricky hits the brakes, and I realize I'm making everyone nervous. Instead of it being a warning, I feel cornered.

Ethan's expression hardens, eyes dark, jaw tense. "You better calm the fuck down and lower your tone, or I'll beat the boy straight out of you. You're only digging yourself into a hole."

I know he's right. Rage will get me nowhere.

My elbows hit my knees. Head in my hands, I grind the heels of my palms into my eyes until I see stars.

After a few deep breaths, I lean back and, with as much patience as I can muster, ask her, "Please come here?"

Without hesitation, she climbs into my lap, resting her cheek on my shoulder. We're worlds apart, and I know what I need to do. It doesn't matter that Ethan is next to us. Some of what I'm about to confess, I've told him during our *therapy* sessions.

With my voice low and arms wrapped around her, I say the words I've run through my mind hundreds of times.

"I've thought a lot about us and still can't place where my regret begins. Maybe as early as the day we met, and I brought you into my fucked-up world thinking I could lead a double life. Either way, there's nothing I regret more than hurting you." Tears blur my vision, and I blink them away. "I never recovered from the night Emily took you to Kyle's party, intending to show you who I truly was. That's no excuse, though. I ended up harming you, and I'll never forgive myself."

Bile rises in my throat. Emily's plan sure as fuck worked, but the ricochet was severe.

"I should've stopped then, but the shame was unbearable. I made promises I couldn't keep and only worked harder to hide my addiction. I was in denial and barely functioning, and you never abandoned me." Agony splinters through me. "I was killing you, Aurora. When I left and told you to stay, I meant it. You deserved it. I was the problem." My head spins, and I breathe through it. "I never intended to return. I got your messages and calls. I watched on the door cam as Emily helped you move out. I didn't spend that time with anyone. I spent it alone in Kyle's pool house, where I knew no one would search for me." I swallow the painful lump in my throat. "Trying hard not to wake up."

Her heart pounds against mine. She tries to lift her head, but I embrace her tighter.

"Let me finish. Okay?"

She weaves her fingers through my hair, always comforting me.

"I emailed my lawyer to give you everything. He must have contacted Kyle, because the next thing I remember is fighting him, LAPD, and EMS, and then waking in UCLA

Medical. By the time my seventy-two-hour hold was lifted, you had blocked me, and I knew I needed to leave you alone."

She trembles in my arms, and her body racks with quiet sobs—my sweet girl.

What I can't tell her, or anyone, is that after I was in the hospital, Kyle was up my ass worse than ever, worried he'd lose his paycheck. My mental instability and addiction made it easier for him to control me, and I wasn't bringing Aurora back into that.

I only broke my vow to distance myself when I saw her with Ethan, and I had been drinking. Through it all, I never stopped. Why would I? My life was more miserable than ever.

Until Ethan.

Until he restructured the team, put Kyle in his place, and gave me hope.

Now, it's all being ripped away from me. Again. "My life is empty without you. I understand what you need and want to give it to you, but I don't know how without losing my fucking mind."

She stays silent and, lost in thought, I watch the city go by.

Her fingernails graze my scalp. "It's golden," she plays with my hair and mumbles.

She hums the lyrics, "All of you, all of me, intertwined," a song more about her than me. It's everything she is to me, and I shut my eyes and focus on her soft voice. "Daylight, daylight, daylight," she sings.

My rigid muscles relax, and I can breathe easy again. I'm no longer drowning.

When she speaks, she doesn't mention my confession or

my meltdown. One thing I love about Aurora is her big heart. Believe me, I know I don't deserve it.

"What if you were more involved? Come home with me. Meet with my agent. I'm sure she knows I'm pregnant by now. She's called several times. Be there with me. We planned to do this fake dating charade anyhow."

I steer clear of situations and places I can't control, especially when it comes to Aurora. That aspect of me remains unchanged; I've simply discovered more effective strategies.

Exhibit A: The house and penthouse I purchased to corral her into a living environment dependent on me. Again.

Exhibit B: The bodyguard I hired to oversee any other area of Aurora's life I'm not privy to. I've also done something similar in the past without Aurora knowing

Yeah, I've yet to learn some lessons—perhaps never will —and her letting me have a say in her career gives me the sense of control I need right now.

Because I don't have a choice. She's going to New York either way.

"Fine, but Ricky goes with you, and you agree to move into the Santa Monica house."

Sitting up, she cocks her head to the side, her gaze twinkling with mischief. "What bedroom do I get?"

Her sinful eyes and smile drag me out of my dark mood. "Whichever one I'm in."

Of course, Ethan has to chime in. "I hope you plan on getting a bigger bed."

"I hope you plan on seeing a lot of my dick."

THIRTY-THREE
AURORA

This meeting with my agent is an absolute clusterfuck. I regret pulling on my big girl panties and gathering everyone in a room, virtual or otherwise, to hash everything out. Luckily, Felicity, the public relations wizard that she is, handles my pregnancy, the bickering between Jackson and Emily, and the addition of Ricky with ease.

"I refuse to be involved in anything where this giant dick is in control." Emily nods toward Jax.

"Emily," Felicity says. "I understand this is difficult for you, but the reality is, Aurora is my client, and she chooses to have Jackson involved as her partner. It's phenomenal for publicity, and unfortunately, you'll have to take it or leave it. Jackson is here to stay."

We're seated on the couch in my small, shared condo, and I intertwine my fingers with Jax's. Ricky stands behind us, arms crossed over his broad chest. Emily is in a chair beside me while Felicity is on the laptop positioned on the coffee table between us.

A tight, unnatural smile stretches across Emily's lips, her eyes cold. "*Is* he here to stay?"

"Yes, Em."

After Jackson's confession, my mind is made up. I'm not backing down from this. If this is what he needs, I'm seeing it through. We can work this out.

My heart is broken for him, for us, and a heavy sense of guilt weighs on me. I should've done *something*.

Instead of believing he was partying and cheating on me, I could've woken to an officer telling me he'd ended his life. That would've devastated me.

I never want that to happen.

"So you lied about him not being the father. You lied about not getting back together. And you lied about not moving in with him. Why?"

Tears gather in my eyes, and my face heats with humiliation. I wish I didn't have to lie to her about Ethan, but I'm not sure I trust her anymore, especially with the way she keeps hurling accusations.

When I don't answer, she continues. "He walks back into your life, and you drop everything. For *him*? Do you enjoy the way he controls you? Pushing away your friends, trapping you, deciding when and where you work?" She gestures toward Ricky. "He even has a spy following you."

"Em..." My voice sounds weak, and the room spins. What is wrong with me? Why does this keep happening?

Jax draws me to his chest. "Emily, as usual, you're wrong." He directs his focus to Felicity. "Can we wrap this up? Aurora needs to eat."

Ricky hands me a bottle of water, and I flash him a grateful smile.

Felicity and Jackson discuss whatever documents his agent and PR team need.

"Our biggest hurdle is coming up," she says to me. "I have a designer in mind who'll work with your pregnancy.

We'll talk more when we meet in New York. You two keep doing what you're doing to attract the paparazzi. Maybe indulge in some PDA during dinner. After fashion week, I'll do my best to schedule everything on the West Coast."

Felicity signs off, and that's it. One giant problem defeated.

But another still glares at me from five feet away. I understand why she's furious, I do. We're canceling several commitments, which means reduced income. I get it. But that doesn't mean we need to end everything.

I drain the water bottle and rise from the couch on shaking legs. I turn to my best friend since middle school. "I'm sorry. I really am."

She curls her lip. "No, you're not, but you will be. And when you're stuck at home with a baby while he's out partying and fucking around, don't come crawling back to me."

Her words are poison-tipped claws, gnawing at my deepest fears and insecurities. Tears flood my eyes, and my stomach cramps, but I refuse to break down in front of her. I grit my teeth and keep my head high as I stride to my room to pack every bag I own.

Then, to my complete surprise, a deep, slightly accented voice says, "You're a real bitch, you know that?"

My gentle, polite bodyguard must loathe my best friend —or *former* best friend—to break his usual stoic demeanor.

Jax chuckles and leads Ricky into the bedroom. "Pack only what you need, babe. I'll hire someone to move the rest."

I nod, my throat tight and eyes averted. I can't look at him right now. If I do, he'll see my torment.

We sit inside the SUV in silence, positioned at opposite ends of the backseat. I haven't stopped thinking about

Emily's spiteful words and the insecurity she unleashed with them.

My life is a mess. I lost my best friend. I won't always be a model—it was only luck that I was noticed. What if Jackson loses interest in me after I have the baby? What if it becomes too much for him? He'll always have women available to him. The same goes for Ethan.

I shake my head, dispelling those negative thoughts. This mindset isn't how I want to live. It has been an unimaginable day, and I'm tired.

A month ago, I couldn't fathom this being my life.

Pregnant. Back with Jackson. Ethan finding out about the baby, and he's single. Both wanting to live together. A falling-out with Emily. Jackson confessing to being in a hospital instead of partying and cheating. Jackson disowning Kyle.

What's next? An alien invasion?

The car comes to a stop and snaps me out of my musing.

"What are we doing here?" I ask as I look up at a *tattoo shop*.

Jax gives me that boyish smile. "Where do you want it?"

That's not cryptic or anything. "Where do I want what?"

"Where do you want your name?"

My brows nearly hit my hairline. "My name? On your body?"

He nods. "Where do you want it?"

I know there's no sense in arguing with him when he has a wild idea, yet I make the effort anyhow. "You don't have to do this. It's not necessary."

"I'm going to regardless. I've never cheated on you. I've wanted you since I first saw you, holding hands with a rookie." A slow smirk spreads across his face. "I'm an asshole. I've been a terrible boyfriend, but I never touched anyone else. Emily is right about me wanting to control our relationship, but she's wrong about me screwing around. So, fuck her and choose. Anywhere but my dick. I'm hoping to use that later."

I release a deep sigh. "How about you pick? And I'll order food."

An hour later, I'm feeding Jackson hand-cut fries while the artist brands my name on his chest. He lies shirtless on the table, gazing at me with hearts in his bright-green eyes. His sandy-blond hair is messy from running his fingers through it, and dark stubble highlights his sharp jawline. His jeans sit low on his hips, washboard abs and well-defined muscles on full display.

He's mouthwatering and crazy and all mine.

It's the perfect snapshot that strategically makes its way onto social media, thanks to Jackson's PR team, along with a cropped picture of our fingers intertwined with the word *Daylight* tattooed on the inside of his ring finger.

It all feels like a fairy tale—a smutty, fucked-up fairy tale.

Later, I wake from a nap to him emerging from the steamy bathroom, wearing only a towel around his waist and a pleased smirk. Maybe it's the pregnancy hormones, but I could trace every cut muscle with my tongue.

"Why are you so hot? It's not fair."

And he'll remain hot as hell while I become a blimp. That should be illegal. *He* should be illegal.

I can't take my eyes off his impressive body, honed from spending every day on the ice or in the gym. Broad shoulders, bulging pecs, abs for days, and that V-cut that makes women do stupid things.

Then, there's the scatter of tattoos, which now include my name.

He stops on his way from the bathroom to his closet. Bending down, he places his hands on the mattress. "You're insane. You know that, right?"

"I'm pretty sure that's you." I press my lips to his and run my fingers through his damp hair.

"Insane for you," he breathes against my lips.

Our kiss is unhurried yet filled with intensity, tongues intertwining with soft moans.

The room is bathed in the warm glow of the setting sun, and even though I have a million things to do before leaving, this is all that matters.

"I like you this way," he says between kisses. "Sleepy, relaxed, in my bed waiting for me."

Different from the last time we were together a few days ago, there's no rush, no all-consuming hunger to reconnect.

"I like you this way too." I lick along his jawline to that spot under his ear that has him stretching his neck for more. "Happy, relaxed, coming home to me."

Trailing open-mouth kisses along his throat, I hear his breathing speed up, feel the rough swallow and the bob of his Adam's apple, see his hands fist the sheets, and suspect he's as affected by me as I am him.

The tent he's pitching is also solid evidence.

"You want me." I loosen the towel around his waist and let it fall to the floor.

"I always want you. *Always*."

His voice is husky, and arousal stirs low in my belly.

I run my tongue and lips over his neck then move down to his chest. He rises to give me access to his stomach, and I make my way lower. I peer up at him, unable to contain my naughty thoughts.

His fingers tangle in my hair. "Damn, those eyes will be the death of me."

I wrap my lips around the head of his cock, sucking and licking like a lollipop.

"And that fucking mouth," he groans.

Leisurely, I trace my tongue over his length, finding every ridge and vein. I take him in my mouth, inch by inch, until he hits the back of my throat.

His hips flex, and I relax my muscles and swallow around him.

"Jesus, fuck, baby."

The sounds of his moans and dirty words only make me wetter.

I increase suction, stroking his shaft in sync with my lips, and gently massage his balls.

It's not long before he swells in my mouth, and I taste the salty tang of his precum.

"Baby, you gotta stop. I wanna fuck you."

He tugs my hair, and I release him with an audible, wet *pop*. I toss my shirt to the floor and lie back on the bed.

He growls and tightens his grip on my thighs, yanking me to the edge of the mattress. "And you wonder why I'm so insane for you? You suck the sanity right out of me."

I smile and lock my legs around his waist. "I guess I better stop then...for your sanity."

"Fuck no. Let me die with your lips wrapped around my cock."

He lifts my body to meet his, biceps bulging and forearms flexing. We're both wet from me giving him head, and he enters me in one, smooth motion that has us both moaning.

My breasts bounce with his powerful thrusts, and, knowing his eyes are on me, I pinch and pull my nipples.

Pleasure shoots straight to my core, and I squeeze around him.

"God, you have the best tits," he chokes.

"I bet they'd look even better covered in your cum."

He slams into me, deeper. "Fuck me. Are you trying to make me come?"

"That's the goal...*yes*," I moan when his hips meet my ass with a hard thrust.

I grip the sheets above my head and dig my heels into the small of his back.

"You're doing a damn good job, baby." He angles his hips and hits that spot that has me clenching around him. "But if you want my cum, you need to soak my cock."

THIRTY-FOUR
JACKSON

SHE STARES straight into my eyes, lust shining in her pleading gaze. "Fuck me. Make me come, Jax."

She's erotic and seductive and mind-blowing and freaking me out.

Not that I don't love it. It's hot as fuck, and my cock is aching to give her what she's begging for.

But it's different.

When we began dating, she'd only had sex once, and the asshole ruined it for her. She was nineteen, shy, and intimidated by me. It took weeks for her to warm up to penetrative sex, which was fine.

Now, she's grabbing her tits, taunting me, and demanding what she wants.

She's different.

I slow my pace, wanting to prolong this moment. I've always been enamored with her, attached to her as if she's my lifeline. I've been obsessed with getting her back.

Finally, she's in my grasp. I'm balls-deep, and being with her is more intimate and incredible than ever, but doubt creeps in. The fear of losing her has gripped me stronger than ever.

She's allowing me to be a significant part of her life, placing her trust in me, but she's also slipping away. She has other people and a developing career to support her. Ethan will do anything for her.

Since ditching me, she has become more independent, flying solo and doing fine. No matter how much I spoil her, how many places I buy for her, or where I tattoo her name, she can leave.

She's not dependent on me. She may *want* me, but she doesn't *need* me.

I gaze at her, vulnerable and open beneath me, mine for the taking, and I want to be buried deep inside her until neither of us can walk. Until I no longer know where I end and she begins.

But I want it *all*. Desperately. Mind, body, soul, every part of her.

"Jax."

My eyes connect with hers.

"What's wrong?" she asks, winded and annoyed.

Careful not to apply any pressure on her stomach, I lower myself over her, resting on my forearms and intertwining our fingers above her head. "This feels different."

"It's you."

My brows pinch together. "You don't feel it?"

Her smooth legs wrap higher around my waist. "I feel *you*."

I stare at her, dumbfounded.

Her flirtatious mood dissipates, and her face contorts into an expression of confusion. "Wait, are we not talking about sex?"

Is she talking about sex? I pause mid-thrust, trying to clarify my thoughts. "I mean...how is it me?"

"You're bigger and harder now... "

Now that I've stopped drinking.

She doesn't need to say it for me to get the meaning.

Her walls flex around me in emphasis, and I don't know if I should be proud or embarrassed. She has always been small. I figured it was her.

"I didn't mean sex, but thanks for that. I'll never drink again, that's for sure." I lean in and kiss her lips. "I meant *us*. This bond between us. It's different. Stronger, but not at the same time. You know?"

She scowls. "Not? How?"

"You're less attached to me while I'm becoming more attached to you."

"That's not true." She releases my hand to run her fingers through my hair. "Don't overthink this. Please. I want to stay with you. Leaving for New York has nothing to do with lacking attachment to you. You have hockey. I have modeling. But that doesn't mean we can't have each other."

Her words sink in, and it's almost enough to satisfy the greedy monster within me.

"Will you stop working after the baby comes?"

Her arm flops to the mattress dramatically. "Seriously? Are we doing this right now?"

"Yes. I need to know before you leave." I give a sly smile. "While I have you trapped beneath me."

I pull out, then slide in as deep as I can. She sucks in a gasp, and I do it again with more force. She writhes her hips and meets my thrusts.

Then, I stop. "Answer me."

"So manipulative," she whines. "I'll work less and on the West Coast. Happy now?"

I understand it's difficult for her to give up her independence, but I need more than a compromise. I'm selfish.

"I want you to travel with me. With us."

Kind of hard not to include Ethan, since he'll be there. Not sure how that'll pan out.

Fucking in secret? Shared hotel rooms? Separate nights?

"We'll figure it out," she says. "For now, can we get back to business?"

She squeezes around me, and it's phenomenal, but I'm not finished.

"God, another reason I'm addicted to you." I leisurely pump into her tight-as-fuck pussy. "One more question, then I'll let you have my dick's undivided attention."

"You're lucky you're hot."

I kiss her neck, then her jaw, then her lips. "Will you have my baby next?"

Her eyes widen, and her brows raise. "What?"

She tries to sit up, but I have her pinned.

"We've been together for two days, Jackson."

"No, two years. A few months apart mean nothing." I grind against her clit and bite her pouty bottom lip. "I want a baby with you."

"You've reached a whole new level of insanity, O'Reilly. Is there a badge or a bonus or—"

I cut her off with a slam of my hips, my cock hitting deep.

She releases a lusty moan and wraps her legs around me. "Keep doing that, and I might give you anything you want."

I do it again then stop, and she whimpers.

"I'm being serious. I want you. I want this. I want a life together."

She glares at me, and I glare at her.

She sighs, and I know I've got her.

"I'll make a deal with you. If you promise never to do what you told me earlier and stay sober, I'll give you the life you want."

The feeling is indescribable. Elation. Euphoria. *Hope*.

"As long as I have you." I can't guarantee more than that, but I know I'm not fucking this up. I grin and whisper in her ear, "I'm going to fuck a baby into you so hard...as soon as this one vacates."

She grows tighter and wetter, and I pound into her with renewed energy. When she comes, it's with my name on her lips and her cunt drenching my cock, sending me into the sweetest oblivion.

THIRTY-FIVE
ETHAN

We have three games this week, including a home game tonight. I'm swamped. It has only been a few months. I'm still familiarizing myself with the team and staff. I have to work twice as hard until we're synchronized. The next game, the players, the organization, the playoffs—it's always on my mind.

Except for right now.

I can't stop thinking about Aurora and our baby. I find myself wanting to know how the meeting with her agent went. Is she eating? Does she still have morning sickness? Does she need anything? I wonder what she's doing with Jackson.

I have a strong suspicion it's the same I'd be doing if I was with her.

My thoughts move in that direction—to her candy taste and honey scent, to having her in my lap, to those damn expressive eyes as she peers up at me from her knees.

And God, the way she clings to me as if I'm hers. And I am. The little brat has me wrapped around her finger.

I've never been easily distracted by a woman. I've only

ever focused on hockey. If it didn't pertain to hockey, it wasn't relevant.

There was a brief period of about two seconds when I considered devoting my time and attention to my wife, to salvaging our marriage.

But that was about as appealing as testicular cancer.

This thing with Aurora? It's not physically possible to ignore. The loneliness of her absence intensifies with every passing hour.

I didn't even sleep last night. I stayed awake, trying to resist the urge to text her while she was with Jackson. I catch myself mentally scouring my schedule for any opportunity to fly to New York to see her, which, considering I have eighty-two games in six months, seems highly unlikely.

Still, the thought of a distraction-free night in bed with her is tempting enough to warrant me making time.

"Seriously?" I glance down at the pulsing erection that fully supports the idea of Aurora sprawled naked beneath me. I have assistant coaches and managers, after all. I could convert those fantasies into reality and let them do my job—not a game, but a few practices won't hurt. Right?

The moment I reach for my phone, I realize how utterly fucked I am.

> Me: Come see me.

> Baby girl: Not a hi, hello, how are you?

> Me: You can tell me all that when I see you.

> Baby girl: I'm with Jax. Aren't you getting ready for the game?

> Me: Tell him he has practice.

> Me: Come see me. Now.

> Baby girl: And you don't have practice?

> Me: I'll have someone run the first half if you come see me.

> Baby girl: At the arena?

> Me: Yes, have Jackson show you my office.

A few minutes go by without another text, and my stomach knots with disappointment. She's with Jackson and doesn't want to see me.

I'm about to give up and toss my phone to the side when the cockblock himself texts me.

> Captain Diva: Fuck off.

> Me: I heard you missed team breakfast this morning.

> Captain Diva: So?? I was balls-deep in your girl.

> Me: Maybe your balls need a rest on the bench tonight.

> Me: You have an hour. Don't bring her through the locker room.

I have nothing against being seen with her, nor am I embarrassed by her, but I'd prefer to keep our relationship away from the team.

Having a woman in my office on a game day is not a good look, especially a swimsuit model dating my captain.

But I won't lie—the forbidden aspect of this has ignited some taboo kink, as evidenced by the steel bar in my pants.

> Baby girl: On our way *blowing kiss emoji*

My smile is fucking ridiculous.

Not even an hour passes before the most irresistible woman walks into my office.

Her hair is in a high ponytail, reminding me of the night we met. She wears a smaller version of Jackson's jersey made into a dress, coming to her mid-thigh, along with those white high-top Converse she seems to love.

She's young and carefree, every bit the temptation I have no business touching or wanting. Yet, my child is growing inside her, and honestly, I couldn't be prouder of how epically I fucked up.

"Hi, hello. How are you? Lock the door," I say in greeting, closing my laptop and setting it on the side table.

"Is this a booty call? In your office? Really, Ethan?"

I love the way she says my name. There's always a hint of seduction or teasing in how she lets it roll off her tongue, as if she's savoring it. I love it even more when she's moaning and whimpering it.

"That depends."

She drops her bag in a chair and saunters toward the leather Chesterfield couch I'm sitting on.

She bites her lip, her whiskey eyes full of flirtation. "On?"

I reach for her, grip her hips, and draw her between my open legs to kiss our baby.

"How quiet you can be." I keep my voice low and guide her to straddle me.

Settling on my lap, she wraps her arms around my neck and tangles her fingers in my hair. She has these cute freckles along her nose and golden flecks in her brown eyes.

I stare at her and wonder how I got so fucking lucky.

"I'd do anything for you," she whispers, her voice full of seduction.

She's only flirting with me, but I'm pretty sure my heart stops. She scares the shit out of me.

Aurora having feelings for me—wanting and needing me—changes the game. I'm not ready for that, and I doubt she is either. She's not leaving Jackson anytime soon, if ever.

He's one manipulative and lovesick bastard. I struggle to grasp the outcome of this situation, but I already know I'm incapable of refusing her, Jackson or otherwise.

I give her ponytail a playful tug. "I want your address, schedule, and Ricky's number before you go."

She grinds her ass over my erection, and arousal curls low in my stomach.

"Sounds as if you're gonna miss me, Blackwood."

"Always. Now, kiss me. I've got about twenty minutes and want to spend the entire time buried in you."

"Yes, sir."

Her pillowy lips are soft, and her tongue tastes like a Jolly Rancher.

I slide my hands up her silky-smooth thighs and over her curvy ass, lifting her dress to find a pleasant surprise.

"No underwear?" My lips slant into a pleased smirk upon hers. "My dirty girl."

"I took them off before we left. They're in my bag."

She bites my neck while her fingers work my belt buckle. Her desire for me is a huge fucking turn-on, and my dick throbs.

"Fuck, I love you." The words escape without a second thought, and my body tenses, panic flashing through me.

Thankfully, she doesn't seem to notice the slipup. She lowers my zipper and continues to kiss my neck, and I exhale a shaky sigh of relief.

She frees me from my boxers. With her hand gripping my shaft, she notches the head of my cock at her entrance and slides me inside her warm, wet cunt.

Sucking air through my teeth, I hiss at the intensity of having her stretched around me. Next to my ear, her breath hitches, and she makes these hot as fuck whimpers with every inch she takes.

I fist the back of Jackson's jersey for leverage and flex my hips to meet hers. "You like riding my cock, baby girl?"

"Who wouldn't?" Her ass meets my thighs, and she releases a shuddering sigh. "You feel incredible."

Goddamn, what is she doing to me? I'll remember her words until I'm old and senile.

"Put your arms behind your back, baby. I need to fuck you."

Without hesitation, she obeys, always eager to please me.

I bind her wrists in one hand and clasp the back of her neck with the other. "You're my favorite thing. Don't forget that."

Because I'm about to fuck her as if she's not.

Before she can respond, I pound into her, and she bites my shoulder to stay quiet. Thank fuck I have a suit coat to put over this shirt.

The noise of our bodies coming together with every powerful thrust is muffled by our clothes, leaving only the sounds of our pleasure.

"So tight. So wet. Fuck, you're a dream." I bite my lip, but as hard as I try, I can't stop the shit that tumbles from my mouth. "This pussy was fucking made for me."

She widens her knees to take me deeper. Her cunt gets wetter, her legs shake, and her hips writhe with my strokes. "Ethan," she cries.

Jesus, the way she calls my name could make me come alone.

Knowing she's close, that she's loud when she comes, I grip her chin and throat and shove two fingers in her mouth, demanding, "Suck."

Her body quakes, and her pussy locks around me, milking every inch of my cock. She whimpers and moans against my fingers, her teeth sinking into my skin. And fuck, my balls ache to unload.

On the brink of ecstasy, I bury my face in her neck. I gasp for air and shatter into a million pieces, never to be put back together the same again.

"Fuuuck..." I grit my teeth and slam into her one last time, then a few more while my dick jerks inside her.

I never want this to end.

We catch our breaths, coming down from the high, and my cock kicks with aftershocks. She rakes her fingers through my hair, and my chest swells with everything I'm desperate to avoid.

I take her face into my hands, lifting her lips to mine. "You're fucking perfect."

She returns my kiss. "So are you."

My head is filled with wild, ludicrous words I fear will slip out.

Instead, I kiss her with those words on the tip of my tongue, pouring every ounce of emotion into her. I caress her arms, back, and tiny baby bump until we're out of time, and she's sliding on her underwear.

I tuck in my shirt and fasten my pants. "I like knowing your panties are soaked in my cum while you're wearing his jersey."

She stares at me, her mouth hanging open, a twinkle of mischief in her eyes.

The biggest grin ever spreads across my face. Damn, I'm going to miss her.

THIRTY-SIX
JACKSON

"Your hair is a wreck, asshole."

Ethan walks past me on the player's bench, and my words spill out in a bitter rush. My emotions are all over the place. I'm finding it difficult to control the irritation in my chest, and my heart and mind are racing.

"Don't like it?" He accepts an iPad from the assistant coach with a nod.

The underlying implication doesn't escape my notice.

"I fucking hate it." Do I, though? Or is it the dark storm brewing in my head that's talking? Can't say I *enjoy* him screwing my girlfriend—without me.

Maybe no one else would notice, given his inability to use hair product, but he's out here with sex-hair. Not only that, but his face is flushed, and he's late. He's never late.

And he's happy—another rare occurrence on game day.

He leans against the boards with his back to the ice and faces me, his attention on the iPad. "That's too bad. Your girlfriend loves it."

"Does she? Does she also love the"—I glance at my wrist

—"three minutes you take *styling* it?" My irritation morphs into a self-satisfied smile.

He shakes his head while reviewing the rosters, his smug smirk firmly in place. "Unlike you, I don't need an hour in front of the mirror to get the job done. My *style* is quite successful. Ask your girlfriend." He grins so wide, his face might split.

My heart batters my ribcage, and I rub at the ache in my sternum. A wave of nausea passes through me then leaves as quickly as it came, taking the chest pain with it.

"You two have similar hair," Grant says, oblivious to our situationship or my mini panic attack.

Ethan and I turn on him in unison. "Shut the fuck up."

Heads swivel our way, but the arena is loud, with music blaring through the speakers and the crowd building in the stands. It's doubtful anyone can hear other than those close. Even if they do, we're only hazing one another, something the team has become accustomed to.

Grant gestures between us. "Coach's hair is darker and longer, but you both have that messy look."

I may have been making out with Aurora in the parking lot, partly to annoy Ethan and partly because I didn't want her to go. Doesn't matter—my hair is always perfect.

Ethan and I exchange a glance of shared amusement, breaking the tension.

I'm not even sure why I'm irritated. It's not as if I didn't plaster myself all over Aurora before she went into his office, knowing full well what he wanted.

With a shit-eating grin, Ethan grumbles, "Thicker. My hair is much thicker."

My eyes want to roll right out of my head. "I'm not worried. You'll go bald soon. What are you, fifty?"

"Again, your girlfriend doesn't mind."

"Again, you can fuck off."

Grant bumps his shoulder into mine. "Hey, who's that guy with Aurora?" He inclines his chin toward the family section behind us.

I twist around, following his gaze.

My brain is slow to catch up, almost as if I can feel it rotating in my skull, and my heart rate spikes at the odd sensation. It's reminiscent of a bad high.

I breathe through it, telling myself I'm reacting to Aurora leaving and seeing her is a reminder. That's all.

In my dazed state, I spot her sitting next to Ricky, his arm casually draped over the back of her chair. His head tilts toward hers, soaking in their conversation. A flash of humor lights up his face, and he playfully tugs at her ponytail.

If you're into rugged masculinity, Ricky's a decent-looking guy, with jacked-up muscles and neck tattoos. He gives off the vibe of a Viking or the president of an MC.

He's not Aurora's type. At least, I don't think. I would've never expected Ethan either, but he has that arrogant-asshole attitude she seems to go for.

I scoff. "That's her bodyguard."

Ethan slams the iPad onto the boards, shooting me an icy glare. He's more agitated by Ricky's behavior than by my earlier insults. I guess he blames me for hiring him.

"Relax. No worries." Wait. Are my words running together? Or is that in my head? Was I supposed to say that out loud?

Ethan's death glare remains undeterred, and his brows furrow deeper. "What's wrong with you?"

"Me? I'm not the one jealous of her bodyguard." My

speech is pressured, as if the words are too big for my mouth, and I swallow hard.

Am I having a manic episode? Aurora leaving might do that.

My respirations accelerate, and now, I'm freaking out thinking about it.

Coach and Grant share a glance. I shouldn't have busted Ethan's balls where others could hear, but the irony of the situation isn't lost on me. He's about to explode while I'm not bothered by Ricky at all.

Ethan walks around the back of the bench and squats behind me, pinning me with his stern gaze. "What did you do?"

What did I do? Hiring Ricky? "Would you rather she didn't have a bodyguard?" My face heats, and my body breaks out in a cold sweat despite the frigid air.

"Shut the fuck up." He lowers his voice. "Your pupils are dilated, and your words are slurred. Your mouth is running more than usual. What did you take?"

Confusion turns into defensiveness, although I've done *nothing* wrong. "Seriously? I've been with Aurora."

He adjusts his stance, settling in, and a wave of déjà vu hits me. I've seen this episode before. It's where Coach kicks me out of morning practice because I'm hungover or maybe still drunk.

Only this time, I'm completely sober.

"What did you do last night?"

I cock my head to the side and lower my brows. "What do you think I did last night?"

"Did you go out? Did you have people over?"

"Fuck no. I was in bed, enjoying my girlfriend." And plotting ways to tie her to me permanently.

His eyes soften, as if he believes me. That'd be a shock. "Then what is wrong with you?"

So there *is* something wrong with me? I'm not the only one sensing this psychotic break I'm having.

Not that I'm telling him that. He'd never allow me around Aurora and the baby if he thought I was a nutcase. "I must be sick. I don't feel well."

"Don't feel well, how?"

Is that patience I hear in his voice?

"It comes and goes. Racing heart, nausea, dizziness..."

He scrutinizes my face, and my stomach twists, fearing he won't trust me.

"And you haven't taken anything?"

Tears prickle my eyes. With a sharp shake of my head that rattles my brain, I exhale forcefully. "I swear."

Ethan stands, calling to the trainer, and Grant passes me a water bottle. "Drink up. It's October. It's flu season. You possibly caught something."

Electrolytes and smelling salts do the trick. My mind clears enough to perform, and I score two goals. But the second goal has me bent over dry heaving, and Ethan pulls me.

"Sit your ass on the bench."

Heat prickles at the back of my neck, spreading over my scalp. I bury my face in my hands, gasping for air and battling the acid rising in my throat. The trainer rushes over, dropping to a knee beside me and rifling through her medical supplies.

"Did you take a little blue pill, or five, last night?" Ethan asks as the trainer packs ice on the back of my neck.

I lift my head enough to shoot him a glare. "You wish. Interesting that you know the color. Something you wanna share, Coach?"

The trainer stifles a chuckle. Ethan huffs, shakes his head, and clenches his jaw.

I sip water as the ice cools my overheated skin.

Not wanting to worry Aurora, I resist peering over at her. She can read me like her favorite book. She'll know something is wrong.

My gaze drifts toward the suites above. I can't see him, but Kyle's watching. He'll be furious I'm not playing. His box is full of politicians and other *influential* figures. It's where he pretends to be a proud father while making shady deals.

Ricky and I discussed the prospect of him being at this game, which is why Aurora sits in the family section behind the bench instead of the suite. I highly doubt Kyle is foolish enough to try anything at the arena, given public appearance is his top priority, but I wasn't taking the risk.

Shaky again, I signal for the trainer. "Can I get something for nausea?"

Her eyes dart to Ethan. "It's against protocol, sorry."

"Since when?"

With her hands on her knees, she leans in. "Since Coach fired the entire training staff. No meds unless you break a leg or crack your skull out there, his exact words."

Fuck. I guess I'm sitting out.

Thankfully, we're winning, because my focus is subpar. I couldn't tell you a single stat to save my position. Not only is this queasiness kicking my ass, but I'm dreading what comes next.

Soon enough, Aurora will leave to visit her grandmother before flying to New York.

The thought has me giving in and scanning the rows of team jerseys, searching for one face. I'm terrified she'll be gone, and I'll be left empty, alone, and struggling to get out of bed.

Then, there she is, her vibrant smile easing the ache in my chest. She's chatting away with Ricky, but as soon as she catches me watching, she stops and locks eyes with me.

"Love you," she mouths across the sea of people, and everything disappears—my racing thoughts, the crowd, the game, all blissfully silent.

My breath stutters, and my heart skips a beat, and it has nothing to do with this meltdown I'm having.

She flashes me a sheepish smile, and I playfully narrow my eyes.

Really? She tells me she loves me during a game? Before she leaves?

She chuckles and blows a kiss my way. I make a heart with my fingers, placing them on my chest, and mouth the words back to her.

A powerful strike to my helmet shatters the moment. "I don't pay you to flirt. Pay attention."

I eagerly watch the minutes tick away on the jumbotron. I'm going to get fined for what I'm about to do. Ethan will have me shooting goals until I can't see straight and skating laps until my ankles break. But I don't give a fuck. He'll understand one day, I guarantee it.

When the final whistle blows, the cheer of victory doesn't even register. I throw off my helmet, the icy air rushing against my sweat-slicked hair, and toss my gloves.

I grab my stick—a player never leaves his twig—and bolt for the tunnel, my eyes on Aurora.

She stands to leave, and my world shakes.

My confidence wavers. I can't do this. I can't be without her.

Ricky pushes through the crowd, Aurora gripping his arm.

I pass security and stop at the edge of the first row. Disregarding the fans, I cup my hands around my mouth and yell, "Aurora! Aurora!"

Her face turns a bright shade of pink, and she makes her way to the barrier between the players' tunnel and the stands.

I hand my stick to a guy between us who's desperate to get my notice. "Here, move." Shit, that's another fine. Worth it.

He steps back, and I have Aurora in my grasp, carefully lifting her over the barrier.

"What are you doing?" She smiles, and laughter rolls through her voice.

"You're going to tell me you love me before leaving me? Seriously?" I set her on her feet but refuse to let go.

"I wanted you to—"

"Stay. Please. I can't do this without you." Too impatient, my words rush out, filled with desperation.

"Jackson…"

I release her from my embrace and cup her face in both hands. "I'm serious. I love you. You love me. Stay."

"I'm already behind. I'll be gone for three, maybe four weeks tops."

Daggers of sharp pain pierce through me. "I need you." My throat is tight, and tears prickle my eyelids.

"I. Love. You." She stresses each word. "We'll be okay."

I drop my hands in despair. "I won't be okay."

"You're Jackson O'Reilly. You'll be more than okay."

I draw her close and inhale her sweet scent. "I just want to be yours. Fuck the rest of this."

"Let her go, lover boy."

This can't be happening. Not again. My head falls back in frustration, and Aurora jolts away from me.

Kyle stands not two feet away, flanked by two other men—men he undoubtedly wants to impress by using me. This is where I paste on a smile, shake hands, tell jokes, and invite these pricks to an after-party.

Ricky places himself between Kyle and Aurora, and she grabs the back of his jacket.

She should be holding me. Her trust should be in me. The familiar weight of hopelessness crashes upon me, and panic floods my veins. I can't do this. I can't go back to the loneliness, every day being on edge and praying for it all to end.

Ethan rounds the corner into the tunnel, the team behind him. His stony eyes connect with mine and flit to Aurora. I can hear that deep voice telling me not to be a fucking idiot, cupping my shoulder and reminding me I'm better than this.

There will be no forced smiles or after-parties. No descent into darkness—he'd probably reach down and rip me out of the abyss by the throat and shake the crazy right out of me.

Snubbing Kyle, I face Aurora, but it's too late. There's distrust and hurt in her eyes.

She puts a halting hand on my chest and mutters, "Bye."

That's all she says before she leaves with Ricky, whose icy glare is fixed on Kyle.

"Great game, son!" Kyle postures and slaps my pads, blocking me from chasing after her. "I have a few people I want to introduce you to."

I knock his arm away. "I need to be in the locker room."

He steps into me. "We need to talk," he says through

gritted teeth, his threatening voice matching the fury in his eyes.

I don't want this confrontation in front of fans, cameras, and my teammates, and neither does he. This is another one of his manipulation tactics, and if I don't comply... I don't even want to think of the aftermath.

"Fine. After I change."

THIRTY-SEVEN
ETHAN

Eager fans crowd the corridor, and security bustles around, adding to the excitement and chaos. Yet, it's all inconsequential compared to my emotions.

What the fuck is happening right now?

I've never felt so out of control, and without control, I'm no better than my idiot captain.

Prior to the game, I couldn't resist the urge to be with Aurora, the intensity of my desire overpowering all rational thought. I almost let words slip from my lips that I have no business saying. I tried to tell myself it was merely some post-nut psychosis.

Then, I was annoyed when I saw Ricky getting close to her. That shit doesn't fly with me. Jackson's the only exception. Before I could wrap my head around my jealousy, Jackson was running his mouth in front of the team.

I still have no idea what's going on with him, but it eats at me. Maybe it's a physical manifestation of his panic over Aurora leaving, but something isn't right.

Earlier in the season, when he showed up to practice hungover and I found out the staff was medicating him, he only shrugged when I sent him home. Until, finally, I pissed him off enough. Today, my insinuation that he was using again genuinely upset him. Plus, it'd never happen with Aurora present.

There's something more going on here.

The game ended, and Aurora was the first thing on my mind, this gnawing urge to reach out and take what's mine. For a hot minute, I wanted to be a twenty-year-old player running into the tunnel to kiss my girl. How ridiculous is that?

I grow increasingly irritated, watching Jackson publicly claim her while I sit on the sidelines. Why can't it be me too?

Because this is what I chose. Because I'm thirty-five, coaching her boyfriend's team, and newly divorced. Fuck.

I enter the tunnel with that depressing thought to find Kyle close to Aurora and Jackson. I see Jackson's internal battle, the weight of his defeat visible in his slumped shoulders, and my possessiveness returns with a vengeance.

The world is testing my limits, pushing me to the edge.

Anger courses through me and adrenaline floods my veins. I clench my jaw and ball my fists, struggling to hold back the impulse to protect what's mine.

My racing heartbeat reverberates in my ears, drowning out all other noise. Every muscle in my body is taut, begging to take control.

But I'm powerless against Kyle. Security won't intervene with the police commissioner. Approaching his son may be manipulative, but it's not unlawful. I'd love to rearrange Kyle's face, but I can't risk losing my job or getting arrested. My only choice is to ensure Aurora's safety.

She stands behind Ricky, using him as a shield, and I know I need to comfort her. Jackson's not thinking clearly.

I quicken my stride, but before I reach her, she straightens her posture, lifts her chin, and walks away. The sight of her displaying such strength fills me with pride.

That's my girl. Don't take shit from anyone.

I hate this for Jackson. It makes me sick when the asshole blocks him from following her. I want to intervene, but I'm torn. Jackson needs to handle Kyle himself. I've done it enough for him.

If Jackson doesn't cut ties with Kyle completely, his father will continue crossing boundaries and taking advantage of him. Kyle contributes to Aurora's insecurities, and Jackson will lose her.

And that abusive piece of shit isn't coming anywhere near my child.

Ricky puts a protective arm around Aurora's shoulders, sealing the deal. That's my job.

"Aurora," I call out and wave the guys into the locker room without me, disregarding my fear of their reactions.

She faces me, her whiskey eyes glistening with unshed tears. Her pain overrides logical thought, and even with the crowd gathering, I know I can't let her slip away.

I take her hand in mine, guiding her around the corner and out of sight. I gather her in my arms, and she rests her head on my chest. Beneath my suit coat, she clings to my button-down, her heart pounding against me.

I cup the back of her head and kiss her temple. If anyone saw, there'd be no mistaking the intimacy between us.

"Everything'll be all right," I assure her.

"He's going to relapse."

Even as she says it, and I can't deny she knows him best, I don't believe it. I can't fathom Jackson risking her.

And as much as I want him healthy and functioning, I

can't let her set aside her dreams to accommodate his dependency. It traps her and teaches him nothing.

"I'll keep an eye on him. You can't let this stop you. You deserve to shine." It's the absolute truth. No matter how badly I want Aurora with me or how much Jackson relies on her, we have to let her go.

The buzz of the crowd grows louder, and I sense a dominant presence approaching.

Ricky steps aside, revealing a frantic Jackson, still in pads and skates. He's around 6'3" barefoot, 6'9" on skates. He towers over all of us and captures everyone's attention.

"I knew I'd find you with her when you weren't in the locker room." He aims his words at me, but his fierce gaze remains fixed on Aurora.

Despite the taboo nature of our relationship and the prying glances, he leans in, takes her face in his hands, presses his forehead to hers, and closes his eyes.

She still clings to me, and I put an arm around his shoulders to provide them with some semblance of privacy.

"I'm sorry. Shit, I know that looked bad. My head's fucked up."

She trembles against me, and I hold her tighter.

"Don't do it, Jax. Whatever he wants, don't."

He gives her a lingering kiss. "I won't. I swear."

I clasp the back of his neck. "You better not."

He lets her go and puts an arm around us both. "Yes, Coach."

We stay embraced in one another's arms longer than we should. Longer than socially acceptable.

Yet, I can't bring myself to pull away.

THIRTY-EIGHT
JACKSON

"What do you want? I can't stay. We're en route to Vegas."

I guzzled a post-workout protein shake, hoping for some energy to clear my head, while I struggled to listen to Coach's end-of-game speech. In a rush, I showered and changed then reluctantly went to find Kyle in his suite—*my* suite.

He's not drunk, but it's early.

A group of men huddle around him, confidently sipping cocktails without a care in the world. Their voices ricochet off the walls, adding to my throbbing headache. It's that loud, overly enthusiastic, arrogant cover that politicians seem to be bred with.

To Kyle's dismay, it never passed down to me, neither through him nor my maternal grandfather, a prominent senator.

I'm an all-around fuck-up in his eyes.

"I know. That's exactly what I wanted to discuss. We're following you. We should hang out tonight. Remember the last time we hit Vegas? Huh?" He puts on a forced smile, projecting his words for all to hear.

He makes me fucking sick.

I shake my head, worsening the migraine, and I wince. "That's not happening." I lower my tone, not wanting to ignite an argument. "I've got an important game tomorrow, and you know Coach won't let me play if I show up hungover."

His eyes narrow. "I'm willing to bet," he pauses for dramatic effect, "a beach house you do."

I try to remain unaffected, but my body betrays me. My knee bounces, and my fists ache with the need to lash out, to release this pent-up frustration.

"That's *my* trust fund. Given to me by *my* mother." My words vibrate through clenched teeth, the tight muscles in my jaw blending with the headache pounding behind my eyes.

"It doesn't matter. I remain your trustee." He raises his chin, dismissive and superior. "You're not allowed to purchase real estate without my consent. You already own two additional properties. It's not in your best interests."

Kyle doesn't give a fuck about my *best interests*, a harsh truth I learned a long time ago while he was beating the shit out of my mother then ditching me at a boarding school after her death.

Pain pierces my temples, the pressure becoming unbearable. "Those two properties I bought independently. I haven't used that trust for anything else. You're the only one who makes use of that account."

"Hockey is an expensive sport. Not to mention multiple private schools and the cost of keeping you out of trouble. I have to monitor you at all times. It adds up."

He gulps bourbon, and my mouth goes dry. I roll my neck, attempting to ease the discomfort.

"We can delve into that tonight. Perhaps you can convince me of this beach house. Although, I'm sure it has something to do with you getting a gold digger pregnant—allegedly." He tacks on with a pointed stare.

He doesn't need to know anything about the baby, and I keep my mouth shut.

But he presses the issue. "Another matter we must address. You're not ready for the responsibility of a child. It needs to be dealt with."

My stomach swims, and I swallow the bile in my throat. "That's none of your concern."

He slaps his palm against the table, and heads turn our way. "You're letting this girl strip you of everything. Wake the fuck up."

His jealousy of Aurora is blatantly obvious, and I don't know how I missed it before. Most frightening is his focus on the baby. But why? What threat does having a child pose?

It's not about money. I have plenty without Kyle, and I have Ethan's help, although he's unaware of that. Kyle believes this baby is mine.

And that's a problem, but I can't tell him the truth. He'll find a way to make it public, to ruin Aurora and Ethan, to kill our relationship.

Seven months. He'll be out of my life once I turn twenty-six and gain full access to my trust. I need to stay sober and keep my composure. Then, he'll have no leverage to prolong the conservatorship.

"She doesn't know anything. She doesn't know about the trust and has her own income."

"Please. Don't delude yourself. Her measly pay is spare

change compared to yours." His tone shifts, and he clasps my shoulder. "Let's enjoy ourselves tonight. We can hash this out later."

There is no hashing this out. This disagreement isn't about the property or money. It's about power, control, and my fight for freedom.

And as I sit here, locked in a battle of wills with Kyle, I can't help but wonder how much longer I can endure this suffocating existence.

"Don't touch me," I growl, knocking his hand away. "I want no part in your idea of fun. If you want me to arrange something for you and your entourage, fine. But that's all I'll do. Where do you want it? The Hard Rock again?"

"That sounds perfect, son. We can meet there and talk about this house you're interested in. Let's ensure it's a memorable night, shall we?"

Kyle wears a smug grin, confident of his victory.

My twenty-sixth birthday can't come fast enough.

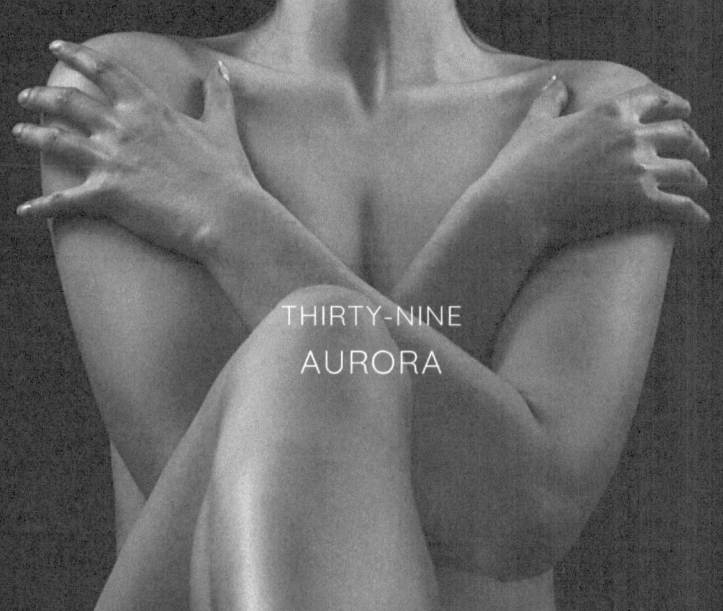

THIRTY-NINE
AURORA

Gram throws down another pair of aces. She may be in her seventies, but the woman is ruthless and sharp as a tack. "You have a picture of your man?"

My bags are packed, and Ricky is waiting in the car. Visiting my grandmother is the last stop before heading to New York.

And she's mercilessly killing me at rummy.

I grab a card from the stack, trying to hide my smile. "My man?"

Gram raises a challenging brow. "Yeah. I know you've got a man. You got that look."

"What look, Gram?"

"The one that says your man knows what he's doin' in the sheets, and he does it often."

I burst out laughing. "Gram!" She has become more loose-lipped as she's gotten older. "Who says I have *a* man?"

"More than one? Hell yeah. Get it while the getting's good. That's what I always say."

Her face radiates happiness, a stark contrast to her previous state. It means the world to me to see her aware and healthy.

After my grandfather died and she had a stroke, I didn't think she'd get out of bed, walk, or speak again. She lost all motivation.

Between her excitement over the baby and the new assisted living facility, she has made significant improvements. She receives physical or occupational therapy daily and sees the doctor once a week, not to mention all the social activities the staff provides.

I recline in my chair. "When do you say that? I've never heard it."

She gives a dismissive wave. "Pfft. All the time. Now, show me some pictures. A girl's gotta eat."

"That's not how the saying goes." I shake my head with a chuckle. "You're quite feisty today. What new meds are you taking?"

"Aurora Belle Embers, my princess." She lays her cards on the table and folds her arms over her chest. "Stop avoidin' me. Tell me about your men if you don't want to show me."

Yup, I was named after cartoon princesses. Not at all humiliating, especially when you're awkward.

I take a deep breath and blow it out slowly. "I have no pictures of the baby's father, but we're seeing each other."

She tilts her head and purses her lips.

"You know what? I'll Google him. He coaches the LA hockey team."

I go for my phone, stomach full of butterflies. I never allowed myself to search for Ethan, never intended to contact him and was too afraid I'd find him living the perfect life with a wife and a bunch of kids.

I pull up Google and type in "Ethan Blackwood hockey coach."

As I suspected, I'm bombarded with various articles and

pictures of his former life in Boston and his transition to LA. Several photos show Ethan with his ex-wife, a flawless blonde by societal standards.

Hockey Barbie. She's beautiful, successful, and part owner of the Boston team.

Seriously? Why can't she be a hag or even a puck bunny?

A daunting sense of inadequacy curdles in my gut. He told me she was having an affair, but that provides little consolation. If she hadn't cheated, would he have left?

His ex-wife is in a league far above me. She's generationally wealthy and independent while I'm inexperienced, insecure, and to be honest, a hot mess.

I glance down at Jackson's hoodie I've been wearing for the past week. Despite having loads of lingerie from modeling, I still sleep in his oversized T-shirt. Lately, it's whichever one he wore that day. What can I say? His scent brings me comfort.

My go-to style is Converse and leggings, and my hair is typically in a ponytail or messy bun.

And I have panic attacks.

Jesus, I'm a wreck.

"Give me that!" Gram snatches the phone and scrutinizes the picture of Ethan and his ex-wife. "He divorced?"

I nod. "Yeah."

"Then stop being a sourpuss. He's attractive. Doesn't seem to smile much."

"He does with me." Wow, that was super defensive, even to my own ears.

She reaches out and pats my hand. "There you go. Is he good to you?"

"In a way. He's busy, but he has made time for me since

finding out about the baby. He knows I'm seeing someone else and still wants to live together."

Gram cuts right through the bullshit. "He's older. More focused on his career and less worried about commitment."

"I guess." I shrug, not exactly happy about her comment on commitment. "He's thirty-five."

"Okay, I trust you know what you're doin'. Be careful with my grandbaby."

"I am. Nobody is taking this baby from me. Don't you worry."

She returns my phone, a smile of excitement on her face. "Okay, let's see the next guy."

Here we go.

I avert my gaze and shuffle the cards, chewing on my lip. It's difficult to tell her I've reconciled with Jackson. She has already been through enough, and I hate to disappoint her.

But I can't hide this. Jackson only has one speed. Fast and hard. All in. He's not going anywhere.

I pull up a recent photo of us at the beach. It's cute, with me sitting between his legs, his chin on my shoulder, his hand on my stomach.

She takes the phone and glances down then up, as though I'm playing a trick on her. When I'm silent, she studies the picture.

"Can't say I approve, but I also don't know him." She releases a heavy sigh. "What does he think of all this? Your modeling, pregnancy, and dating other people?"

"He's adjusting. It was difficult for him when I left today, but he's ecstatic about the baby and close with Ethan. The trouble is, he wants me by his side, not traveling for work."

She lets out a contemplative humph.

"What?"

"He has always wanted you under lock and key. All to himself." She frowns. "Don't let him suck the life out of you again."

I take a moment to reflect on her words. Now that I know the truth of Jackson's whereabouts at the end of our relationship and what he was struggling with, I realize his core behavior hasn't changed much. He has always been controlling.

The difference is now he's sober, which makes him less volatile. I thought he was cheating on me. He was mentally unstable and battling his addiction.

Can I live with Jackson's obsessive behavior? Maybe. It's not as though I don't have my own faults.

But the real question is, can I deal with a relapse?

Not with a baby.

It hurts not to love him unconditionally. It feels like a failure. Only those who've witnessed a loved one lose themselves to addiction can understand the anguish of letting them go.

Guilt is a heavy burden to bear, especially knowing how reckless he is, but I'm not putting a child through that.

"I've changed. I'm not that naïve girl who believed she found lightning in a bottle. I'm not dependent on him, and I'm not afraid to walk away. I have more than me to think about."

Gram gives me a warm smile before slamming her cards down. "I win. I was waitin' for you to finish."

Savage.

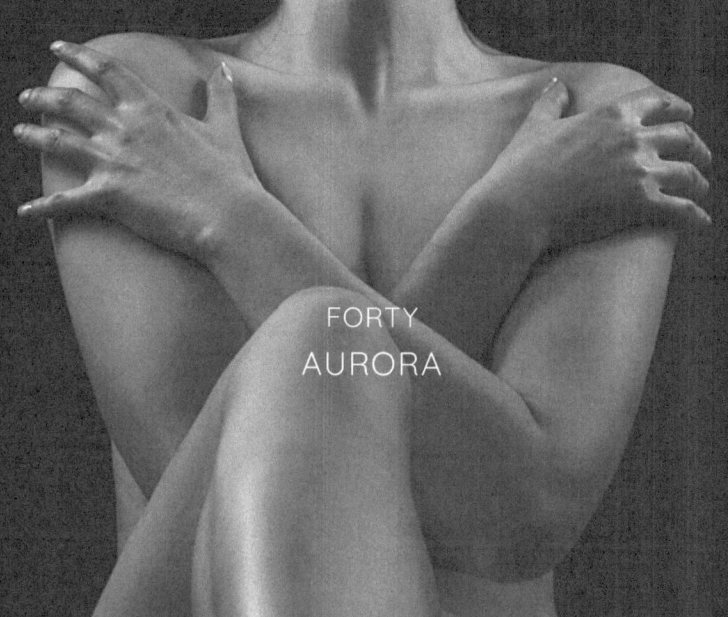

FORTY
AURORA

Ricky and I land in New York in the early morning hours.

This is my first trip without Emily. She's the organized and outgoing one. Ricky's a tremendous help, but he's not my assistant, and we're still getting to know each other.

After the second time I fumbled to find my ID, phone, and boarding pass, he took everything from me to check in himself. At our destination, he grabbed all my bags, including my carry-on and backpack, threw them over his shoulder, and led me out of the airport by my hand.

He never once complained or made me feel inadequate. He even let me sleep on him.

He's a take-charge kind of guy.

When we arrive at the Tribeca loft, our home for the next month, I'm exhausted and nauseated. Apparently, the baby doesn't enjoy flying.

Ricky assists the driver in bringing the bags up, insisting I rest in the locked vehicle until he returns for me. I know he must be tired too.

Once we're inside, I apologize for being a pain in the ass.

His brows furrow tightly. "I was deployed in the military as a medic. I can handle your anxiety."

That has me giggling. I must be sleepy. "Did you just compare me to war?"

He turns toward the kitchen. "Never had anyone drool on me in battle."

I laugh even harder. "I did not drool on you!"

The loft is boutique-style, with exposed brick, floor-to-ceiling arched windows, modern amenities, and three bedrooms. Odd, since we usually stay in a hotel or a studio. Then I remember Jackson is part of the picture now, and this is likely his or his team's doing.

Ricky comes back with a package of sliced apples. "Eat so you're not sick." Then, he inspects the entire place before settling for the bedroom opposite mine.

Despite longing to collapse into bed, I sit against the headboard, eat the apples, and scroll through my messages.

> Ethan: I miss you already. Text me when you get settled. No matter the time.

> Me: Miss you too. We're here.

Next, I skim through Jackson's essay of texts, shaking my head at the difference between the two. I can't even keep up with everything Jax wrote. I'd be worried if I didn't know he was on a flight with Ethan.

> Jax: I miss you already.

> Jax: I need you.

> Jax: I love you.

> Jax: Returning home to you felt like my world had finally come together.

> Jax: I'm fucking proud of you. You deserve it. You don't deserve to deal with my baggage. I'll work on that.
>
> Jax: I want to be with you. You make it all worth it.
>
> Jax: You're more than worth it.
>
> Jax: I sound obsessive, but I'm legit sick over you leaving.
>
> Me: I love you. Everything will be okay. Call me when you get up.
>
> Me: And you are obsessive! But I can't wait to see you.

Something nags at my brain, but I'm too tired to think. I know I shouldn't get sucked into his orbit. I know this is moving too fast, but Jackson's a freight train. There's no stopping him.

I rub my eyes and drop my phone on the nightstand.

A shrill noise slices through the stillness. I swear, I fell asleep minutes ago. My heavy eyelids wage a fierce battle against the grip of sleep while my mind works to separate dream from reality.

I ignore it and bury my face in the cool side of the pillow, willing myself back to sleep. But the caller is determined. Harsh vibrations rattle against the bedside table, each buzz growing louder and louder.

With a flail of my arm, I blindly search for the furious noise.

I find it, silence the ringing, and fall into the plush pillows.

The reprieve is short-lived and, groaning, I roll onto my side. "You've got to be fucking kidding me."

Disoriented, I grope for the device, squinting against the blurry brightness of the screen.

Jackson, I surmise, struggling to keep my eyes open. Who else but my obsessive boyfriend would demand my attention at such an ungodly hour?

I press the phone against my ear. "Jax," I croak, my voice thick and scratchy.

"Honey, it's Emily."

In her tone, there's sympathy, and it sends a jolt of adrenaline through my foggy mind, dispelling any remnants of sleep.

Grams.

No. The nurses would've called me.

Maybe they tried, and I rejected the call.

I blink several times to clear the haze, dread creeping up my spine. "Em? What's wrong?"

Weak sunlight filters through the windows, and I realize it's light out. I must have slept longer than I thought. What time is it in LA?

"God, you don't know." A note of panic laces her words.

My heart bursts into a hard pounding. My body trembles with fear, and I swallow the thick lump in my throat. "Know what? Is it Grams?"

The door creaks open. Ricky enters wearing a grim expression, and his gaze shifts from mine. He sits on the edge of the bed and slumps forward, burying his face in his hands.

"What's going on?" I cry, my voice cracking. "Someone tell me."

Emily releases a defeated sigh. "Sweetheart, check your phone."

With shaky hands, I pull my phone away from my ear

and skim through the onslaught of messages. I can't make sense of what I'm seeing.

There are texts from Jackson, Felicity, Ethan, and unknown numbers, but what catches my attention are the hundreds of IG notifications.

My finger touches the icon, the pictures flood the screen, and my heart stops dead.

The air ceases in my lungs, and I clutch my chest.

From the phone, I faintly register Emily's voice.

I stare into midnight-blue eyes.

He reaches for me. "Aurora. *Aurora.* Breathe."

No. I shake my head. I don't want to.

The world spins. I fall into Ricky, and everything tumbles into darkness.

FORTY-ONE
JACKSON

I YANK OPEN the heavy door. A drawn-out creak of the hinges pierces my throbbing head, and I wince. The locker room comes to a standstill. Judgment. Disgust. Darting eyes.

Fuck them. I'm not in the mood.

I take a seat on the bench in front of my designated cubby, and the weight of their collective scorn presses down on me.

Next to me, Grant refuses to meet my gaze. His rejection only adds to the loathing eating away at me. I get it. I fucked up.

I skirted curfew and missed the team bus. I'm late and hungover, and my entire body hurts.

Someone could've woken me, or maybe they tried. I wouldn't know. I was dead to the world and lost my phone.

A broken film reel of fragmented memories of last night flit through my mind. I remember a stream of texts and a drunken attempt at calling Aurora. An unending flow of alcohol started with a sip, became wildfire and vengeance in my veins, and hit me harder than I ever expected.

I'm a fucking idiot. No, I'm more than an idiot. I'm an absolute fuck-up.

After several long minutes of icy silence, besides the occasional sounds of tape being applied and the rustling of uniforms, I can't take it anymore.

"Did someone fucking die?" I snap, my voice raspy, bitterness lacing my tone. I sweep my glare across each player, waiting for one of them to muster the courage to confront me.

Anything but this silence.

I'd rather the entire locker room beat the shit out of me than drown in my thoughts.

"Other than your relationship?" Grant mutters, not even allowing me the dignity of a glance.

My heart twinges, and my stomach plummets, but I cage the pain and wrestle with it.

I did nothing wrong. My relationship isn't over. It can't be. I won't let it be.

Denial. Denial. Denial. The word breaks through my lies, and I push it down.

"O'Reilly, you're out. Hoosier, you're in for O'Reilly." Ethan's tone is cold and detached.

Here we go again.

My knee bounces with agitation, my eyes locking on *him*.

She has every reason to be with him, and I bet he couldn't wait to tell her how much of a fuck-up I am.

Ethan and Aurora. Endgame.

I rub the inner side of my ring finger with my thumb, the sting of the new tattoo anchoring me.

It's not over. She's mad, but we'll work through it. He can't have her. He *can't*.

A violent cocktail of resentment, withdrawal, and self-loathing jolts through me, and I'm on my feet, fists clenched. "You're benching me? Why?"

His sharp gaze meets mine, brimming with disappointment and disgust, deepening my hatred—hatred for myself.

He cocks his head and narrows his eyes. "You missed curfew and you're late, all so you could get drunk and chase tail. I hope it was worth it."

"Fuck off. I don't chase tail."

"I stand corrected. Missed curfew and arrived late after getting wasted and spending your night fucking puck bunnies. Is that better?" he shoots back, sarcasm heavy in his tone.

My blood boils, shadows linger at the edge of my vision, and I'm on him before anyone can stop me.

"Is that what you fucking told her?" I grit through clenched teeth and shove him.

He doesn't move. He doesn't fight back. He sneers and shakes his head with disdain.

I lean in. "I'm gonna wipe that fucking smirk off your face."

Nothing.

I rear my fist back, and pandemonium erupts. I'm restrained and struggle against an arm around my throat, pressing into my windpipe, and hands clutching my arms and shirt.

Grant gets in my face, his expression mirroring the same hatred I see in everyone else.

I scoff. "You'd seriously defend him over me? What a fucking joke."

Ethan stands behind Grant, chest heaving and fists balled. I bet he wouldn't hesitate to take a shot if given the opportunity. I wouldn't mind the unconsciousness, a respite from this shitstorm.

I raise my chin. "Hit me. Fucking do it."

He ignores my taunts. Instead, his words strike me with the force of a sledgehammer. "No one had to tell Aurora anything, you fucking idiot. It's all over the internet. You're fucking done."

Ice flows through my veins, rage shifting to panic. "What the fuck are you talking about?"

A dark storm rages in my mind, and my body trembles with fear.

What the fuck did I do? I blacked out.

"Why don't you sit down, shut up, and figure it out while the rest of us prepare for the game?" Ethan switches to coach mode, walks away, and ends the confrontation.

Gone is the man who kneeled beside me yesterday, patient and concerned. The man who spent nights with me on the ice, coaching me through sobriety.

"Get the fuck off me." I push aside my crushing humiliation and break free from the players holding me. I rummage through my bag for my phone, only to remember it's missing—same as the last twenty-four-hours. "Motherfucker." I throw my bag to the side. "Let me see your phone." I'm desperate, pride be damned. "Please, Grant."

"How many pictures of your wild night do you want to see?" He fiddles with his phone before shoving the screen in my face.

A sharp pain slices across my chest, and the sound of my heartbeat rushes in my ears.

Everything makes sense and falls apart at the same time.

There on the screen, the front page of TMZ showcases the greatest mistake of my fucked-up existence.

"*Jackson O'Reilly — Two-Timing and Double-Teaming.*"

In the picture, I'm sitting on a couch in the Hard Rock

penthouse, flanked by two half-naked women. One is laughing at something outside the frame, and the other has her hand on my knee.

No. No. No. No. No. I'm going to be sick.

In front of me are bottles of liquor, red plastic cups, piles of cash, lines of white powder, and baggies of pills.

Fucking awesome.

Intoxicated and high, I'm captured leaning forward, oblivious to my surroundings and about to take another line.

My eyes lift to catch Ethan's stony gaze. There's no gloating, only devastation.

You're fucking done.

It's over. I know it. He knows it.

The wave of realization hits me like a wrecking ball, crashing into my sternum, cracking my ribs, fracturing my heart, sucking the air from my lungs.

I stagger to the restroom, drop to my knees, and purge my roiling stomach until it's empty, alternating between retching and stifling my sobs.

She'll never take me back, and fuck, I don't deserve to have her.

I crumble against the wall, gasping for air. Hot tears burn my eyes, and the pounding in my head intensifies. My shivering body hunches forward, and I bury my head in my knees. I want to fucking die, end this torture, but my brain scrambles to make sense of it all, to absorb the gravity of my mistake.

Not a mistake. An annihilation.

How many times do I need to do this? When will I learn?

It only took one night to destroy my entire life. No, one drink.

It doesn't matter what brought me there.

I felt the rush, the intensity, with the first sip. The euphoria was almost orgasmic. The weight of my issues fell away, and as the night went on, I was numb.

Nothing mattered but that moment, that high. I surrendered to oblivion. The boundaries of reality faded, and I found solace in the escape it provided.

I was Jackson O'Reilly, revered hockey god and the life of the party. I was invincible.

Yet, here I am, alone and on edge.

No one is rushing to my aid—not my teammates or supposed friends.

Not Ethan, who I've become close with.

And definitely not Aurora.

She'll never speak to me again.

ACKNOWLEDGMENTS

First and foremost, thank you to my family for their patience while I spent the last two-plus years writing this series and for putting up with my ADHD whims. This wouldn't be possible without your support.

Next, this series would've never come to fruition without the love of the Kindle Vella community—both my readers and other writers who guided me along the way. To my readers who've been with me since Vella—through every edit, oopsie daisy, trial and error, and quirky author note—thank you from the bottom of my heart. Without you, this series would've died with Vella. Now, some of you brighten my Patreon and day with your heartfelt comments, fueling my drive and chasing away my imposter syndrome.

Thank you to all the editors I've had along the way, because I'm a bit of a worry wart. Ellie Sandoval, who did my first Vella edit, thank you for your thoroughness and patience. I'm sorry I couldn't tone down Jackson. He will forever be a creepy stalker. Okay, maybe not *forever*. A strong possibility, though. Emmy at Studio ENP, thank you for the positive feedback and lightning-fast edits. EJ at EJL Editing and Alexa at The Fiction Fix, I'm looking forward to continuing to work together in the future.

Photographer Michelle Lancaster, thank you for Anthony *chef's kiss* and to Lori Jackson for the stunning cover and for dealing with my nit-picking.

Much gratitude to my super PA and all-around

wonderful person, Courtney McNeil, for all your hard work and willingness to drop whatever you're doing to help me out.

To my ARC readers and Grey's Promos, a million thanks for taking a chance on a new author. You rock!

And to my lovely readers, I hope you enjoyed reading *Triple Power Play* as much as I enjoy writing Jax, Ethan, and Aurora. After working in crisis stabilization for over a decade, writing became my therapy. Through writing, I found a way to keep my chaotic brain happy and entertained while weaving my interest in psychology into complex characters. When I couldn't sleep and my mind was racing, I'd write on my phone. I never intended for any of it to be published. Yet, here we are. Life is wild!

Thank you for joining me on this journey! I can't wait for you to read book two. Ethan is on the cover, and it's even hotter than the first—if that's even possible. The next book is twice as long, with more spicy goodness, twists and turns, and surprises! Did someone say threesomes?

ABOUT THE AUTHOR

Jessica Lyn is a dark romance author who loves hockey, the mountains, and snow. She lives on the Oregon Coast with her family and a never-ending list of pets.
Her stories, initially chart-topping Kindle Vella serials, are influenced by a decade-long career in psych triage.
Outside of writing, she's into reading, traveling, crime docs, and a strong cup of tea.

CONNECT WITH JESSICA

Facebook | https://www.facebook.com/profile.php?id=100095221866597
Instagram | https://www.instagram.com/authorjessicalyn/
Amazon | https://bit.ly/3ZTI5Ah

Made in United States
Troutdale, OR
07/08/2025